Sugarless

Terrace Books, a trade imprint of the University of Wisconsin Press, takes its name from the Memorial Union Terrace, located at the University of Wisconsin–Madison. Since its inception in 1907, the Wisconsin Union has provided a venue for students, faculty, staff, and alumni to debate art, music, politics, and the issues of the day. It is a place where theater, music, drama, literature, dance, outdoor activities, and major speakers are made available to the campus and the community. To learn more about the Union, visit www.union.wisc.edu.

Sugarless

James agruder

TERRACE BOOKS
A trade imprint of the University of Wisconsin Press

Terrace Books
A trade imprint of the University of Wisconsin Press
1930 Monroe Street, 3rd Floor
Madison, Wisconsin 53711-2059

uwpress.wisc.edu

3 Henrietta Street
London WC2E 8LU, England

1   3   5   4   2

Printed in the United States of America

Library of Congress Cataloging-in-Publication Data
Magruder, James, 1960–
Sugarless : a novel / James Magruder.
p.   cm.
ISBN 978-0-299-23380-8 (cloth: alk. paper)
ISBN 978-0-299-23383-9 (e-book)
1. Coming out (Sexual orientation)—Illinois—Fiction.
2. Bildungsromans. I. Title.
PS3613.A3473.S84   2009
813'.6—dc22
2009008142

Lyrics from "Company" and "You Could Drive a Person Crazy" written by Stephen Sondheim
are used by permission of Herald Square Music, Inc., on behalf of Range Road Music, Jerry
Leiber Music, Mike Stoller Music, and Rilting Music, Inc. Lyrics from "The Telephone Hour"
written by Lee Adams are used by permission of the author.

This is a work of fiction. While, as in all fiction, the literary perceptions and insights are based
on experience, all names, characters, places, and incidents are either products of the author's
imagination or are used fictitiously. No reference to any real person is intended or should be
inferred.

For my mother,

my brother
Edward,

and my sisters
Margarette, Alison, and Marlyece

Sugarless

∾ 1 ∾

Until the day I made two girls cry in speech class, I always thought I left no impression. My stepsister Carla, also a sophomore, broke the news at the dinner table.

"Ricky made two socialites cry today," she said, smacking the serving spoon flat onto the mashed potatoes. The *pud* it made matched the phlegmy sound of her voice.

I looked up from my plate. Carla and I didn't acknowledge each other at school. She was a burnout with low-slung torpedo tits. I was cautious, featureless, a bus stop stand-alone holding his breath, beneath anyone's notice.

"Georgie Porgie, puddin' and pie, kissed the girls and made them cry," said my mother in singsong, handing green beans one at a time to my baby half-sister in her highchair.

"It was all over school, Sue Larsen and Robin Baver bawling in class," said Carla.

"All over Herrick's Lake, you mean," I countered. Carla and her friends got high at lunch in a forest preserve across the street from school.

"It's pretty creepy," she said.

"No one told them to cry. Jesus Christ," I snarled.

The Lord's name focused my mother somewhat. "So tell us what happened in school today, Rick."

"Nothing. I read a story out loud in speech class. It was an assignment. It's called Oral Interpretation, okay? I did a good job, okay?"

"*He* almost cried too," announced Carla, trying to pull her father in, but for now Carl was working through his chuck steak. Instead of holding his fork between his thumb and forefinger, my stepfather ate with it stuck through his fist like a drill bit.

"I was interpreting the story orally. Sue and Robin got emotional."

"Tracy Sawicki told me you really got into it too."

A smear of dried zit cream under Carla's collarbone cracked with the heaves of her fake sobs. She shouldn't have bothered with the cream. Blemishes weren't a problem on the third biggest chest at Wheaton-Warrenville. I could have made instant friends by giving out her bra size, but then kids would know we lived in the same house.

"Nah, I was only pretending to get into it, like Steve does when you're on a blanket in the arboretum."

"Eat shit and die, Ricky," she said, giving me the finger.

My mother shifted her eyes to see whether Carl would reprimand his daughter for her language. When he didn't, she pretended she hadn't heard Carla over Lisa's shout for more green beans and asked me what the story I read was about. I sighed like nothing in my life was worth an explanation and stared at the orange coffee grinders and horns of plenty on the glossy

4

wallpaper. Carl had picked the pattern. My mother called it her Polish wallpaper behind his back. So easy to keep clean, she'd say, making a tiny face.

"It's about a kid who lets his crippled brother die in the woods during a hurricane," I said finally.

"That doesn't sound very nice. Why would he do that?"

"Because he's ashamed. He pretends he doesn't hear his brother calling for help and when he comes back, Doodle is dead and bleeding by a nightshade bush."

"Doodle?" snickered Carla.

The story I read in speech class was called "The Scarlet Ibis." I'd done what Miss Schuette, the student teacher, said to do, which was to pretend I was the narrator looking back on the accident. I was supposed to see and feel everything he described. She said to find a reason why I *had* to tell the story, to make my listeners feel how I had loved my little brother Doodle as much as I hated him and wanted him to die.

Reading aloud I pretended that the words were painted on the back wall of yellow cinderblocks in Room 100. I made eye contact with the foreheads of three classmates, left, center, and right, like Miss Schuette told me to. When it was over and I was heading back to my desk I noticed that Sue Larsen's shoulders were twitching and Robin Baver's mascara was leaking into a Kleenex she held over her nose. From under the clock Miss Schuette was giving me a big thumbs-up sign. Mr. Wegner, the real teacher, kept clearing his throat at the podium. It was obvious that until then I was only a name in his attendance book. He mumbled something about the power of literature, and then it was someone else's turn.

Robin Baver, so popular she could talk to anyone she

wanted, turned around, her eyes like wet beetles. She mouthed, "Thank you." Crying in class at a story a four-eyed nobody read probably made her feel soulful. I hoped that her boyfriend, Paul Hicks, wouldn't think this soft spot of hers was a good excuse to punch me out in gym class. I rushed the door as soon as the bell rang.

"Why don't you read it to all of us after supper?" suggested my mother in her "Let's make this second marriage work" voice. She was big fan of *Redbook*'s monthly features on family togetherness. Carla made a gagging sound.

"I left it at school," I muttered.

"I don't believe you, son," she said mildly, clocking plates to see if the food was disappearing to her satisfaction. "I'd sure like to hear it."

"Went over better than the artichoke speech, huh?" said my stepfather.

I stiffened in my chair. I looked at the thick, freckled forearm guarding his dinner plate, at the dead black nail on his right forefinger. My mother was smiling as if to say, "See, he does pay attention. Now say something nice back." I stared at the stripe of red roots in the part of his fake blond hair until my eyes blurred. I'd dug the box of Miss Clairol out from under their bathroom sink as proof that he dyed it, but my mother pretended it was hers.

To graduate from high school in Illinois in the seventies you had to pass two quarters of what they called Oral Communication. I was presently taking Oral Com II. Freshman year we had started Oral Com I with how-to speeches. One December afternoon, after a girl made origami Christmas ornaments and a jock waxed his skis, I pulled a foil package and a thermos of melted butter out of my book bag to show my classmates how to eat an artichoke.

I wasn't trying to be original. I just liked artichokes, which I'd learned how to eat when my mother was still married to my father and we lived in Downers Grove, a ritzier town ten miles east of Wheaton. I began my speech by explaining the origins of the vegetable, the two different kinds, and how long it took to steam them in a double boiler, a utensil I drew on the blackboard with colored chalk. I tossed away the bitter skirt of outer leaves, then plucked off some edible ones and sieved the meat with my teeth. After detaching the choke in one piece with a knife and cutting up the heart, I invited everyone to come up for a taste.

Not one single person would try it. I was so surprised I walked down the aisle with the plate balanced on my fingertips. Begging isn't pretty. Mrs. Widmar took one to be polite and pronounced the taste "different."

Different is the kiss of death in high school, especially gray-green chunks of it speared by frilly toothpicks. Telling my mother and stepfather about it that night compounded the humiliation, so naturally it was the kind of thing Carl Schwob, the licensed psychologist who held his fork like an ape, would remember and bring up ten months later. He checked to see if he'd got me. I looked to the right, selected an awl from the collection of antique implements my mother had hung on the kitchen wall, and punched a new seam in his skull.

It was Carla's night to clear and load. I went up to my room, sat in my beanbag chair, and tuned my radio to WLS. I could hear my mother and Carl getting ready to go bowling with the McClellans. If my mother was still married to my father, I

7

would be eating real steak, not chuck. My classmates and teachers would know what an artichoke was, and I would know how to wax skis.

I grunted through the door at my mother's cheery goodbye, but then she came in.

"Is the skirt crooked?" she asked, knowing it wasn't. Her frosted pink fingertips glowed against the acid green pleats.

I shook my head.

"I think it's wonderful that God gave you this talent."

God? Did *Redbook* have a religion page? I flicked my metal beer mug trashcan to make it ping. And what talent was she talking about?

"Funny it should be for speech," she continued.

"What do you mean, funny?"

I knew what she meant. I didn't talk until I was nearly three years old. Not even "mama" or "dada" or "gimme," supposedly. Family legend went that I didn't have to, so perfectly were my mother and I able to communicate without words. My father and her mother finally broke us up by sending me down to Grandma's house in Washington, D.C., where I was forced to talk. It was that, or no lunch.

What's funny is that all these years later I can remember my grandmother standing by the open refrigerator door in her long, narrow kitchen, and me pointing at the bright yellow bottle on the shelf in the door. I can remember the tickle of her bracelet charms against my arm as she closed my hand in hers, and the flowery smell of her face powder as she stooped to tell me that she didn't understand what it was I wanted. What I can't remember is saying the first thing I ever said—"I'd like some mustard for my sandwich, please."

Little Rick could talk all along. He just hadn't needed to. Or wanted to. My father thought that was hilarious, especially the "please." As I grew up, and listened to him repeat the story of the historic bologna and cheese in Washington, D.C., I began to take offense. Had he thought I was retarded? Eventually the implications—mama's boy times ten—embarrassed me too.

My mother, stalling at the door, was wanting me to say the mustard line now. I did that sometimes just to cheer her up. She didn't like bowling, I knew, or the pizza after, or Ron McClellan and his permanent five-o'clock shadow. We still didn't need words to tell each other stuff like that. I rolled my eyes, splitting the difference. She shifted her ball bag to her other hand and blew a kiss.

I went down to warm Lisa's bedtime bottle. Lisa was definitely saying "mama" and "dada" and "whazzat?" I had a list of words I was going to teach her, starting with "birth control." I was pretty sure she'd been an accident, and once my mother was pregnant Carl made no secret of gunning for a boy. I liked to think Lisa heard him from the womb and decided to be a girl on purpose. It made her an ally.

I was feeding her when Steve Hendrie came by for Carla. While he waited, I told him about Sue and Robin crying in speech class. He leaned against the wall and pulled at the tooth-brushes of hair at the corners of his upper lip. He used to listen to my stories.

After Lisa fell asleep I went to my room and undressed. I kicked my clothes across the hall into the dirty laundry pile at the bottom of the linen closet. Then I removed the finial from the curtain rod holding the psychedelic rug up over my bed and withdrew a crumpled, crusty baby sock. I set it on top of the clock radio and started jerking off. I didn't think about any-one or anything except how to make it last. It took seven songs on the radio, plus commercials. The first shot hit my collar-bone, not a record, but nearly.

∽◡◠

Steve Hendrie had been my friend first.

After Carl and my mother got married in August of 1974, the month before I started eighth grade, we moved to a brand-new subdivision. Briarcliffe sold seven kinds of house, all with bogus British names. The most popular models were the split-level Richmond and the L-shaped Somerset ranch. Three out of every five houses in Briarcliffe were Richmonds or Somer-sets. I had grown up believing that poor people lived in split-levels and ranches. Rich people had full staircases.

We lived in an Andover. A two-story, four-bedroom Dutch Colonial, the Andover was the most expensive Briarcliffe model, at $45,500. There were only five of them in the entire subdivision. Three pillars graced the front porch, but the window shutters were resin, the porch itself was unfinished concrete, and there was no center hall. The last two houses we lived in before the divorce had center halls, and now my mother had settled for a living room that led right into the dining room without even the possibility of pocket doors. The demotion bugged me even more because she acted like it didn't matter. Less to keep clean, she said.

After a week of watching me mope, my mother pushed me outside one Saturday afternoon while she painted the laundry room and Carl worked at hooking up the central air-conditioning system. Up and down Kingston Drive, flats of lumber waited to become Richmonds and Somersets. Three houses had sod deliveries; their front yards were dotted with grass snack cakes, giant chocolate mint rolls drying in the sun.

The littlest kids were racing down the brand-new sidewalks in their Big Wheels; the ten-year-olds were throwing dirt clods at each other through the ribs of half-built houses.

I walked around the block to Durham Drive with the vague idea of investigating a horse farm behind the south border of the subdivision, but the pillars of another Andover, this one with gray siding, not our goldenrod, stopped me. A boy was lying propped on his elbows on the driveway, a basketball pinned between his ankles. He shaded his eyes and said hey. Steve Hendrie was a year younger, but standing up he was two inches taller. His widow's peak, his brush haircut, and his pointed teeth made me think of the Wolf Man. The dark hairs on his arms made my stomach turn over. Mine were blond and sparse. Steve Hendrie was miles ahead in the race to puberty. I pushed away the image of the Bower Junior High boys' locker room, an all too imminent proving ground, and announced that I lived in an Andover too.

Steve said that his Andover cost more than mine because their lot bordered the Morton Arboretum and their view would never be spoiled. After he told me that his sister Tanya had silver-dollar-sized nipples and that his parents, who were chiropractors, shoved their fingers up their patients' butts to fix their backs, I knew it would be easy to avoid shooting baskets with him. I had only to mention the magazines in our basement for Steve to heave the ball onto the front porch and fall in beside me on the sidewalk.

Covered with two inches of small white rocks, our basement crawlspace was home to Christmas decorations, tax returns, bags of salt pellets for the water softener, and Carl's porn. He had boxes of all the latest magazines, but also every single issue of *Playboy*. He kept the ones from the fifties in individual plastic bags. Collector's items, worth real money, my mother had said, scraping a spot on her pants with a thumbnail when I brought up the subject of what I'd helped carry down the basement stairs during the move. She never said I was supposed to keep out of them.

I led Steve to the box of the most recent *Penthouse*s and *Viva*s and *Oui*s; their pictures were raunchier. His knees collected a layer of fine rock powder as he hunted for beaver. When he twisted to reach for more, he'd swat at the light bulb string, thinking an insect had landed on his neck. Sitting apart, I played host, on supposed lookout for Carl. The real fact of the matter was that apart from the rare man-plus-woman photo spreads, known as *Playboy* pictorials, my basement pleasures were literary. Steve would zip through the pictures while I pored over Xaviera Hollander's Happy Hooker column and the Playboy Advisor. In those days, *Penthouse* also published a separate magazine of personal experience letters called *Forum* that I couldn't get enough of. No detail that the writers described to reach their identical destination—a mind-blowing, world record orgasm—struck me as extraneous or repetitious. I read letters in the gloom until my eyes hurt. Carl had books too: Casanova's complete *Memoirs,* all of Henry Miller, and *Fanny Hill* lined up on shelves by his workbench. I didn't bother with them, but one September afternoon, with Steve mouth-breathing in the crawlspace, I opened a volume of drawings called *The Erotic Art of Japan* that was sitting out next to a cracked fish tank.

The contrast between the blank faces of the Japanese couples and the angry, diving animals beneath their robes made me physically sick. Every pubic hair on the women's quivering pussy lips was a separate, bristling spear. The hard cocks, every vein a river, every pee hole a gash, were a shock, as were the aggressive squats and jets of squirt. Turning the pages, I saw giant black dildos, an octopus sucking between a woman's legs, a boy spread-eagled on a standing bald-headed monk, and everywhere the same blank, unreadable faces watching me.

I threw the book down like a hot potato. Thumbing through it, Steve said he'd rather look at real people. "Me too," I shouted with relief. I preferred the soft-focus pictorial shots, women swishing cotton drapes between their legs or unhooking their garters in meadows, mustaches tickling nipples, sunlight baking a man's butt fuzz.

For months of Saturdays, I watched Steve Hendrie tent his trousers in my basement. I watched his teeth, white as the rocks beneath us, the soft purple creases at the corners of his eyelids, darker in the morning or when he was sleepy. The same purple was streaked in the folds of his elbows and the backs of his knees. I was thirteen years old and praying for the hair on my arms to get dark, and everyone and everything was sexed up. Or maybe it was the silicone seventies that were oversexed, I don't know. But I do know that because I was thirteen, I thought sex began with me. That the Japanese had been doing it, and doing it all those crazy ways for hundreds of years, was the most upsetting thing.

∞∽∿

Steve was a grade behind me at Bower, so we were only neighborhood friends. Cute, with a mouth on him, he'd been able to sweet-talk Carol Dudek and Kim Lacefield into the arboretum the summer before high school. My sex life began on an old blanket, spread out in an alfalfa field. The four of us would thrash around until we heard the ice cream truck coming down

Westminster Street. Steve and I had to fight for it, but we were finally allowed bare tit with our hands. That got boring, especially with Kim, so the real goal was getting a finger in. If we propped their legs apart with our elbows, we could at least get an eyeful of where to bank our fingers along the edge of their terrycloth short shorts. The girls wouldn't go near what we had, but we were permitted to hump it against them. We'd roll and crash, they'd slap, and I'd feel Steve's back solid against mine. I liked that part best without really understanding why. Both girls wanted Steve, but Carol's C cups gave her first dibs. This went on for maybe six weeks, until some high school boys lured them away with a bottle of Boone's Farm.

Summer nights Steve and I would pitch a pup tent in the Hendries' backyard and run like bandits all over the subdivision. I secretly called us the Andover Boys. We raided gardens and pretended that carrots tasted better with dirt on them. We knocked over swing sets, tossed lit lunch bags of shit from the horse farm onto front porches, knifed kiddie pools, and drove chained dogs crazy with rocks and firecrackers.

Then came cocktail hour. I had a collection of miniature liquor bottles, empties gathered by my father at the end of his business flights. ("Just one more way in with the stewardesses," huffed my mother.) I had nearly sixty, arranged on a bookshelf, another distinctive touch to my bachelor pad. I'd funnel booze from the high broom closet shelf into six little Smirnoff vodkas and take plastic cups, cans of soda for mixers, and a peanut butter jar for a cocktail shaker. From one of his babysitting jobs—he was mad for money and sometimes filled in for his sister—Steve had swiped packets of brandy alexander and grasshopper mix, in case we ever got any girls to sleep out with us. We didn't have the liqueurs on hand for these advanced concoctions, but we impressed ourselves with an ability to plan ahead. We'd swig three drinks apiece and flop on our backs until it was time to piss together through the fence into the arboretum. I'd sneak a sideways look at the tiny motion of Steve's right hand pulling back his foreskin.

Twirling one of the rabbit-head drink stirrers my father had brought me from the Playboy Club downtown, Steve sometimes asked me why I didn't live with him.

"Divorced kids always go with their mothers," I'd answer patiently.

"But still . . . stewardesses. He's a real swinger, your old man."

I guess he was a swinger. He wore a Capricorn medallion, but it wasn't a stewardess who did his marriage in. It was a cocktail waitress named Josephine, with kids of her own. Like Steve, my father wasn't circumcised. He'd been born at home, not in a hospital. That was something of a secret—born at home, not his foreskin.

"He travels an awful lot. It wouldn't work out if I lived with him. What if I sprained my ankle or something?"

This I would bring up because I wanted Steve to tell me again how his father had bathed him when his ankle was sprained.

"He could get you a nurse, a Swedish nurse with big tits like Little Annie Fannie."

"Yeah," I'd enthuse.

"She'd give you blow jobs."

"Yeah."

"Blow jobs whenever you wanted."

"Whenever I wanted, yeah."

The blow job on demand was Steve's destination for all of our drunken pup-tent talks. At night, zipped in our sleeping bags, no light for magazines, we'd talk about blow jobs end-lessly, and I would think Steve was testing me. I would hope Steve was testing me. I could hear crickets and the safe explosions of air conditioners changing cycles in the backyards, and I knew he had a boner too.

~⁊⁊~

Carla came home hours after Carl and my mother got back from bowling. I could hear the two of them arguing about it downstairs on Saturday morning. Carla, too wild for her own mother to control, had only been with us for two months, and I was getting used to the hiss my mother put on the words "set an example."

But Saturday mornings were tense even before Carla. Briar-cliffe's exclusive Andover turned out to be a corner-cut piece of crap, so the Honey-Do list on the refrigerator had grown as long and tough as a dandelion root. The basement was always flooding, the sump pump backed up, the bathtub pipes leaked into the kitchen ceiling, the porch was cracked, the windows rattled, there wasn't enough insulation, the grout was falling out of the shower tiles, etc. Whatever tone or tactic she adopted to get him off his ass, Carl always had something better to do on the '69 Renault. He had spent the summer fixing it up for his precious Carla. Now it was October, and it still sat in the driveway, hillbilly style, its front end on cinder blocks, driving my mother nuts.

I looked out my window and recalled the spectacle of Carl's chair-breaking mother and sisters popping out of the Renault like snakes from a can, an hour after the wedding was over. They'd gotten lost on 294 from Indiana. The patterns on their sleeveless dresses weren't the psychedelic paisleys my mother and her friends favored; they looked like they were wearing tablecloths. Their hair didn't swirl up like soft ice cream—even the gray-haired one had long drifts of ropy curls. Flapping elephant-ear arms, Carl's relatives looked like extras on *Hee Haw*. When my mother hugged them hello, she was swallowed up like a raisin dropped into rising dough.

I went downstairs. As I was about to pass him in the den to get to the kitchen, he shouted, "What time is it, Marie?" If he was up, I should be up.

"A quarter to ten," she answered. She was cleaning Lisa's bib.

Getting out my cereal, I could see him in the booger chair, his hairless tits and stomach pushing through the lapels of his green bathrobe. I called it the booger chair because he picked his nose in it while he watched TV. The armrest was bumpy with his crop.

"Is Carla up yet?" I asked.

My mother shot me a look. "Do you want some bacon?"

"You mean there's some left?" I said loudly. Carl had gained weight on her cooking.

She took a plate from the oven. "Do you know where she went last night?" she murmured.

"She and Steve tested mattresses."

"Oh, honey, that's just not funny." She put her head in her hands.

Lisa, already tuned to household moods, started to whimper from the floor, where she was playing with some plastic bowls. I hoisted her up and blew bubbles in her neck.

My mother was having a tough time with Carla: the tight tops, the hip huggers that showed her pussy crack, the glitter eye shadow, the smoking, the Aerosmith cranked high for hours at a time, her disinterest in school or in minding Lisa, her ability

17

to lie for hours on the couch without even a magazine for distraction, the lag in her response time to all statements and questions. Carla wasn't malicious, my mother concluded early on, she was *indifferent*. She was a shrugger at life, doing just enough to get by, which was far more dangerous. My mother didn't have to put it into words, but with the tag line "not living up to his potential" trailing me through seven schools, she was terrified that Carla would lure me into the cave of her bad behaviors.

"Maybe they went to his grandmother's," I said, not caring if that made her feel worse. No one had put a gun to her head to remarry.

Steve's grandmother Hannelore was German, from Germany, and she kept Nazi banners and medals and stuff in an old desk drawer. She lived right across from the front entrance to Briarcliffe in a home called Martin Manor. When Steve and I were still friends, we'd visit Hannelore because she was good for ten dollars and whatever Steve could find in her hiding places. My job was to distract her by asking her to teach me German words. Holding up a knickknack, I'd say, "Was ist das?" like Colonel Klink. Steve's mom said her mother hid money because of the German "hyperinflation." We had inflation now, tied to the oil embargo—whatever that was—but Steve's grandmother told crazy stories about buying one pear with a grocery bag stuffed with paper money.

My mother dropped the subject of Carla and Steve. "Do you have a lot of homework this weekend?"

"Geometry, that's it."

"What are you going to do today?"

"Dunno."

"I'll bet you're going to add to your collection."

"Maybe," I said, smiling in spite of myself.

"Why don't you take Lisa with you in her stroller? It's a beautiful day out."

"It's a mile each way."

"I trust you with her."

"I'm taking my bike."

"You don't have to be embarrassed, Rick. She's your sister."

"Half-sister," I corrected her. I drained the milk from my cereal bowl and walked to the door to the garage. I would have died to admit it, but I liked taking care of Lisa; it wasn't her fault that she was half spawn of Satan. I just wasn't in the mood that day. I'd heard pages rustle in the powder room. The booger chair was empty. I wanted out before he stunk up the whole house.

∽↝

I gave up hunting for my bike lock and decided to walk to Wax Trax. Things went missing in the garage, which was heaped with car parts and cases of motor oil. Carl had talked my mother into buying a side of beef as a hedge against inflation, so now we had a meat freezer and a regular freezer. I counted four tackle boxes and thirteen fishing rods, some still in their K-Mart bags. Carl was fixated on a fish called (here he'd drop his voice) "the muskie." Related to the pike, the muskellunge had razor-sharp teeth and could grow to sixty pounds. Carl would bore us with news of when they were biting on Lake Superior. I'd have gladly gone fishing with him so I could push him overboard and watch the muskies devour him the way termites buzz through houses in cartoons.

Briarcliffe was at its ugliest in the fall. The sky was a greasy yellow-gray pillowcase, the lawns were hatched with dead

19

sod squares, and the lava rocks were piled like turds around the bases of dinky trees wired to the ground. Walking past the Hegnas' house, a Richmond, I thought about the night I helped Steve babysit there. We poked holes through the foil pouches of Mr. Hegna's Trojans with needles, then went into the family room and took our clothes off. We had talked all that week about wrestling in the nude. The idea was that I needed practice for winter gym, which I despised. I was a freshman then and Steve was still at Bower. Even Xaviera Hollander wrote that boys experimented with each other during puberty.

At the end of the Hegnas' block I turned onto Butterfield Road and walked along the gravel shoulder, passing Briarcliffe North, Arrowhead, and the white brick gates to High Knob. A three-pillared Andover was one thing, but High Knob houses, in clapboard and stone, not vinyl siding, started at $90,000 and their yards had huge old trees flaming with color. I spotted some burnouts in army jackets smoking around a drain culvert, so I zipped between cars to the other side of Butterfield. My mother didn't have to worry about Carla's bad example. I didn't smoke or cut class. I was a C student, halfway down the aisle closest to the door. I had nothing in common with Carla except—assuming they'd gone that far already—giving Steve Hendrie a blow job.

Before we wrestled that night at the Hegnas', Steve had shown me the mechanics of his foreskin, popping the head, which matched the purply color of his eyelid creases, in and out of the skin bag. I felt like I was watching a sped-up filmstrip of a flower blossoming. Maybe he took my silence to mean I thought it looked gross, because he said that his uncut dickhead was more sensitive than mine and so he'd always get more pleasure out of it. Then he said that the wide vein running up

20

the top of my shaft looked weird. That bugged me, but I didn't try to get even by saying his penis looked like a dog dick or the end of a doobie. I just wanted to lie down on him.

It wasn't that I *let* him win the match. I was paying attention to the feeling of his body on mine; the moves I tried were designed to put as much of me in the way of his boner as possible. After he pinned me, his knees gripping my chest below my armpits, I didn't expect him to force his dick into my mouth, even if I knew he knew I'd let him.

It wasn't how I wanted it to go. I thought if I concentrated on using what I'd learned about giving head from the *Penthouse Forum* letters, he would give us the room to be in a man-plus-man pictorial. I wanted to gauge the effects of what I was doing, hear his sounds, catch the look on his face, feel the length of him against me, but the pumping derrick of his back and haunches held me in place. When it got too difficult to breathe, I made gagging sounds.

He was too far gone to care. Basically, he fucked my mouth. I kicked my legs up in an effort to throw him, but he held on, and my right leg slammed down hard on Nancy Hegna's Fisher-Price Schoolroom. The major bruise on my calf was nothing next to the bloody nose I got when, after trying and failing to cough up his load—a futile face-saving gesture—I suggested Steve blow me in return. After all that talk, I had assumed the act was something both Andover Boys wanted to do.

Carla hadn't come between us. Steve and I hadn't been friends for a long time. He dogged her torpedoes from the first day at the bus stop. Four days into sophomore year I heard my mother answer the doorbell and say with genuine surprise, "Steve Hendrie! I haven't seen you in an age. Look at you! When did you get so big?"

In Wax Trax I gave my best impression of nonchalance. I checked out the Fritz the Cat T-shirts until I made eye contact with the cashier. I nodded politely at the row of bongs behind his head, and he said, "How's it going?"

On my way to the back of the store, I stopped at E in the rock section and pretended to study an Emerson, Lake, and Palmer album until the other customers passed my security clearance. One time I'd had to wait an extra half hour until a girl in my American history class left with the Eagles' *Hotel California,* an album I didn't think deserved lengthy contemplation. Moving down the row I spent a minute with Jefferson Starship, then Kiss, and on to Led Zeppelin. I hesitated over the stenciled black-and-white cover of the first Manhattan Transfer album—too close for comfort—and pulled out *War Child* instead.

I carried Jethro Tull around the corner, past the swinging poster stand, and set it in the front of the rack marked "Broadway." I glanced left and right, and then at the cashier. If anybody saw what I was looking at, I could shove the load of records back and sidestep to R & B with *War Child.*

Wax Trax had the sense to separate original cast recordings from film soundtracks. The music sections in Sears and Montgomery Ward mixed them together, putting *The Good, the Bad, and the Ugly* next to *Guys and Dolls.* I pushed my wire-rim aviator eyeglasses onto the bridge of my nose. My stomach fluttering with covetousness, I flicked the first white plastic divider forward and began:

Annie Get Your Gun, Anything Goes, Applause, The Apple Tree. Breath. Flick.

The Boy Friend, Brigadoon, Bubbling Brown Sugar, Bye Bye Birdie. Breath. Flick.

Cabaret, Camelot, Can-Can, Candide, Carnival, Chicago, A Chorus Line, Coco, Company. Breath. Flick.

Dames at Sea, Damn Yankees, Dear World. Breath. Flick.

Finian's Rainbow, Flower Drum Song, Follies, Funny Girl, A Funny Thing Happened on the Way to the Forum. Breath. Flick.

I knew when it happened, even how it happened, but not why it happened. That June I'd watched the Tony Awards on television. I had never been to see a play and was only dimly aware of what Broadway meant, but the musical numbers on the show cast a spell. There was a bizarre Japanese song with screens. There was a song from a musical called *Chicago* with a man who stripped down to his boxer shorts surrounded by girls with white feather fans. The show ended with the finale to *A Chorus Line.* The glittering white and gold costumes, the top hats and chrome mirrors, the high kicks of the dancers that went on forever—it all made the hair stand up on my neck. I moved to the floor in front of my mother and Carl so they couldn't see me bawl. I was never a crier.

Before those Tonys I followed the top forty on WLS and WCFL, bought 45's like Led Zeppelin's "D'yer Mak'er" and Manhattan Transfer's "Operator" every once in a while, but instantly afterward my allowance had a purpose. On my next trip to Wax Trax I crept to the back of the store and found *A Chorus Line.* Then I bought *Chicago,* then *The Wiz,* then *Pippin,* then *Grease.*

I would set the records in a row around the perimeter of my room and listen to them in their order of purchase, A sides first, then B. Though tempted, I never skipped the slow songs, and I didn't play favorites. The biographies of the composers and stars on the album backs or in the foldouts dropped the names of other shows, other glamorous strangers, some male, some female, whom I was destined to invite home. My room gradually filled with friends, friends who knew each other and had only been waiting for me to throw them a party.

No one needed to tell me how weird this was. My mother called it my latest collection, but this one I knew I would never outgrow, as I had my airline decals or my animal stamps or my *Peanuts* books or my Wacky Packages. Carla listened to Aerosmith, I listened to *Cabaret,* doing extra chores to support a weekly $8.32 addiction. "I'm getting this for my grandmother," I'd say if a salesclerk looked at me funny. "It's for my mother's birthday," I'd say to the burnout bandits who might waylay me on the trip home to Briarcliffe.

I got out easy that Saturday. The new cashier was on the phone to Ticketron the whole time he rang up album fourteen: *Company,* whose mod slyness had been taunting me for weeks. *Company,* whose cover, electric purple with red-orange geometric letters, gave nothing away.

Back home, Carl's feet were sticking out from under the hillbilly Renault. I went into the kitchen to make a ham and cheese sandwich, purposely delaying *Company's* entrance to the ball. From the chirr of the plumbing, I knew Carla was finally up. My mother shouted from the top of the stairs to say that my father had called and I should call him back.

"Later," I yelled.

"I think you should call him now."

"Later," I repeated, and again she said I should call him right away. I walked to the stairs making fart noises with the squeeze mustard and asked her why.

"Just call him. He wants to talk to you."

"Tell me what he wants, Mom. *God.*"

My father was getting married again. Not to Josephine the cocktail waitress, but to Julia, a Southern belle—his words—he'd met on a business trip to Louisville. She was pretty, she came from an old family that was going to make him an honorary Kentucky Colonel, and she couldn't wait to meet me. A Kentucky Colonel, he explained when I made no reply to this piece of excitement, got invited to the best parties on Derby weekend and could watch the race from the infield.

He wanted me to say something. I wanted to say that ten weeks of knowing her might be no guarantee, since my mother and Carl had dated for ten months and look what happened. Instead I asked him if she was pregnant.

What shocked my mother he tended to find funny. This he found very funny. I could tell my acknowledgment that he was fucking his belle was a relief. It was like I approved. I asked him if she was a stewardess. He laughed harder. Carla walked by in a towel with a bottle of nail polish and signaled that she had to use the phone. I rolled my eyes. She made the jerk-off motion with her hand.

I had an alarming thought. "You're not moving to Kentucky, are you?" I asked. My mother and Carl and I had taken a horrible car trip to Hodgenville, Kentucky, the summer they got married. Mammoth Cave was freezing and Lincoln's Birthplace was a gyp because they moved the log cabin from its original location and it was under a plastic dome so you couldn't go in. Worse, through a gap in the accordion doors separating our rooms in the motor court, I watched for a minute while Carl screwed her. The top sheet jerked down his back while he pumped, and her right foot had twisted its way out of the covers and lightly smacked the metal bed frame.

"No, I'm staying put. She's going to move to New Jersey with her kids. I'll get a bigger house."

"With a center hall?"

"What?"

"She has kids too?"

"Three little ones, two boys and a baby girl named Susannah." His voice made three ready-made kids sound like an incredible bonus offer.

"Oh Susanna, oh don't you cry for me," I said.

"That's right."

"What happened to *her* husband?"

"Well, son. He died."

"Sorry," I mumbled.

He and Julia would fly up from Louisville in a few weeks to meet me. We'd go downtown to dinner at the Pinnacle, the revolving restaurant on the top floor of the Prudential Building. I decided I would stick him with the price of a lobster, and maybe shrimp cocktail too.

Robin Baver stopped me before class on Tuesday and tried to explain. We were standing by the trophy case near the front entrance to school. The football pin and the green and gold ribbons twisted through her French braid meant that her Wolverette uniform was on under her patchwork leather coat. We had way too many pep rallies.

"Rick, what you . . . that story you read on Friday about the scarlet, the scarlet—bird, I mean the way you *read* that story, well, you saw what happened."

"Go Wolverines," I mumbled, reading off the felt banner draped over the glass-fronted case.

"What?" she said.

"Thank you, Robin," I said in a tone girls of her rank expected. Wolverettes were equal to cheerleaders.

"Congratulations on a job excellently well done," she continued. She wouldn't need my Homecoming vote for two years. "How did you do it?"

She wasn't trying to get away. I kept sneaking glances at the reflections in the case to see if anybody noticed her talking to me. I widened my eyes to indicate that I didn't know how I'd done it. Robin shifted her books and leaned in. She had a phone number inked on the back of her hand. "It felt good to cry, you know?"

"Crying is good for you," I said. "That's what Truemper told us in health class." Only a man like Mr. Truemper, who had lifted weights at the Munich Olympics and was built like the Tasmanian Devil, could say it was good to cry.

She nodded. "Boys have feelings too."

I ducked my head, not wanting to be a Wheaton-Warrenville boy with feelings. I began humming *phone rings door chimes in comes company* to myself. I had forgotten my Oral Com II triumph because I'd spent all weekend, and Columbus Day, memorizing what I could of my new record. Before I put *Company* on for the fifth time in a row, I shut the rest of my albums in the closet and cheated on them with my first solo date. I couldn't help myself. I had already decided I wanted to move to New York, be one of another hundred people who got off of the train, and drink Sazerac slings.

Robin was tapping my arm.

"Rick, the reason I cried was because . . ." She pulled in her lower lip for a second. "My little brother Dave has Down's syndrome, Rick. And I just love him to death. But sometimes I . . . I . . . sometimes for me it's just like the boy in your story. . . ."

Robin didn't know what to say now. I shrugged.

"Sometimes you love him to death."

She gasped, and I thought she was going to cry again, but then she looked at me like I was the wisest man on the planet. That was a laugh when I didn't know what a Sazerac sling or

Down's syndrome was, but I guessed it meant retarded. Drooling. Flippers. Pee smells. The short bus.

"It's okay, Robin," I said. "I understand, really. I won't tell anyone."

I did understand. It was risky for Wolverettes to have retards in the house.

"That's why I had to tell you. When you read that story, Rick, it was like you were reading my story. It felt like . . . it felt like you were inside me."

We were both backing away from that disaster when the bell rang.

At the end of speech class, Wegner asked me in front of everybody to come to his office during B lunch. Miss Schuette was smiling behind him to let me know this was a good thing.

The cramped Performing Arts Office was tucked under the auditorium stairs, so the ceiling sloped like a ski chalet. Beyond the teachers' desks was the AV closet. Seeing two spring musical posters on the wall, *The Sound of Music* and *You're a Good Man, Charlie Brown,* reminded me that my records might be ganging up on *Company* at home. I vowed to go all the way back to *A Chorus Line* and patch things up. I cleared my throat. Mr. Wegner emerged from behind a rolling cart with a filmstrip projector on top. He seemed skinnier up close, and his hair was greasy, a total sin in the seventies.

"Richard—or do you prefer Rick?" he asked.

"Rick, I guess. I don't care."

He pointed me into a chair. An eyetooth crooked forward like a piece of candy corn. "Have you ever thought of joining the speech team, Rick?"

"No. What's the—"

"The reason I ask is that your oral interp on Friday was very successful. You connected to 'The Scarlet Ibis' and communicated that to your audience. Miss Schuette and I both had the same idea about getting you on the team."

I had no activities. If speech team emanated from this office, then it was like drama club or swing choir. The kids who did these things were called "play fags," as defined a group as the jocks, the socialites, the burnouts, and the Jesus freaks.

"Not if it's like debate," I said, acting as if I knew something about it. My father's debate skills had gotten him a scholarship to a business college in Washington, D.C. Wegner said no, speech team was more creative than debate, another alarm bell. Creative boys had feelings, or boys with feelings were creative. Whichever way, there weren't enough of them on the team.

Mr. Wegner explained that there were nine events and that the team rehearsed after school and went to tournaments on Saturdays. If, for example, I read "The Scarlet Ibis" and practiced two more short stories, I could compete in Prose Reading. If I read poems out loud, that would be Verse Reading. In the partner events—Humorous Duet Acting and Dramatic Duet Acting—two students got up and performed a scene from a comedy or a serious play. An Original Orator gave an eight-minute speech about a national problem. Here Wegner mentioned a senior who had won third place in the state the previous year for his oration on teen suicide. I nodded and agreed that suicide was a problem.

The closest thing to debate was Extemporaneous Speaking; an extemper drew a question at the tournament—Should Congress restore the draft? Should the United States change its policy toward the Philippines?—and then had an hour to make up an original speech to answer it. Insane as that was, extemp sounded less terrifying to me than Original Comedy, which was eight minutes of telling jokes. The two most famous alumni of Wheaton Central High School, our rivals up Naperville Road, were the football player Red Grange and John Belushi. Less well known, said Mr. Wegner, was that in the late sixties John Belushi had been state champ in Original Comedy two years in a row.

Miss Schuette came in and put her hand on my shoulder. I smelled egg salad in her lunch bag.

"So, Rick. Are you going to join us?"

I was her success story. That was okay, even though I had no school spirit and still couldn't picture speech team. Kids talking for trophies?

"I only know 'The Scarlet Ibis,'" I said. "If you gave me two more stories to read, Miss Schuette, I'd think about it."

Mr. Wegner and Miss Schuette looked at each other.

"We have two strong prose readers already," said Wegner. "Ellen Bintz and Cheryl Ito."

"Oh. Well, I'm not smart enough to make speeches in an hour and I don't know any jokes."

"That's fine, Rick," said Miss Schuette. "We have extemp speakers, and Joe Bacino has a wonderful original comedy."

Joe Bacino, star of all the school plays, was as fat, hairy, and out of control as John Belushi. I didn't want to be like him either. We all looked at each other. The left side of Wegner's neck was a skid of oatmealy bumps, zits long scarred over.

No strings good times just chums company.

"Chuck and I . . . Mr. Wegner and I thought you should try D.I."

Wegner hadn't mentioned D.I. It sounded like something the March of Dimes collected for.

"There's H.I. and there's D.I.," Wegner said. "Humorous

Interpretation and Dramatic Interpretation. It's like duet acting except you play both parts. Sometimes you play even more parts."

"I don't get it," I said.

Miss Schuette jumped in. "It sounds kooky, Rick, but you shift from one character to another. You play Romeo *and* Juliet and shift back and forth—"

"I'm not playing a girl."

"Bad example. It's more like Dr. Jekyll turning into Mr. Hyde and then back, over and over. Watch me."

Miss Schuette demonstrated. A lady with a Southern accent started an argument with her daughter Laura about cutting her typing class. Miss Schuette turned at the waist and rotated her head a tiny bit when she switched characters. Laura's voice was breathy, higher than her mother's, and she was taller, because her eyes looked down when she talked. The mother's shoulders sagged and she moved her arms more. It was the definition of schizo.

Miss Schuette broke off with a "Ta-dah!" I asked her who won the argument.

"Argument?"

"Between Laura and her mother."

Miss Schuette had sucked me in, and she knew it.

"It's a draw, Rick. The mother—her name is Amanda Wingfield—drops the business college idea because Laura's ashamed of being a cripple. But Amanda refuses to let her think she's crippled. It's from a beautiful play called *The Glass Menagerie.*"

That made three cripples. Doodle in "The Scarlet Ibis" and Robin Baver's brother Dave and Laura the typist. I thought about typing, the one class Carla wasn't flunking. And my

32

mother had typed Carl's psychology dissertation when they were dating.

"But you have to memorize the lines," I said.

"That's the easy part, Rick," gushed Miss Schuette. "And you never forget them. I went all the way to nationals with *Glass Menagerie.* It was the most wonderful year of my life."

"Rick was referring to himself," observed Mr. Wegner, reeling me in.

"The only play I've read is *Julius Caesar* last year in Intro to Lit. And I didn't understand it really."

They looked at each other again.

"We have a cutting—"

"He means a scene," Schuette interrupted, "one we think you can do to help out the team." She opened a blue folder on her desk.

"For this scene," said Mr. Wegner, "I want to tell you that you're going to have to get your parents' permission to perform it."

"My dad lives in New Jersey," I mumbled.

"Your mother, then."

I shrugged—piece of cake—trying to outrun the blush. Divorced kids don't like to have to point it out.

"It's from a play called *The Boys in the Band.* It's controversial. It's about a group of homosexual men," he said. "They live in New York City."

I stared again at Wegner's bad skin, smelled egg salad, heard kids shout in the hallway. *I could understand a person if a person were a fag* was a lyric from *Company,* from the song "You Could Drive a Person Crazy," the fourth track on side A, between "Sorry-Grateful" and "Have I Got a Girl for You." It was also my *favorite* song from my *favorite* album. In that moment, I let myself have a favorite. I took a deep breath to test how that felt. It felt electric purple and red-orange, not scary at all.

"Cool," I said on the exhale.

Wegner handed me three stapled mimeo sheets. I folded them into my math book. He told me to read the scene and give him an answer after I got permission.

Joe Bacino was standing outside the door holding a rubber dagger and a bunch of plastic grapes. He gave me a funny "Who are you?" look. I announced that I might be on the speech team and dashed away.

∽∾

My mother was ironing under the basement stairs. The finished shirts were hanging on a cord that stretched from a bolt in the crawlspace wall to a nail in a strut. She used to say she liked to feel like the old woman who lived in a shoe when she ironed. I didn't know what that meant, but when I was a little boy I loved tucking myself under the board and smelling my father's clean shirts while she rocked on her feet listening to the portable radio.

I explained the mechanics of speech team and Dramatic Interp as I understood them. She was thrilled, predictably, that I would have an activity. Her own face was plastered all over four volumes of her yearbook: volleyball, Spanish Club, Nursing Club, chorus. The content of *The Boys in the Band* didn't seem to perturb her.

"Do you know what homosexuals are?"

"Duh," I scoffed. My father had covered sex with me back in fifth grade, failing only in clarifying how the penis found its way into the vagina while both the husband and the wife were sound asleep. Homosexuals were old and prissy, like Paul Lynde.

"What do you wear to the tournaments?" she asked, digging at a cuff with the tip of her iron.

"I dunno."

"A suit? Or a sports jacket and tie?"

"I said I don't know, dammit."

"Don't take my head off, Rick," she said calmly. "I'm sure you're supposed to look nice. Be sure and find out, okay?"

"So I have your permission?"

"If Mr. Wegner feels it's appropriate, then you have my permission. You go to a good high school, son. That's why we live here." She sprinkled water on a sleeve like she was salting potatoes. "One of the characters is married, you said?"

"Alan is married to Fran, but Michael, the other character, is a homo. Alan and Michael went to college together, and Michael has always thought Alan is a homo too. But because Alan calls his wife on the phone at the end of the scene and they get back together again, it turns out he's really not a homo. It's from the sixties."

"And you play both parts?"

"Alan *and* Michael. Weren't you listening?"

She set the iron on its heel and crossed her arms. She looked me up and down, frowned at my shoes. A frosted side curl flapped loose from her cheek like a fishhook.

"You're going to need a suit for your father's wedding."

"I wasn't invited."

"Funny funny."

"He met her at a *party*."

"He met me at a party too. Parties are where people meet people."

"You were a nursing student." She had dropped out to marry him, but she said they all did that back then.

She moved to touch my arm, but I stepped away from the board. Her index and middle fingers rubbed together. She hadn't had a cigarette since she was pregnant with Lisa. She salted another sleeve.

"It was a mixer nevertheless. Promise me one thing, Rick. Promise me you won't get drunk."

"I haven't been invited!" I protested. I drank seven glasses of champagne at my mother's wedding. Our Ginger Creek neighbor Mrs. Lucia nursed my hangover while my mother and Carl went on a glamorous honeymoon weekend at the Wisconsin Dells.

"Carla drank more than I did."

"Carla didn't throw up in Mrs. Lucia's roses."

I flicked the cord with my finger. Carl's cheap shirts swayed on their hangers. Ten feet away was a playground of porn my mother didn't like to think about. She was also too naive to identify the pot smell reeking out of the rec room Carl was building for Carla at the other end of the basement. Carla toked there between breakfast and the bus stop.

Too late now to tell my mother these things. After they separated and my father got himself transferred back to New Jersey, she'd had her pick of the rich single Chicago men Rhea Lucia and the Ginger Creek gals fixed her up with. She said they were too old, so she joined this group called Parents Without Partners. Because she was beautiful, with only one kid instead of four or five, the men were on her like flies on shit. Every weekend I stood in a hamburger line with other sunburned kids tricked into a picnic. The dads were always throwing the balls too hard. It was at Potowatomie Park that she met Carl Schwob, supposed handyman with dyed hair and a pipe and a psychology dissertation that needed typing. Another great advantage, she claimed, was his potential to earn sixty dollars an hour in private practice. That hadn't happened. He evaluated drunk drivers for the Illinois Highway Administration. If he thought they could stay sober, he let them have their licenses back. He was an all-around huge mistake, but no way could she admit it.

"Why do you iron his shirts when they're polyester?"

"They're cotton blends."

"They don't deserve it."

"Funny funny."

∾∽

I removed James Madison from his perch, and after some deliberation, William Howard Taft, and set them a foot apart on top of my dresser. They would be the focal points for my Dramatic Interp. When I was Alan, I would look at Madison. When I switched to Michael, I would turn my head and talk to Taft.

I guess I had a "collect 'em all" personality. Every week in 1973 a four-inch president, from Washington in a blue and gold Continental Army uniform to Nixon in a gray suit and tie, went on sale for forty cents at the Jewel food store. On the shelf above the shelf with my miniature liquor bottles, the thirty-six chief executives lined up like beauty contestants on a set of molded Styrofoam risers, with four Greek columns notched into the back row for a more republican effect. I was the class shrimp in grade school, so Madison, the shortest president, was my favorite. Taft was the fattest, buried in a piano crate.

Mimeo sheets in hand, I began to read aloud. I yelled when there were exclamation points. In the scene, Michael accuses Alan of being queer and of sleeping with a third friend from college named Justin Stuart. Ten years later, at a birthday party,

37

he taunts Alan into calling Justin on the phone to tell him that he has always loved him. Alan denies everything but finally dials a number. "I love you," he says, and then Michael rips the phone out of Alan's hands and discovers that he's talking to his wife, Fran, and not to Justin Stuart. The scene ends with Michael apologizing over the phone to Fran.

Michael had most of the lines, so for him I used my regular voice. He was so nasty that I didn't bother going to the telephone cabinet downstairs to look up *sodomite* and *pederast* in the big dictionary. I substituted *asshole* and *dickhead* in my mind. For Alan, I pitched my voice as low as I could manage, which slowed me down. I couldn't use my hands yet, but after a couple of times through, I could sort of imagine doing this in front of kids from other schools. It wasn't sad like letting Doodle die in "The Scarlet Ibis," no one was going to cry, but there was screaming and the definite drama of bad language.

I never stopped to consider why Wegner and Schuette, strategizing in their troll-house office, matched me to *The Boys in the Band*. Michael was mean, but accusations like "You were in love with Justin Stuart!" and "You slept with Justin Stuart!" excited me. *Love,* and men *sleeping* together, not forcing their dicks into each other's mouths, were ideas that *Playboy* pictorials and *Penthouse* letters didn't accommodate. *Exclusive you, elusive you, will any person ever get the juice of you?* ran through my head, and I made another racy connection. *Company* was ready to go on my record player as a reward for my first D.I. rehearsal.

"Talking to your dolls?"

It was Carla, in from the cold, with her red cheeks and her cigarette-smelly jacket with the fake-fur cuffs. She called my presidents dolls, and my shirts blouses. I wouldn't give her the satisfaction of knowing how crazy that made me, but she knew anyway.

"Hey, this is my room, get out."

"What's that in your pants?"

"Get out!"

"God, is that a boner, Ricky?" she squealed. *Ricky* was another thing she knew I hated.

It was. I jerked the pages over my crotch, and she choked with laughter. When I moved to shove her out of my room, she shrieked at me not to touch her with my little boner. I slammed the door so hard the liquor bottles clinked and my presidents tumbled into the shag like it was the St. Valentine's Day massacre.

⚮

In two days I had the scene memorized, and Miss Schuette scheduled a coaching session for Friday. Waiting on a bench around the corner from the speech classroom, I watched a custodian polish the hall floor with a giant two-brushed buffer he could barely control. Now and then it would slip away, bump against a wall, and buzz off on another diagonal. I pictured it running amok during school, dragging kids through its brushes and streaking the floor with blood and matted hair. Then it would roar through the front door and chew up the line of Wolverettes practicing out on the lawn. It would shoot their green and gold poms through its gullet and into the air like a Roman candle, then zoom across the street to the Herrick's Lake parking lot and feast on Carla, too stoned to run.

I heard a strangled scream. I moved around the corner and peeked through the glass on the left side of the door to Room 100. Brian Tadder had a knife in his hand and was threatening

39

a boy I didn't know. They were shouting as Brian backed him to the wall. Then they suddenly stopped to look at Miss Schuette, who was at a student's desk. She said something and they took new positions. Brian sat down on two chairs pushed together, and the other kid moved right. Brian said something, whipped out his knife, and the other boy screamed again. Then I noticed that Brian Tadder didn't have a knife in his hand. His fist was holding air.

"They're late," a girl sighed behind me. "I'm supposed to give Ty a ride home."

She introduced herself, but I already knew who Mindy Kendig was, a junior so born-again she had album covers to prove it. Mindy was one of the seven Musical Kendigs, a Christian family that sang all over the world. Millie, Margie, Monty, Madeleine, and Mindy lived with their parents in High Knob in a huge house with a belowground pool. Mindy, the baby, played the violin, never wore pants, and got straight A's.

It was impossible not to find the idea of the Kendigs hilariously dorky, except Mindy was sweet and friendly to everybody, kissing lepers just like Jesus. I pointed into Room 100. "What is going on in there?"

"That's *The Zoo Story*. Dramatic Duet Acting. Brian has the knife now, but watch, he's going to give it to Ty and force Ty into killing him. It's a big surprise."

"Wow."

"They're really good. Last week they won second place in Elgin."

"You do speech team too, Mindy?"

"When I can, I do an original oratory on the Doomsday Clock."

She motioned with her violin case for me to sit with her on the bench. I was caught, for the first time, in a potential candid shot for the *Timberline,* our yearbook. I waved to the pyramid of Wolverettes out on the lawn in front of us. Robin Baver was in there somewhere.

"What's the Doomsday Clock?"

Mindy's eyes got as big as ten-cent gumballs. "Basically, Rick, time is running out. Wars, famine, poverty, disease, nuclear proliferation, Communism, the depletion of our natural resources, greed, and basic human nature are destroying the Earth."

"Wow."

A basketball sailed out of the open gym door, plonked on the window, and bounced our way. Mindy skipped to meet it, her wavy blond hair swinging in time with her skirt. The sweaty JV-er was pleased to have Mindy Kendig return his ball. Brian and Ty were shouting again in the speech room. This was after-school life.

Mindy sat back down. "The United Nations created the concept of the Doomsday Clock in 1960 as a warning. The planet has basically five minutes left to live, so my oration is a reminder to people that unless we take strong measures against these forces, it will all be over before we know it."

"Are there any solutions?"

"There is only one real solution, Rick," she said softly. "Jesus." She tucked her hair behind her ears, eager to hear my witness and save me from sin.

This was the thing, and no small thing it was. Birthplace to Red Grange and John Belushi, Wheaton, Illinois, the middle-class county seat of my adolescence, was—and remains—a center of American Christian Fundamentalism. The Reverend Billy Graham built his Faith Center on the campus of Wheaton College, where the students signed pledges not to dance, drink, smoke, gamble, swear, or fornicate. Their gooey piety dribbled down to the high school level.

There were hordes of Jesus freaks at Wheaton-Warrenville, some of them presentable like Mindy, others so far gone they sang hymns in the lunchroom and passed around pictures of aborted fetuses. Peer pressure to "let go and let God" got intense. Monday homerooms would hum with the news of who had accepted Christ over the weekend at Campus Life, an off-site club devoted to Bible study and persuasion through pizza. The image of arrogant football jocks collapsing in tears, or hip-huggered sluts crying out to be saved in somebody's family room, provided both grist for spoof and a scary warning for the suggestible. Jesus could happen to anyone in a flash, and did all the time.

As a nonentity, I had escaped the hallway zealots. Jesus wasn't my personal savior or my very best friend. Mindy blinked. I blinked. Finally she said that she and Mr. Wegner were in conflict over her oratory. Mindy knew that the ills of the world were but the selfsame devil with a gazillion faces and that letting Him into our hearts was the only way to turn back the Doomsday Clock, but Mr. Wegner preached the secular gospel of church and state separation. Jesus had to go. Mindy argued that America was founded as a Christian nation and was living in a state of advanced apostasy, but Mr. Wegner preached tolerance.

"So what are you going to do?" I asked, impressed by her vocabulary, if not her bind.

"If I can't bring Mr. Wegner to Jesus, then I'll just have to keep praying over it, Rick. The Lord will show me the way." She started jiggling her car keys.

Bring a teacher to Jesus? Students didn't convert teachers. I resisted telling her she was insane, because it was nice to be talking to someone out in the open.

"Do you have a coaching session now?"

I nodded. "Dramatic Interp."

"That's a freaky event." She giggled.

"I know."

"Ty is going to make me late."

"Should we go knock on the door?"

"No," she whispered. "Baby Christians need lots of attention. Or they backslide."

"Ty? I didn't know," I whispered back.

"Two weeks ago at Lisa Halsey's. Oh, Rick, to see a young man like Ty cast away sin and make His spirit indwelling is a precious miracle, a harvest of hope, oh let us praise Him," said Mindy, running her words together like a syrup. It was creepy to hear her call Ty a "young man" when they were the same age.

"What sin?"

"Ty Vandenhoop was an habitual user and abuser of marijuana cigarettes until two weeks ago."

I had to laugh. I couldn't help it. She sounded like a nurse in a drug movie. Stung, she leaned away and let her hair hide her face. To make amends, I told her I wished she could convert my stepsister, who was a total burnout.

"What's her name?" asked Mindy, without enthusiasm.

"Carla Schwob."

She yanked my arm and I cracked my head against the wall. "I know Carla!" she cried.

"You do?" I couldn't see how that was possible.

"Carla Schwob is my tormentor. She whipped a soccer ball at my head yesterday in gym class. I have a bump right here."

Mindy was patting a place above her right ear. As she stood, her purse got caught on the neck of her violin case and knocked it onto my feet. "This is incredible! This is God at work!"

"Huh?" I said, bending over to pick up the case. My own bump was starting to throb.

"I was praying for her only last night, praying for her to come to know Jesus. She's in so much pain, Rick. She needs to be rescued from her prison of pain."

"She is not *in* pain, Mindy. She's a pain in the ass."

"All pain is a prison, Rick. She is calling out. Oh, the Lord has answered my prayers by having you and me meet here today. God is so good!"

In five minutes, Mindy had my phone number and was floating out to her car with a sheepish-looking Ty Vandenhoop, plotting her next mission impossible: Carla Schwob's soul.

◦◦◦

That night my mother and Carl went bowling with the McClellans, Carla slimed out the door with Steve, and I put Lisa to bed. Before I went to my room to start the party with my records, I removed the pink carousel of Ortho Novum pills from Carla's top bureau drawer. Reading the prescription in reverse on her mirrored dresser tray, which was dusted with incense ash, I considered throwing the pills in the garage trashcan. That way she'd have to ask who took them. Then I toyed with flicking a few off the windowsill or down the heating duct to muck up her cycle, but thinking it through, I worried that she might conceive and hatch a flipper-finned cripple that I'd have to babysit.

In the end, I stuck to my original idea and slipped them under my mother's pillow. I got results, but not as planned. In the middle of the night, the light went on in my room and Carl pulled me out of bed. "You think you're so smart, you think you're so damn smart," he kept shouting until I was fully awake.

I fell back against the wall and slid down to curl into a ball. When my eyes adjusted to the light, I could see that he was naked except for his tightie whities. My mother appeared in the doorway and cried, "Don't you touch my child." Carl pointed his dead fingernail at her and thundered that this was his house, that I wasn't worth hitting but if he wanted to he could put me through a wall. He loved to say he could put people through walls.

Above his waistband, on his hairless, farina-colored food bag, I noticed two new disgusting things. Instead of a small oval, his belly button was big, circular, and grayish. It looked like a cross-section of a dead hot dog. Even worse, four inches west, over in the appendix area, hung a long, red skin tag. On each of his breaths, it wiggled like a kidney bean. I thought of him mashing it against my mother under the covers, and the gorge rose at the back of my throat. I spoke to push it down.

"What did I do?"

The pill carousel cracked against the wall. Carl crossed his arms and waited. It was weird how all the hair was sheared off his calves. My mother went to him, the hem of her black chiffon nightgown grazing his knees, and I realized they had started to have sex when they discovered the pills. That meant there was a rubber ring smeared with jelly stuck up inside her. I closed my eyes.

"What a sneak you've turned out to be," said Carl.

"Me? I'm not the one on birth control."

She had been with us for two months, but it was clear that Carla, stoned and shruggy, queen of detention, thrower of soccer balls, rec room and Renault recipient, could do no wrong, and I could do no right. If anyone had cared enough about me at the time to ask why I hated him, I would have said it was because he was a hypocrite.

"Beware the green-eyed monster," Carl intoned.

I looked up at this taunt, but closed my eyes at the sight of his skin tag winking at me. "You think I'm jealous of that slut?"

"Could anything be more obvious, you sneak?"

"You tell me, Dr. Schwob."

Carl took a step forward, and it was one of those times I thought I could smell him. He smelled like a sack of wet, fermenting leaves. My mother pulled on his arm and said I was her child and she would handle things her own way. I hummed my escape, *Phone rings door chimes in comes company,* until they left my room.

As I tried to get back to sleep, I could hear my mother crying through the wall. That made me feel rotten, but only up to a point. The court documents would later describe "a rapidly deteriorating home environment," a tasteful, nearly neutral phrase.

3

The morning after the Ortho Novum standoff my mother and I drove to Yorktown. I needed a suit.

My coaching session with Miss Schuette had gone well. First she gave me a real telephone so I could test its weight and remember how I held it when I made Alan's call. Then she took it, and I practiced being Michael snatching it away. Then she pushed the phone aside and had me mime picking it up, dialing, and holding the receiver to my ear. Finally she chalked two X's on the back wall of Room 100, closer focal points than Presidents Madison and Taft, and told me to go ahead.

About the dialogue she had little to say, except to interrupt once and tell me to pronounce *pederast* like "ever last," not "Everest." She also wanted me to pitch Alan's voice even lower, so the second time through I pretended I was my father making a presentation to the National Association of Dairy Farmers—which was what he did sometimes.

She clicked a stopwatch to start the third run-through. Eight minutes was the D.I. time limit. At the end, when Michael says to Fran "My love to the kids" and hands the phone back to Alan, Miss Schuette jumped up from her seat. "Why did you do that?" she exclaimed, clapping her hands.

"Do what?" I said.

"Get that catch in your voice?"

"Catch?"

"The little sound you made in Michael's voice at the end, as if he was going to cry—was that on purpose?"

"I'm not sure," I stammered, tugging my sweater down. I was worried I had a boner.

"What do you think Michael is feeling at the end of the scene?"

This was a terrible question, as bad as "What is the theme of this poem?" in English class. Miss Schuette's fingertips were resting in a point on the tip of her nose, like she was praying. I coughed to gain time. "Uh . . . I think he's upset, because he's lost the fight. He's wrong about Alan . . ."

"Go on," she said, flapping her cardigan open like she was starting a striptease. The light panels above us started to buzz.

"And so he's sad, maybe, because he's not ever going to have kids, and Alan gets to go back to being normal with Fran. . . . Is that all right?"

It was more than all right, she said, it was *interpretation*. I would go straight into the lineup for the Oak Lawn tournament. Her answer, when I asked her what boys wore to compete in, was a smiling threat. "I'm not like other coaches, Rick," she said. "I'm not going to pretend that speech team is about getting comfortable with public speaking and that it doesn't matter what you wear. It does matter. I dressed to win, and I won. Champions wear suits, Rick. *Not* pants and sweaters, *not* sport coats with sweaters, but suits with ties."

My mother let me listen to WLS on the way to Yorktown, a pacifier for the baby who'd tattled about Carla's pills. She had nixed Oakbrook and Fox Lake, claiming their anchor stores weren't nice enough. Neither of us needed to say it, but it felt like my father was with us in the car. It was his job to buy his boy a suit, and I would be wearing it to his wedding, and the Yorktown Mall was close to our last house, the Ginger Creek Tudor with a center hall, a circular driveway, sixty-foot trees, five bedrooms for three people, and a master suite with walk-in closets and double sinks. After my father left, I lived there alone with my mother for fifteen months, the male mascot in a sorority house for Mrs. Lucia and the other wives, some divorced, some not, some on their way. This wasn't Women's Lib; they came over with Sara Lee and wine and craft kits—plaster figurines to paint, papier-mâché angels to build, pine boards to age with screwdrivers and sandpaper, colored glass to wrap with lead and solder into window ornaments, shadow boxes to fill with beads and dried flowers as they listened to Dionne Warwick albums and Carole King's *Tapestry*. That's when I learned to mix brandy alexanders and grasshoppers. Mrs. Hetzel, teaching me the box step one Sunday afternoon, wondered once whether I wouldn't rather go outside and play with her boy Kurt. I said I was perfectly happy right there. "Did you hear that?" she kept repeating. "He's perfectly happy." After that she called me Perfectly Richard. My mother lost touch with the ladies after Carl. I recall the tight mask of her face the day she opened a box of hand-me-down baby clothes for Lisa sent from Ginger Creek, as far-off and foreign now as the Philippines.

I wanted to check out Chess King, but my mother insisted on Madigan's, a fancy store where the sweaters on the tables rustled with hidden tissue paper. My choice was a pale green cotton gabardine—her term—with wide notched lapels, baggy bell bottoms, and a six-button vest. In it, I felt like one of the crap-shooting strutters on the cover of my *Guys & Dolls* album.

But my mother was against it. She called it a zoot suit, a demeaning rhyme that offended my ears. Her finalist was in slate blue wool, a Nino Cerruti, with cleaner lines—another unfamiliar term—and a four-button vest. Nothing happened when I put it on. I looked like a turtle, I looked like a guidance counselor, I looked like every four-inch president from Woodrow Wilson to Nixon. I stood on a platform in front of a three-way mirror, and we discussed it while I snuck glances at the back of my head.

"It has a lining, Rick," my mother said, lifting up a side vent to show me a flag of white and blue striped silk. "Feel this."

"I'm not wearing it inside out."

"The zoot suit is unlined. It's *shiny*. It's just not the same quality at all."

"Stop calling it a zoot suit. It sounds gross."

"Trust me, I'm an old lady, that's what they're called."

"I look like a businessman in this."

"Well, in the zoot suit, you look like a—"

"Like a what?"

"Like you're trying too hard."

"Too hard to do what?"

"Never mind. This suit can go more places, Rick. You'll get more wear out of it."

"Yeah, but I'm the one wearing it. This one is boring."

Left unspoken was the $119.00 printed on the glossy tag tickling my fingers, a fortune, more than half a child support payment, the most ever spent on me for any one thing. I didn't know where the money would come from or what Carl would do if he found out. The zoot suit was only $74.00.

The cords in my mother's neck suddenly stood out like umbrella spokes. She was making an awful face.

"What is it, Mom?"

"Oh, honey. You're handsome."

"What?" I said, feeling a spike of dread.

"You were a darling little boy, but now you're a handsome young man. You look like your father."

"Mom, would you stop?"

"You've been hiding out under that hair."

"I'm not cutting it."

"Did Miss Schuette say you needed a haircut?"

"Let's pick a suit."

"You're growing into your father's face. You've got his eyes, and his chin. The girls better watch out."

"Stop it, Mom. I told you!"

"You could be in a catalog."

I stomped hard on the platform to shut her up. In the mirror I saw a shopper react to the noise. My mother had never made comments like this, *ever*. If you asked a stranger, or the Madigan's salesman, to describe me, this is what he'd say: straight brown hair, halfway down my neck, center part; caveman forehead, no eyebrows, big ears, short, squat nose, thin lips, watery blue eyes, pimple patches around the lower lip and cleft chin; aviator glasses listing to the right from a busted nose pad.

She was hugging herself against the mirror, her breasts squished between her arms. I thought of her nightgown brushing Carl's bare knees, her foot smacking the bed frame in Kentucky. It was like her compliments were a way of saying she wouldn't be able to protect me from Carl; from now on I'd have to rely on my father's looks to get what I needed. I suddenly didn't want any suit. I didn't want to be a champion; I could compete, or not compete, in clothes I already owned.

My mother sighed and shook out the green suit jacket in her hand. "Honey, you look good in both of them. But the blue one has more class." Pretending the choice was still mine, she rubbed the sleeve between her fingers as if she were soaping a stain and said under her breath, "Don't worry about the money, Rick."

"I'm not," I said through clenched teeth, wanting to hit her for guessing right.

She patted my arm. "There's a reason certain things cost more, that's why we came to Madigan's."

Because the Oak Lawn tournament was only a week away, the salesman said they would have to rush the alterations, even more money. But now I didn't care how much it cost her to retrofit me into Ginger Creek Rick, the boy I'd be if she and my father had stuck it out together, Perfectly Richard who might have had a shot at handsome. I left her at Madigan's to pick out a shirt and tie combination and limped over to Monkey Ward's to get album number fifteen. I'd hurt my foot on that platform.

～◡◡

The next day Carla tipped a bottle of fuchsia nail polish onto the den sofa, playing into my mother's hands. For three years she'd been itching to reupholster the green and sawdust plaid on Carl's faux Danish modern. It needed to match the lamp shaped like a Revolutionary War musketeer, the crewel-kit pillows of the Betsy Ross House and the Governor's Mansion in

Colonial Williamsburg, and the armchairs covered with drums and eagles.

Her good humor as she left for Jo-Ann Fabrics was infectious. Somehow Carla and I found ourselves playing rummy five hundred in the den. Steve was off shampooing Hannelore's carpet. Carla thought he was a jerk for caving in to his grandmother, but I told her he'd return from Martin Manor with enough money to buy the opal bracelet she wanted from Service Merchandise. Carla gave me a funny look, maybe wondering whether it was a good thing I kept track of what she wanted.

She beat me a second game, and I tossed her the *TV Guide* in a fake snit. Sunday TV always sucked: puppet shows, sports, westerns, and the lamest cartoons. She leaned over in the direction of the television set and placed a hand on the floor. Her breasts swayed heavily as she fiddled with the UHF dial, hoping to find a monster movie on Channel 32, and I felt a stirring in my crotch. Except for the turtleneck and hip huggers, Carla had assumed a standard on-all-fours porn pose. Suddenly realizing that she had a foxy body, I grunted with surprise. She turned to look at me, and her hair fell across her eyes. She shook it free and pursed her lips with a question—another cover of *Viva* look.

I wanted to stroke her tits, take her from below so her hair tickled my forehead and cheeks. I wanted to stand her against a barn in the sunshine, snake my hand between her legs. I wanted to arch back into a pile of hay as her lips grazed the hairs that started below my navel. I wanted to do all the things I'd read about in the basement, the things I was supposed to want to do.

"What?" she asked.

Her phlegmy voice killed my fantasy. I sat up and nodded at

the TV. Even allowing for the fuzzy reception, the screen was jumping to the shout of a hundred gospel voices.

"Keep this on." I said. "It's *The Jubilee Showcase*."

"Religion is dumb."

"No, this show's funny."

The Jubilee Showcase, broadcast live from a church in Chicago, was like tuning into a different country. Rows of black people in long purple robes clapped and swayed behind a line of four men growling into microphones. Sweat dripped from every face; hands pushed up into the air to keep the ceiling from caving in. Old ladies with big hats jumped in their pews, and little girls with lace doilies pinned between their pigtails freestyled their way into the aisle, their gloves like bouncing cotton balls on the ends of their arms. It wasn't church; it was like one of those cartoons where the natives dance around a boiling pot of explorers. "Oooga booga," I said, "oooga booga booga," and started to crack up.

"It's ignorant to make fun of black people," said Carla.

"Change the channel, then," I said, instantly ashamed.

She flicked a joker at the set. "That's just one of the hugely fucked-up things about Wheaton-Warrenville. No black kids."

Like the show, her comment was from another country. There was no way to predict what having more than two black students would do to my high school, but it couldn't be good.

She began a game of solitaire. "We had a church like that down the block. Everybody was always happy coming out all dressed up. Dressed better than the honkies, that's for sure. Those men were *fine*. I caught shit for going to a funeral there in sixth grade. It's so goddam boring here, all these stupid trees, you can't walk to the store, nobody's out at night, everybody's in love with Elton John or—"

"Who died?" I interrupted, not wanting her opinion of my music.

"My friend Rutina Mountain." She kissed the index and middle fingers of her right hand and touched them to her forehead. "Bitch had leukemia."

What did the gesture mean? What kind of a name was Rutina? How was *fine* different from handsome? Why was her friend a bitch? What was a honky exactly? It dawned on me that before Carla came to screw up my life on Kingston Drive, she had her own life someplace she liked better, a dinky brick row house in Calumet City, part of the total South Side tar pits maybe, but her home nonetheless.

On the TV a preacher was praising Jesus with hoarse, ragged inflections, like he was sawing a plank. "Why did you come here, Carla?" I asked. I wasn't being mean. I hated Briarcliffe trees because they weren't big enough. Carla hated trees, period.

She shook her hair back again and began to tug at the bottom of her turtleneck. I cleared my throat as she ran her fingers along the waistband of her jeans. Then she jerked up the turtleneck.

Three inches above her navel were letters cut into her skin. R E G I. The delicate pink scars floated on her abdomen like the threads of coral in one of my mother's bracelets. "Oh my god," I breathed. "What is that?"

"It's my boyfriend's name. You can touch it if you want," she said.

I shook my head.

"I used one of Regi's knives. He cried like a baby when I showed him. June fourteenth was the last day I got to see him."

"You're here because of—that?"

"Well, there's that, sure, everybody freaked, but it's more be- cause Regi got caught robbing a 7-Eleven. My dad told the judge he'd take me out of Calumet City and raise me if they dropped the charges."

"You committed a crime?" I asked, impressed.

"I dropped a Slurpee to distract the cashier, no huge big deal. I was an accomplice. Go on, touch it."

She pushed out her stomach to meet my hand. I expected the letters to flame like burning ridges, but they felt more like celery strings.

I had a dozen questions. "Is Regi black?" came out first.

"No, but it wouldn't matter if he was, 'cause I love him."

"I thought you loved Steve."

She sucked her teeth. "God, you're a dork. Steve's—just Steve. He's a freshman for one thing."

"He sells drugs," I said, thinking that might add to his ap- peal. The rules had changed so quickly.

"Yeah," she replied indifferently, as much a queen in her own way as Robin Baver. The day Steve showed me the pot and pills he'd hidden in a tennis ball can, I almost threw up with nerves.

"Regi said I should date other guys. He doesn't get out of juvie until June of 1979."

"That's the month we graduate."

"That's right, and then we'll get married, and then we're going to Florida."

"Wow. Do you ever hear from him in—in juvie?"

"Not directly, which is better, 'cause they'd censor him."

"What does Steve think? About Regi's name there, I mean.

Carla brushed her solitaire game into a pile with her leg. She leaned back against her father's plaid sofa, drew in her knees, and began combing out the tassels on the gold oval rug with her nails. "It's not his favorite thing about me," she finally answered.

I tried to be blasé too. I untangled a tassel of my own and looked back at *Jubilee Showcase*. A group of white singers was on, seven beeswax tapers crooning in front of the purple-robed choir. They didn't pitch and rock. They swayed gently as they sang a sappy love song to Jesus.

Something looked familiar. Carla figured it out right before I did. "It's those goddamn Kendigs!" she screamed.

"The Musical Kendig Family," I shouted. "Millie, Margie, Monty, Madeleine, and Mindy!"

"Gross! I hate that Mindy, she makes me want to puke. 'Jesus loves you, Carla,'" she lisped. "'He holds you in the palm of His hand.' Look at all that makeup she's got caked on."

"She's in your gym class, right?"

"She won't even use tampons. She uses those mattresses. Like Marie."

I bit my tongue and looked at the TV. I didn't like Carla calling my mother by her first name. The camera had zoomed in. The girls wore matching white dresses with gold sashes, and their faces were shiny. Mrs. Kendig's long hair was braided on top of her head like a loaf of holiday bread, but her daughters wore theirs down. Monty, at the marimba, had a blow-dried bubble. Mr. Kendig held his microphone steady in front of his blond mustache, but his other hand was lashing the cord like a lariat. Singing harmony with her father, tears dripping down her cheeks, Mindy tapped a tambourine against her palm.

I couldn't hear the lyrics over Carla's retching noises. Because Mindy had been nice to me that one time, I thought I should defend her, but Carla had a dead girlfriend, the name of her fiancé carved into her stomach, and a police record. I listened to show tunes. I was starting speech team. I didn't know any black people.

The Kendigs finished. Everyone in the church fell into each other, kissing and hugging. The preacher shouted out a blessing, the organ roared into action, and the Kendigs and the blacks threw up their hands and started dancing in place.

I flipped off the television. "Carla?"

She looked at me sideways.

"I showed my mother your birth control pills, and she showed them to your dad."

I expected more than another roll of the eyes.

"Really. What did they say?"

"What did they say to you?"

She shrugged. "Nothing." Then she kicked me, but not hard. "Hey, stay the fuck out of my room, asshole."

"I will."

"What did you do that for, anyway?"

"Because I'm a dork."

"That's right, you are." She stood up and began to tuck in her turtleneck. "What do you want for lunch, dork?"

"I can make a sandwich."

"No, I'll make lunch."

She put some hot dogs on to boil, and I pulled a box of pizza rolls out of the freezer.

∽∾

Not until a boy with a yellow pick wedged in his Afro howled, "Nigger, let go my TOE!" and burst into tears did I understand just how weird speech team was going to be. The boy dropped his head to show he was finished and then bopped back to his chair, his knuckles knocking each desk he passed while the rest of us clapped for him. Nobody else in the Oak Lawn chemistry lab seemed to find his fit unusual.

Every room in the old-fashioned, brick-layer-cake high school was a pen of kids telling stories, reciting poems, doing scenes, speeches, or comedy routines. Each school entered two students in each event. In D.I. Stacy Granbur, a Wheaton-Warrenville senior from Arrowhead, was 14A, and I was 14B. Bulgy, with custardy skin and white eyelashes, Stacy was so famously diabetic she was allowed to eat candy bars in class. On the bus, she said her piece was from *David and Lisa*. I pretended I'd heard of it.

We had numbers so the judges wouldn't know which kids went to which school. I was going to perform *The Boys in the Band* three times, twice before lunch, once after. 8A, a skinny girl with braces and a striped dress, had started my first round, interping a woman and man called Abby and Eben in a scene from a play called *Desire under the Elms*. (I wrote the titles on my schedule sheet, as Miss Schuette commanded.) Abby smothered their baby with a pillow so they could move to California. It was scary, but not as bizarre as 26A, "Nigger, let go my TOE!" from *The River Niger*.

"14B."

I walked to the front of the room. I buttoned, then un-buttoned my suit jacket, wondering whether open or closed was better. Schuette hadn't weighed in. The suit itself was a hit; Mindy had gushed, and another boy on the team asked me whether it was Pierre Cardin. "Nino Cerruti," I mumbled. Then, shaking my hand as if I'd passed some test, he introduced himself as Eric Smola in a juicy radio voice. He was an extemp speaker; his wide, square briefcase was filled with issues of *Newsweek, Time,* and *U.S. News and World Report*. He confided, as if revealing part of a secret code, that *U.S. News* was the least biased of the three.

I turned to face my first audience. I pushed up my aviators, remembering Miss Schuette's warning never to touch them during a performance. From the Periodic Table of Elements on the back wall, I chose focal points: Li for Michael and Ne, at the other end of the chart, for Alan. The lady judge nodded to begin.

Later on, everybody would ask me whether I ever got nervous doing my interp. I always said no. The idea behind D.I. was to suggest the characters, not become the characters. It wasn't acting, Miss Schuette always said, it was interpretation. Nevertheless, suggesting Michael and Alan, I wasn't Richard exactly, and so I didn't get nervous. I only had to be Richard for twenty seconds, during the introduction Mr. Wegner had written for me:

Homosexuals are sad and lonely young men, and it is the lives of these men that Mart Crowley portrays in his tender yet dynamic play The Boys in the Band. (pause) *Alan has just left his wife Fran and has come to New York seeking help and consolation from his old friend Michael. When he arrives, however, he discovers a side of Michael he never dreamed existed.* (pause) The Boys in the Band *by Mart Crowley.*

I'd say it with the pauses, then, as coached, drop my head quickly, raise it slowly, find Alan's focal point, and begin.

Alan's voice cracked that first time at Oak Lawn when I pitched it down to say, "Mickey, I'm leaving," but I remembered the lines, and I didn't mix Alan and Michael up in the shouting match before the phone call, as I'd feared I might. My eight minutes were over fast. Reclaiming my chair, I could hear my pulse pounding in my ears. I wedged a finger under my collar and tested the heat of my neck. My mother had been right about wearing an undershirt.

22B went next, with a cutting from a play called *A Streetcar Named Desire*. Maybe because this girl was doing three characters, two sisters and a husband stuck between them, I had trouble following the action. One sister talked like a hillbilly, and the man spoke every line with his fists glued to his hips. A couple of times, switching characters, the girl adjusted her glasses; fright spun her eyes like marbles behind her big octagonal frames.

By the time she finished, I was sitting straight up in my chair. I was better than 22B. The *Streetcar* girl had set out from some other dark suburban house that morning; she'd gotten up, curled her hair, listened to WLS while putting on her prairie skirt, eaten cereal, said goodbye to whichever parent had dropped her off at School 22, and mumbled her scene on the bus just like I had. She'd filled out her critique sheets, found the chem lab, and was doing her D.I. But the difference between us was that I was better, *mine* was better. I would be ranked ahead of 22B, at least fourth out of five kids. Fourth place meant I would earn two points.

No longer an abstraction, like Jesus or democracy, points would accrue to me, and I had two more chances that day to get more of them. I would be ranked. I would have a tally. A first place in all three rounds would add up to fifteen points, a perfect score. That day's champions were still a mystery, nine top-secrets pinging through the halls of Oak Lawn High until they were unmasked during the awards ceremony. The thought of it knocked me out.

My first round finished with a scene from a play called *The Bad Seed* in which a mother forces her little girl to admit that she killed her friend Claude for his penmanship medal. The daughter, Rhoda, finally confesses that she pushed Claude in a lake and beat his hands with the heel of her shoe when he tried to climb back onto the dock. It was dramatic, but listening to a teenager talk like an eight-year-old girl creeped me out. I also couldn't imagine what was so special about a penmanship medal that you'd kill for it.

The judge wished us all luck and released us. Filing past her, I counted the five pink sheets on her desk—Dead Baby, Nigger Toe, me, *Streetcar,* and Dead Claude. I silently thanked Li and Ne on the back wall.

We had ten minutes before the second round. In the hallway, 8A turned to speak to me. "You were really good," she said.

"Huh?" I was focused on finding a bathroom so I could blot my face with toilet paper. Some pimples might have crested during my scene.

"*Boys in the Band.* Super duper," 8A said. Her braces were the rubber band kind, and her eyes were dark brown, almost black. Her striped dress was shinier up close.

"Thanks. I'm glad I didn't screw up any lines."

"It was very cool. You're not in my other rounds today. I checked already."

"Your scene was cool too," I said. "Especially when the guy sang 'California, Here I Come.' That was sad. I could never sing in front of people that way."

"Eben's a blast, all right." She smoothed her black bangs. "I'm Dina Demacopoulos. I go to Shepard."

"Where's that?"

"Palos Heights," she said.

I nodded blankly.

"South suburbs," she added.

I told her my name and high school, and said this was my first tournament. She said she hated me, and I believed her until she laughed.

Lunch in the cafeteria was nerve-racking. Schuette wasn't around to lean on, so I was a tacky Briarcliffe sophomore sweating inside a brand-new suit. Mindy made me describe my impressions so far. I turned scarlet and stuttered out something about how weird it was to wear a tie in a chem lab. When Joe Bacino ragged on Eric Smola for pointing out that my focal points were lithium and neon, I was able to edge out of the spotlight and eat my bologna and cheese sandwiches. "With mustard, please," I thought, tucking my mother's smiley-face note into my vest pocket. I smiled back at it, even if it was sad how my having an activity could make her so happy. I watched *The River Niger* guy dance on a table. His teammates clapped along, like on *Jubilee Showcase*. When he pushed his butt out, his olive leisure suit stretched like scuba gear. I think he was what Carla meant by *fine*.

Three hours later, Eric, a brainiac waiting on an early decision from Princeton, became the Oak Lawn Regional High School Extemporaneous Speaking Champion for his speech "Reducing Farm Subsidies." Clearly used to the winner's circle, he took his time getting to the stage. The head coach of Oak Lawn shook his hand and draped a silver medal on a red sash over his head. Eric turned to the front, looked out to his team, and lifted the medal to the level of his chin. The overhead light bounced off it like on an Olympics telecast, and I found myself screaming along with the rest of the Wolverines like someone had flipped a secret school-spirit switch in my back.

Ten minutes later, Mindy sprinted down the stairs for her third-place trophy in Original Oratory—the Doomsday speech—and gave the auditorium a heavenly million-dollar smile. I was checking out her trophy, a little gold man gripping a podium on a block of wood, when I thought I heard my own name amplified through a microphone.

The next thing I knew, the team was shouting and Miss Schuette was pushing me into the aisle. Everything was a blur, but I did spot 8A whistling through her fingers before the light and the heat of the stage hit my face.

∞∽∽

At the sound of my father's car in the driveway I snatched my trophy from the center of the kitchen table, where my mother had put it so that Carl would see it when he got back from his analyzing drunks. I didn't want him knowing anything about it. She shot me a look as I slipped around her and out the front door.

"Give it up, Mom. It's too dark out for you to see her," I said.

"Don't sass. Best manners, now. Remember—"

"—who raised me," I finished from the porch.

My father got out of his powder blue Skylark and curled me into his left shoulder. He had already released me before I could decide whether it was good to see him. I had a habit of putting off how I felt about things until the last minute. I shook Julia's hand from the back seat and breathed in the scent of her hairspray. On the way to town, they relived the story of their romance but I was deep in the upholstery, watching the highway lights flash and gutter along the windows. I wasn't really listening. Courtship stories were just cleaned-up versions of *Penthouse Forum* letters. Maybe they had been introduced at a charity dinner for heart disease, but unless Julia wanted to tell me

64

how she could hardly fit her hand around my dad's throbbing uncut tool to guide it into her hole, doggy-style, I wasn't going to pay much attention.

I got a good first look in the Prudential Tower parking garage. I knew not to expect a hoop skirt, but I thought a Southern belle would have her hair up. Julia's was pulled into a knot at the back of her neck. She had almond-shaped brown eyes and a dimple on the downward slope of her left cheek. She looked too ritzy to have three kids. Stepping off the elevator, she dipped her shoulders to signal my father to slip off her coat, instead of gasping at the skyline like my mother used to do.

Like Jell-O 1-2-3, the revolving restaurant was a foodways fantasy of the 1970s, combining the awe of space travel with the slapstick potential of plates flying off tables. To dine at the Pinnacle was on the level of having tickets to *The Bozo Show* or watching batting practice at Wrigley Field. No child who'd eaten there let on at recess the next day that the Pinnacle's rate of rotation was two miles an hour, tops. I hadn't been there since my twelfth birthday, when I'd insisted on a cheeseburger. Now, as planned, I ordered jumbo shrimp cocktail and lobster thermidor. My father didn't blink. Lobster, my mother had taught me, was the ultimate edible.

The wedding was going to be a small ceremony in New Jersey, just family and very close friends, the week after Christmas, and Julia so hoped I would consider being a tremendously essential part of the party.

I fell for her finesse. "I would be delighted to attend," I replied.

"How wonderful, Richard," she drawled. The second syllable of my name came out "chud," and I liked it. "You know you have your father's exact chin."

"Is that going to be a problem?" I drawled right back.

When Julia excused herself to use the bathroom, I stood up before my father did, which she noticed. Beyond the oasis of ferns and dwarf palms dressing the center of the restaurant, the twin antennae of the John Hancock Center were beeping red in the mist. We sat down. My father's eyebrows were going salt and pepper. He was forty-four years old. I dragged some peas out of their sauce and tried to spear them with separate tines.

"What do you think, son?"

"She's pretty."

"She is. And she's a wonderful lady. We're very happy. She wants to make a good impression on you, Rick."

"Duh. Who's watching her kids in Kentucky?"

In the past, if I ticked him off in a restaurant, he'd summon a waitress for a flirt. He couldn't do that now. "Her mother, who is also a wonderful Southern lady."

"You like them with kids, don't you, Dad?"

My anger surprised us both. How long had I been waiting to say this?

"What do you mean?"

"Josephine. Julia. J names and lots of kids."

I wasn't supposed to know about Josephine the cocktail waitress. He clenched his hands. He pulled twice on his nose, as if the gesture might magnetize wifey-to-be back to the table. He drained an already empty tumbler. Another scotch was also out of the question—that was the road to Josephine.

"This isn't the fair time to discuss that, son." He pushed back his chair and bumped the lady behind him.

"Mom said you went to Josephine's kids' ballgames."

"If you'd had a ballgame to go to, I'd sure have gone," he

shot back. After third grade, I'd spent a miserable July in right field, begging after every practice to be allowed to quit.

"Look, son, Julia isn't out to be your mother. She only wants to be a friend to you."

His leap confused me. "What are you talking about?"

"No one is going to take your mother's place, son."

"Duh," I repeated, with heavier sarcasm.

"No one ever could," he said, pissed now.

I pretended to fish for a last bite of lobster. There was only white ooze clinging to the ribs inside the tail. The flip side of the family lore that I didn't talk until I was three was that I was utterly inconsolable whenever my mother left the room. I'd wail like a banshee until she came back from even a tiny trip to fetch clothes from the laundromat down the street. If my father tried to hold me, I'd scream louder and go completely rigid, like I was getting ready to back-dive out of his arms. He joked that his greatest terror was that I would wake from a nap when she was out of the house.

Julia, on her return (Perfectly Richud stood again), felt the tension. She turned to me, freed her bracelets from her forearms, and gave me a bright smile. "Tell me about school, Richard."

I sighed loudly. My father cocked an eye. She tried again.

"Didn't you have some sort of activity going on today? I remember wanting to spend more time with you, but your father said you were otherwise occupied."

Her attempt to engage, her acknowledgment that I was busy, released something in me. I realized that I couldn't wait for the big tournament that was coming up the following Saturday at Wheaton Central, couldn't wait to put on my Cerruti armor and do battle for another trophy, second place, first place. The only way to manage my excitement was to make speech team seem like the most ridiculous thing ever, so I told Julia about the girl with the bad Southern accent, about Dina Demacopoulos's braces, about Mindy Kendig's geopolitical crusade, lithium and neon in the chem lab, and Eric Smola's hairy nostrils. Her laughter spurred me on. I imitated little Rhoda killing Claude with her shoe. I held a dessert fork behind my ear like an Afro pick and bobbed my head like the *River Niger* boy dancing on the lunch table. I told her my stepsister was a white trash slut and Carl's mother and sisters were Two-Ton Tessies. I said I called Carl Mr. Clairol because he dyed his hair. Then I asked her whether she made hominy grits, and how was she ever going to get used to Northern ways and winters when she moved up to New Jersey? Might I be Richard Alexander Lahrem, a Yankee Doodle boy at her service?

My father was choking with glee. I gave him a snide smile, wanting to make him aware that I knew I was putting out for wife number two. He reached for her hand. "I'll be there to keep her warm, son," he said.

"I hope you'll let me see your trophy," said Julia. She dropped two saccharine pills from a tiny silver box into her coffee. They hissed up into foam and disappeared.

"It's a crappy little thing," I replied.

"I'd still love to see it," she repeated.

"It's in my bedroom," I said.

It was not in my bedroom. My trophy was twenty yards away in the coat-check, sharing the left pocket of my parka with a tie and some crumpled toilet paper I'd used to dry off my armpits between rounds. We were traveling two miles an hour and would never get to it.

I looked over my shoulder to catch the waves in Lake Michigan, silver squiggles miles below that I imagined I could see. I pretended to hear them too, crashing on the rocks and piers. I was sorry I'd told Julia that I'd won third place. I hadn't taken my trophy so Carl wouldn't see it. I'd taken it so I could show it to my father, and he hadn't asked.

The next Saturday afternoon, as I was coming through the main entrance to Wheaton Central with Joe Bacino and Brian Tadder, I saw Miss Schuette's head bobbing left and right in a river of students. Spotting me, she charged.

"Rick, where have you been?"

"We went to Cock Robin for lunch," I stammered, holding out my shake cup, afraid that saying "we" might make Joe and Brian think I thought we were friends. It was enough that they'd asked me to go along. We got weird looks from some of the customers, but Joe said suits and ties were the best way to score with the Christian chicks from Wheaton College. He managed to flirt a ketchup packet out of a beanpole reading *I Never Promised You a Rose Garden*. I just laughed at the right spots.

"But your mother made you lunch," Miss Schuette said. "Joe, I hold you responsible."

"It's *Wheaton,* Miss Schuette," he said. "I've been going to Cock Robin since grade school. We're not late or anything."

"Well, Rick just made final rounds," she said.

"Huh?" I said.

She frowned at Joe. "You see? He could have missed finals because he was hanging out at the Cock Robin."

"Did I get in?" asked Brian. Miss Schuette shook her head, patted his shoulder, and told Joe that Original Comedy hadn't been posted yet. Then she grabbed my arm and dragged me down the hall. Joe fell in behind us, and I heard Brian wish me good luck.

At the base of a big staircase in the center of the school, a crowd of kids enclosed by two stories of glass windows pulsed like bugs at the bottom of a beaker. Everyone was pointing up at giant sheets of white paper taped overhead. Messages from the speech gods, each sheet had the name of an event and a room number, followed by a column of numbers.

"Look, Rick!" Miss Schuette shouted over the noise. I followed her index finger past a girl who was sobbing into her hands, the wings of her hair flapping on every intake of breath. The third number under Dramatic Interp, 9B, was me.

The last of my milkshake swirled up in my stomach. "What now?"

"You do it one more time, Rick. You're up against the other five high scorers in the preliminary rounds. You go third, in Room 324, at one forty-five."

"What time is it now?"

"Twenty after. Did you bring a toothbrush?"

"What for?"

"Smile for me."

I bared my teeth.

"First I want you to go to the boys' bathroom and pick that food out of your pearly whites. And then I want you to call

71

your mother on the pay phone and tell her to come watch you."

"No way!"

"She's right down the road."

"She's busy!"

Miss Schuette was gnawing off her lipstick. "Tell her it's the *championship* round. She might not get another chance to see you compete until districts. You want your mother to be on your side every step of the way, Rick." She looked up.

"What are districts?" I asked Joe, but he was looking up too, watching a sheet of paper walk by above our heads. The crowd began to surge in its direction. The paper stopped. A rabbity-looking lady popped out from behind the sheet, flipped it over, and began sticking it to the glass with violent pulls on her roll of tape. It was Original Comedy. Joe gave out a war whoop and shouted, "I'm in, I'm in!" He put his arms around me and jumped us up together. He was taller, so my face fell into his shoulder. I squeezed back just a little as we landed.

When we broke apart, Miss Schuette whispered through spooky two-tone lips, "This sure beats Cock Robin, doesn't it?"

I nodded back, breathless myself. She dropped a dime into my hand and shoved me toward the pay phone.

Other than the sound of the judge's pen scribbling critiques in the back, Room 324 was dead quiet. There was no chatter between interps, and the putty-colored carpet in the foreign language classroom silenced twenty-eight pairs of feet. The desks were modern, with metal legs, blue kidney-bean-shaped tops, and headphone jacks. The left-side bulletin board in the front of the room had a French collage: wedges of cheese, the Eiffel Tower, a man in a beret, long breadsticks; on the right side was a Spanish bullfight poster. I wondered about German, but if I turned in my chair to look for swastikas and beer steins I'd see my mother, and I didn't want anyone to connect us. Walking into the room, she had taken her cue from my pained expression and gone to sit by the window.

First up was a startled-looking girl with hair as long and straight as Cher's doing a piece from *And Miss Reardon Drinks a Little.* Two sisters discuss what to do with a third sister who's going nuts. She's a teacher, and her students have begun taping signs to her back saying, "One of my tits is rubber" and "Please mount me." Then the teacher has to get rabies shots in the stomach for a feral cat bite. The Cher girl's "Nice pussy pussy, nice pussy pussy" sounded nastier than even the rubber tits line, and when she jabbed her belly with the rabies needles and said, "Pow. Pow. Pow," I wasn't the only one flinching.

The next interp was *Equus.* A stable boy named Alan rides around naked at night on horses, but he blinds them with a hoof pick because they watch him have sex with his girlfriend. At least I thought that was what was going on. Talking about the "hot cream" falling out of Equus's mouth, the bug-eyed redhead doing the scene got so worked up that he made his own white spit strands, which was completely disgusting. He fell to his knees at the end and started screaming gibberish. "Equus! Fleckwus! Neckwus!" Then he bugged out his eyes even more and whispered, "And the chinkle chankle never comes out."

I snuck a peek at my mother. She looked like the top had come off Lisa's diaper pail.

Third was 17A, a petite girl with huge, wide-set brown eyes. When called, she slowly stood among a circle of friends who fluttered like petals around her. I saw a Wheaton Central letter jacket on the back of one of their chairs, so she had home field advantage. Central was our rival in everything from football to show choir.

The girl was doing a simple scene about a girl named Willie, whose big sister Alva has just died of "lung affection." She talks to a boy named Tom while they walk the railroad tracks together.

This Property Is Condemned wasn't violent or sexy or mean. Dumb as I was, even I knew it was about death. I watched Veronica Satterwhite do it a lot that speech season, as we often went head-to-head, but I would always run away from it in the middle. It just got too sad. Willie was completely alone in the world. Her eyes would well up talking about Alva, whose boyfriends were the railmen, and I'd stop taking in her words and daydream about rescuing everyone. Veronica, Willie, Alva, Tom, I'd take them all on a trip to safer places—Yorktown, Cock Robin, Wax Trax, a record party in my room, anyplace but that lonely rail yard.

My mind would hook back in when Tom asked where Alva was now. "She's in the bone orchard," Willie would reply. Tom didn't get it, so Willie would say, "Bone orchard, cemetery, graveyard! Don't you understand English?"

Bone orchard. Bone. Orchard. The first time I heard those two words go together in Room 324, they exploded in my head like crossed sticks of dynamite. Skeletons in the trees. Skulls on stems. Apples in coffins. It was the first metaphor that *happened* to me. All season I'd wait for "bone orchard" and explode with intelligence every single time. Like Tom in the piece, it was as if I hadn't understood English until that moment.

Willie's last line in the scene was "It wasn't like death in the movies," and then Veronica would sing a few lines of Alva's

74

favorite song, "My Blue Heaven," swiveling her hips a tiny bit to suggest Alva's performance for the railmen. Veronica's voice would tremble, but she wouldn't cry. She'd blink hard, eyes wet, then drop her head.

That first time, everyone applauded until Veronica was all the way back to her chair. *This Property Is Condemned* was the best D.I. I'd seen in my seven rounds of competition. My mother was biting her thumbnail. She didn't know that I was next. The scribbling stopped. I heard a swish of paper. My critique sheet.

"9B," said the judge.

There was a charged pause. Who would that number be? Boy or girl, black or white, tall or short, cute or ugly, dress or pants, suit or sport jacket? I stood and walked toward the Eiffel Tower. I turned around and created focal points in the back of the room. There was nothing German on the wall. Wheaton Central didn't offer German, but Wheaton-Warrenville did. We were the better high school, and 9B was out to prove it.

The judge nodded. My mother smiled. I scowled for a second, then did my intro, making eye contact with three listeners. Then I lowered my eyes. This was a ritual gesture, something interpers did to focus whether they needed to or not.

I needed to focus. How to compete with the chinkle chankle? Or "My Blue Heaven," which had almost made me cry myself? At Oak Lawn, I'd gotten a first, a second, and a fourth in my rounds, eleven out of a possible fifteen points. Miss Schuette and I had reviewed my critique sheets. "You have a good presence." "Strong finish." "More vocal variety, please, for the Alan character." "Good concentration." "I want to hear *all* your words, Richard, even when you're shouting."

These criticisms were floating in my head, along with Miss

Schuette's last piece of advice at the door: "Remember to breathe." Head still down, I took a breath. The whiff of myself reminded me of the sharp, vinegary smell of Joe Bacino's pits when his arms were around me by the staircase. Joe was in his own final round, in another battle in another part of the war. He was comedy, I was drama, but we fought in tandem. Teammates. I lifted my head and began.

On the drive home from Central, the angel on top of the columned trophy flew between my legs like a giant silver boner. *Dramatic Interp Champion Wheaton Central H.S. October 30, 1976* was etched into a gold strip glued to the marble base. I wanted to be quiet and think about the word *champion*—a word never next to my name—but my mother wanted to know more about Miss Schuette, who'd sort of chewed me out as we were getting into the car.

The finalists had been called out backwards, like at a beauty contest: sixth place, fifth place, fourth place, etc. In D.I. the *Equus* boy finished last, which surprised me. *This Property Is Condemned,* which I thought was best, got only third place, so it was down to me and a black girl who'd done *A Raisin in the Sun.* The moment Central's head coach said over the microphone, "And in second place, from Luther High . . ." my teammates shot up around me screaming. I waited with my mouth open, a skull on a branch in a twisty tree, feeling thumps on my back and tugs on my sleeve, waited until I heard both Richard *and* Lahrem.

We were sitting in the front two rows on the far right of the auditorium. I stumbled to the short brick wall at the edge of the stage and held up my hand. The sudden cool of the trophy made me weave into Mr. Wegner. Above me, Joe Bacino held out his own champion's trophy to clink with mine like champagne glasses. I turned to hide in my seat and saw my mother standing near the back, jumping and whistling through her fingers like a Wolverette. I got a lump in my throat for having left her bag of sandwiches on another team's cafeteria table and gone to Cock Robin.

Ten minutes later, Wheaton-Warrenville finished in second place, six points ahead of Central. Joe and Eric Smola, our third champion of the day, were motioning for me to come onstage with them to get the team trophy, but I was too wiped out to move.

Kids stormed the parking lot. It was going to be Saturday night in a couple of hours. My mother offered rides, but nobody else lived in Briarcliffe. I had just opened the passenger door and pitched my coat into the back seat when Miss Schuette came over. I thought she wanted to meet my mother, but instead she asked me if I'd watched Veronica Satterwhite accept her trophy.

"Veronica who?"

"17A, Veronica Satterwhite, third place, Wheaton Central. You beat her, Rick."

"She was excellent," I said, then added "*This Property Is Condemned* by Tennessee Williams."

"You didn't act like you beat her."

"What do you mean?"

"Veronica Satterwhite walked all the way up onto the stage to get her award. Then she turned to face the audience, and then she smiled. She took her time. Did you notice that?"

"I guess not."

"Do you remember what you did, Rick?"

From the corner of my eye I saw Joe getting into the school bus, his trophy stuck under his arm like a pike. He and his

77

girlfriend, Beth Cook, were going to a rock concert in Aurora that night.

"I won?"

"You won, but you didn't act like it. You held your hand out at the edge of the stage like you were getting a Christmas turkey."

"A turkey?" What was she talking about?

"Like you were accepting charity. A handout."

"The steps were way over on the other side, Miss Schuette."

"Then you walk around to them! I don't care how long it takes, Richard, a champion takes his time. A champion gets up on the stage and acts like a champion." She pointed to the blue and gray tongue hanging out of my jacket pocket. "And a champion keeps his tie on."

By now my mother was out of the driver's seat and had come around the car. Miss Schuette put on a smile and said it was a pleasure and you must be so proud, Mrs. Lahrem. I didn't correct her and say the name was Schwob, and then my mother said how interesting the final round had been, all the children were so talented. Miss Schuette buttered her up by saying parental support was crucial.

The bus driver hit the horn. Miss Schuette closed her sweater around her throat.

"He's going to need another shirt and tie. The next tournament is an overnight."

"Overnight?" My voice cracked.

"A downstate overnight."

"Downstate?" I flopped into the front seat.

My mother gave me one of her looks. "Do you think he needs a hair cut?"

"Mom!"

The driver hit the horn again.

"Shirt and tie first," said Miss Schuette. The muffled cheers of the team inside the bus greeted her sprint. No one was ever going to pin a "One of my tits is rubber" sign on her.

"Your coach is intense," said my mother as we drove past the stone entrance to one more bogus subdivision going up on Herrick Road.

"I guess so."

"I'm glad she's taken an interest, but don't feel you have to do everything Miss Schuette says."

"Uh-huh."

"She means well . . ."

"Uh-huh." If I'd been listening, I might have realized that my mother felt threatened, but I wasn't listening. My mind was on the overnight part of the next tournament. Showers. Beds. Eric Smola. Brian Tadder. Ty Vandenhoop. Joe Bacino. My mother said I'd won first place because I was the best, but I believed it was because I had hung on to Joe's smell and feel while I interped Alan and Michael. That quick hallway hug with him *was* my interpretation final round.

As I raised the garage door, the happiness I felt shriveled under an onslaught of screams. Carl got overtime testing drunks on weekends, so my mother had left Lisa with Carla. She cut the engine and ran into the house.

Lisa was lying in the hallway, the purpled ball of her head rolling back and forth in a spill of toys and shards of a mixing bowl. There was blood on the tiles. My mother pulled a sliver of glass from Lisa's sleeve and lifted her out of the mess. Little pieces caught the light as they flaked off her Donald Duck overalls. Lisa screamed louder at my mother's look of horror, but she calmed down rapidly in the lock of her arms. The three of us were jammed in the powder room, my mother putting ointment on a gash in Lisa's hand when the front door opened.

"What the fuck," said Carla.

My mother rolled Lisa into my arms, and she started to cry again.

"Shhh," I said, leaning down to kiss her forehead. "You're just scared." I watched a thread of Lisa's blood rise from the cut and get caught in the slug of antiseptic jelly. I heard a slap, and then another and another. Carla didn't resist. In between blows, she said she'd only gone around the corner to Steve's to get something. She was gone five minutes. She just had to get something.

"Get what? Drugs? Sex?" my mother shrieked.

"Both," I whispered to Lisa, who inexplicably smiled through her tears.

∽∾

Sunday night Carl said there were two sides to every story. I took this to mean that Lisa wouldn't have gotten hurt if I hadn't called my mother to come watch at Wheaton Central. It was like the wings on my trophy had cut Lisa, not the glass. In the lunch line on Monday, I told Mindy about my champion's homecoming. Violence not being a feature of the Musical Kendigs' home life, Mindy's big blue eyes watered. Robin Baver swished by with her tray and said way to go, Rick. In morning announcements, Principal Dahlbeck recapped our triumph over Central and read out the names of the winners. Three people in homeroom turned around to look at me. Through half-closed eyes, I bobbed my chin like I was grooving to a Doobie Brothers song in my head.

The lunch lady handed Mindy a tray of pizza, applesauce, and green beans.

"Rick, do you think I'm plastic?" Mindy asked, a question out of nowhere.

I held up two fingers for two rectangles of pizza. "What?"

"Do you think I'm plastic? You know, fake. My second-round judge Saturday wrote on his critique sheet that my Doomsday speech had 'a plastic quality.'"

"What did he mean?" My finals judge had written one word on my critique sheet: "Outstanding." Miss Schuette said that was flattering, but not constructive.

"Mr. Wegner said he thought it meant 'not real,' or 'synthetic,' which is a nice way of saying fake. Fake like this pizza."

I looked at the oily brown crumbles dotting the cheese on the dough. Mindy sighed. "This isn't real meat, Rick. It's TVP. Textured vegetable protein."

"It tastes real," I said. "I like the taste." Pizza day was a big deal at Wheaton-Warrenville. Even the burnouts ate it, which was why the line was so long.

"It's soybean. The world is running out of meat. The world is running out of everything except plastic." She yanked a carton of milk from the cooler. "Doomsday is real, but guess what, I'm a fake."

"No you're not, Mindy. You're real too."

"Your sister Carla is real. Maybe if I wore hip huggers and swore at my teachers and"—she dropped her voice—"took birth control pills, I wouldn't be so plastic."

"She's my *step*sister, Mindy," I said, looking to the far corner of the cafeteria, where Carla was scooping bags and cans out of the vending machines. It was getting too cold for the parking lot. Where did the burnouts take their pizza in winter?

"God brought you together for a reason, Rick."

Now, that was too much. I told Mindy *that* sounded plastic and clomped to the speech team table, which was waving at me to come sit with them—another first, like the word *champion* and my name over the intercom. Brian Tadder flicked a vanilla wafer off the orange pancake stool next to him and said, "Your throne, my lord."

At the end of the day I apologized to Mindy outside the performing arts office. I took a deep breath and asked her over on Wednesday to study. It was a lame invitation, since she was a junior and took all enriched classes, but she said she'd love to. I saw Miss Schuette smile into her attendance book.

~~

Because she was beautiful and sweet, and lived in a house with a belowground pool, and had her own car, and had traveled the world with her rich and famous family, and was basically the Anti-Carla, Mindy Kendig's first trip to Briarcliffe felt like a home inspection from Suzy Snowflake.

I was in the upstairs bathroom when the doorbell rang. My mother yelled for Carl to get it, because her hands were sticky; she was making Chex mix for our guest. Carla was walled up in her room with Aerosmith and a bowl of leftover Halloween candy, and Lisa was asleep.

"Rick, you have a visitor," Carl called up the tunnel of the stairway, no sarcasm in his voice. He'd clearly gotten an instant whiff of Mindy's minty freshness.

I delayed my entrance with an extended Stridex session. When I came down they were all in the living room, and my mother, having wiped off the Chex crumbs, was explaining to Mindy that even though the living and dining room suites were Mediterranean, her main stylistic influence, since she was originally from the East Coast, was Colonial. Carl was tapping his pipe against his leg, waiting his turn.

"Hi, Rick," Mindy said. "Your house is super." She squeezed my arm, and my mother smiled at Carl.

"Yeah, I guess. There's no center hall though," I said.

"What's a center hall?"

It figured. The Kendigs were so rich, Mindy didn't know the signs of their success.

We never got around to "studying." My mother showed Mindy everything on the first floor, including the Betsy Ross crewel pillow and the side of beef in the second freezer, but what put her over the moon was the can of bacon grease on the back of the stove. She sat down at the kitchen table with a million questions: Where had my mother learned to cook with pork fat? Did she pour the drippings straight from the bacon pan into the can or did she wait for it to cool down? How many packages of bacon did the grease can hold? Did it ever get solid all the way through? Did she stir the grease before use? Did she strain out the petrified bits? Did everything taste better in it? Did I, Rick, ever cook with it? Did he, Mr. Schwob, ever cook with it? Did it ever go bad? Did it ever catch fire? Had it ever run out? Her most absolutely bizarre question was whether we ever put it on cuts.

Obviously, the Kendigs didn't keep animal fat on their stove. When my mother confessed that during her childhood in the Depression, her family sometimes poured bacon grease on cornbread and called it supper, Mindy had to have a closer look. My mother blotted the can with a paper towel and handed it to her. It was part of an old green canister set, and years of bangs from pans and spoons had scraped away most of the paint, but Mindy held it in her pretty white hands as if it were a casket of jewels.

She breathed in the aroma and didn't gag. "Praise Jesus," she said, bowing her head as she gently gave it back to my mother.

"I put some in the Chex mix," my mother remarked brightly, fumbling for something to say.

Mindy explained that Jesus had recently led her to study the many uses of oil in the Bible. Did we know that it was food, it was light, it was a purifier, an anointer, and a healer of the sick? She quoted from Luke's description of the Good Samaritan binding the stranger's wounds with oil and wine. She declared that our can of bacon drippings was another manifestation of His holy love. "God truly is everywhere," she sighed happily, our kitchen caught in her outstretched arms.

It was some explanation. I thought God's name would send Carl back to the booger chair, and my mother to the laundry room, but Mindy's unfakeable goodness had the four of us eating Chex mix and playing rummy five hundred in no time. The Kendigs didn't think it was a sin to play cards—not that we'd asked. They'd go nuts on the tour bus without rummy, it was the *gaming spirit* that went against God. That started my mother on the traveling angle and Carl on the money angle of the Musical Kendigs. Mindy said that they tithed ten percent of everything, and that their latest record, *Spirit Indwelling,* had sold two million units in the Christian market, and that they'd witnessed miracles in thirty-four countries. Carl had to ask her if they'd ever sung in Duluth, Minnesota; that's where the muskies ran.

His snooze-alarm lecture to Mindy about the wily muskellunge gave me the opportunity to test the boundaries of this good time. From the way she exaggerated the ups and downs of her cards and the many trips she took to the fridge to refill glasses, I knew my mother was on cloud nine. It was a *Redbook* pictorial: her son had friends, smart, pretty blonds who appreciated her decor and her stove-top snacks; card games could happen in her kitchen on the spur of the moment; her marriage was solid, she'd kept her figure, and she had a baby girl to love. As for Carl, I couldn't give him an inch, not even in the creepy canyon that opened up when he referred to me as "last week's champion."

The focal point of Mindy's visitation didn't emerge from the devil's den until 9:15. I hadn't forgotten Carla, even with Mindy portraying her midseason replacement in the chair next to me. I was just hoping she wouldn't show. My mother's happy expression died at the sound of feet on the stairs.

"Hi there, Carla!" chirped Mindy, like she was talking to a hand puppet.

Red-eyed Carla took some time stringing together Mindy, her father, the cards, and the puddled plate of ice cream sandwich wrappers. "Jesus Christ," she finally said.

"Oh, He's here with us too, Carla," said Mindy.

"What . . . the fuck . . . is going on here?"

Carl told Carla to apologize for her language, so I guess that was a start.

I walked Mindy out to her car. This time, instead of getting pissed when she said the whole family needed healing, I agreed with her. As she drove away, her headlights caught a neighbor's cat in the sidewalk. I whipped some lava rocks at it, then looked at the stars, wondering why we had all been put together in that particular house on Kingston Drive by God or divorce or whatever. Two doors down, Mr. Dudak came out on the porch to blow out the candle in their jack o'lantern. It was so wrong that we didn't have one. Carl said they were a waste of money. I sat brooding on the milk box until my butt froze.

Back inside, Carl was watching the news in the booger chair. I crept through the dining room to the kitchen to look at the bacon grease can. My mother was already there, bent over the stove, hands clasped between her legs, silently crying. She didn't see me.

∽⌣∽

My mother and I went back to Madigan's for a second shirt and tie. Repeating the four syllables of Yves St. Laurent's name as I pushed Lisa back and forth in her stroller, I didn't mind my mother bragging to the saleslady that I was going on an overnight speech tournament.

I'd gotten twenty dollars from my father for winning first place at Central. "Julia and I are both very proud of you, son," he'd written on office stationery from New York. The money was burning a hole in my pocket, so on the way home from Yorktown I had my mother drop me off at Wax Trax. The ability to buy two albums at once presented a dilemma. It could be asking for trouble—more time for the cashier to interpret the purchase, double the treasure for the Butterfield Road bandits to seize, and most of all, more grief from the rest of my records, who were upset that I was still going steady with *Company*.

The cashier was familiar. The customers were strangers. The untouchables section was empty, so I quickly got down to business. I savored Broadway A to M, then stepped to the right for N to Z. A tough chick called Sweet Charity was tempting me to buy her. Her right hip jutted out. There was a heart-and-arrow tattoo on her arm. "Please mount me," said the cartoon bubble I gave her.

"You can fuck the Music Man," I thought giddily.

I sensed someone standing across from me on the other side of the rack.

"Hello," said a man. "Show music," he said.

Sweet Charity could be deciphered from her back too.

"No, Jethro Tull."

I dumped Charity, grabbed my decoy, and started for a normal section of the store, but the stranger had already turned the corner of the aisle and was blocking my path. He had curly blond hair and a mustache. He came up right next to me and began flying through the I's. *I Can Get It for You Wholesale, I Do! I Do!, Irma La Douce, The King and I, Kismet, Kiss Me, Kate.* His indifference to them was mesmerizing.

Then, just as quickly, he stopped. "Do you have this one?" he asked, stepping left to give me a better view. It was such a surprising question that I dropped *War Child* without meaning to and said, "Not yet."

The midnight blue cover bore the design of a tree lit by a full moon. Hidden in its branches were drawings of naked women. There were also two couples posed like in a *Playboy* pictorial. In fact, it was like an entire issue of *Playboy* set in a tree. You might miss the bodies if you didn't look closely, but once you'd seen them, you'd never see just the tree and moon again. It was like one of those puzzles that the Campus Life kids carried around at school, a patch of math symbols that magically turned into a block-letter J E S U S if you stared long enough.

"This is a great album," said the man. A ring on his pinkie matched the yellow cursive script of the title—*A Little Night Music.* "The songs are fantastic."

"It's by the same man who wrote *Company,*" I said. I had been tempted to buy *A Little Night Music,* but ever since

Company became the crown prince of my collection, I'd re-sisted adopting a relative.

"Stephen Sondheim, that's right," he said, too loudly, as if he were saying "Neil Young" or "Ted Nugent." I wanted to shush him but he went on. "I think *Night Music* is better. It's more musically sophisticated." It also bugged me that the man didn't use the full title, like he didn't care enough. "On stage I'd call it a draw," he continued, "but then there's *Follies,* which was ab-solutely staggering. *Pacific Overtures,* on the other hand, was not for the masses."

As he handed me the album, my jaw dropped. "You mean . . . you *saw* them?"

He laughed. "That's right."

"Like in New York? You saw them in a theater?" This seemed inconceivable, or against the law.

"Live and in person, Richard."

"You mean, with the same people as on the record?"

He pointed to the three magic words in a little white medal-lion on the top left corner of the album. "With the Original Broadway Cast."

I was about to ask, in a whisper to set an example, what his favorite song from *Company* was, but then I registered the "Richard" and froze.

"I know your last name too," he said. "It's Lahrem. Richard Lahrem. Is that how you pronounce it—rhymes with 'harem'?"

I nodded. That was exactly what my dad said to waitresses when he signed credit card slips. "But how do you know my name?" He was too young for a Briarcliffe parent and too old to be a student teacher.

"Well, it's like this, Richard Lahrem Rhymes with Harem. I gave you first place last Saturday at Wheaton Central."

"You did?"

"Final round."

"No way." I looked at him. He had hazel eyes and a round chin that stuck out a little like a ping-pong ball, and a diagonal scar under his lip. His tan parka was open over a sweater with two bamboo toggles at the throat. "You're a teacher?"

"I teach at Glenbard West."

"That's in Glen Ellyn."

"I live in Glen Ellyn."

"I live in Wheaton. I go to Wheaton-Warrenville."

"I know. I watched you accept your trophy."

"What are you doing here?"

He laughed again. "I know this is hard to believe, Richard, but when school lets out, teachers buy records and groceries, and some of them see musicals in New York with their original Broadway casts."

"I was nervous, so I didn't look at you in finals."

"I understand, Richard. Or is it Rick?"

"Either. Thank you for the first place."

"Well, I got a look at you. You were outstanding."

"That's what you wrote on my critique sheet," I mumbled.

Flattering but not constructive. I wanted to put *A Little Night Music* down, but it wasn't right to mix it in with the S's. Telling a teacher, even one from a different school district, to move so I could file it with the L's wasn't right either.

The Blue Öyster Cult playing in Wax Trax suddenly cranked up super loud. The cashier felt as far-off as Iowa. The man flipped through a couple more albums—*Oliver!, On a Clear Day You Can See Forever, On the Town*—and repeated "You were outstanding, Richard." I suddenly wanted to be a boy who liked Blue Öyster Cult.

Then he lowered his voice to say, "And you were . . . excited."

I didn't know what he meant and said so.

"Doing *The Boys in the Band* made you excited. Like this."

He put his hands in his pockets and pulled his parka away from his body. His boner was like a speed bump pushing out the front of his soft gray corduroys. My hand cramped on the album.

His name was Edward Bolang, but I was to call him Ned. He'd grown up downstate on a soybean farm, near a town called Streator, the youngest in a big, extended family of farmers and schoolteachers. He went to Bradley University on a speech team scholarship, then worked as an actor in New York, doing mostly bus-and-truck before heading back to Peoria for a master's in education. He had been teaching at Glenbard West for four years. The scar on his chin was from a stone a plow threw up at him when he was eleven. I found Streator on a map once, but I never did the math on his age.

Ned was right. Although I had seen teachers get in and out of cars, I had never imagined them anywhere private but the faculty lounge. The first thing I noticed about Ned's apartment was the couch. The eye went right to it walking in. It was the brown of wet sand and had no resistance. A sit became a loll in seconds. If you fell onto it, the cushions would topple like slabs of a velveteen temple and bury you.

I'd be stretching the truth if I said the second thing I noticed then, and remember now, was a vertical stack of three pine crates across from the couch. They held Ned's records. When I realized what I was looking at that first time, I staggered back and smacked into the glass coffee table. Ned, pouring sodas in the kitchen, popped his head around the corner.

"Those are all . . . original Broadway cast recordings," I said, hovering between question and statement.

"That's my collection. Yep."

I kept my records in the order I'd bought them. Ned's abundance required alphabetization. The spines were gone on the most ancient jackets; others were split and flaked and hard to read. I hunted for the fourteen in my party, separated here by dozens of people I had never even heard of—grandparents, great-aunts, third cousins twice removed. Suddenly frightened by the size of the world, I found myself hyperventilating in the N's, stuck in the middle crate on a trio of titles called *New Faces*. The *New Faces of 1952* and the *New Faces of 1956* had to be old faces now, as dead and gone to the bone orchard as Willie's sister Alva. The newest new faces—of 1968—were new when I was in the second grade.

Ned, his desert boots planted in a speckled rag rug, held two glasses. "Would you like to sit down?" he asked. Still staring at the three-tiered treasury, I sank into the fuzzy brown couch. The cushion put static in my hair. My knees knocked my chest.

He said he'd been collecting musicals since he was about my age, so I told him I was fifteen, and he gave me a weird little army salute. He had 267 albums, which still wasn't all there were. He never passed up a used record store, and the super rare titles could be found in mail order catalogs. Rose Records in downtown Chicago had a great selection, and one special store in New York City carried *only* show music. I blurted out that I wanted to go, and he smiled. How I'd get there hung in the air. I shrugged myself out of my coat and pushed it to the far end of the couch.

While Ned went to hang it on the back of a chair, I hauled myself up and over to the window. His building was off the service road parallel to Roosevelt Road, a commercial artery that cut straight across all of DuPage County. I was amazed to see a familiar pink and turquoise neon sign just two lots away. "That's the Seven Dwarfs," I said.

After home games the popular kids went to Rascal's for onion loaf, and after Campus Life the Christians went to the Seven Dwarfs for chocolate-chip pancakes. I had taken my dad there once, but his mood turned when Del, our waitress dressed like Snow White, couldn't get him a scotch, this was a *fountain* restaurant. The yodel music gave him a headache, and he gave Del a hard time about his overdone steak. I ordered dessert, counting the times he looked at his watch.

"The Seven Dwarfs. Where the elite meet to eat," Ned said with a la-di-dah accent. He had whooshed into the other end of the couch, but he knew how to sit up straight in it. Explaining the rhyme, he brushed down the ends of his mustache and said it was a silly line from a famous movie.

"Oh," I said, feeling dumb. I sat back down, trying to grab my ginger ale on the way. I looked from his teeth to his sweater. Some blond hairs were curling over the top bamboo toggle. I failed on a second reach for the glass.

Ned lifted it from the coffee table. The water ring sparkled. "Happy, Sleepy, Sneezy, Doc, Grumpy, and Dopey," he said.

"That's only six. You forgot one."

"I always do. Itchy? Lazy?"

"It might be Lazy," I said, tapping my fingers on the cushion between us.

"I suppose we could ask the hostess, Richard Lahrem Rhymes with Harem."

"Her name is Del, and she's old."

"I've never been inside."

I had to say something. "It's like the Alps. Inside."

"If you're hungry, we could go get something to eat."

This was his offer of escape, I knew it, but eating with a teacher was impossible and I said so. Then he said he wasn't *my* teacher, and all at once the nap on the couch buzzed and the bubbles in the glass he was holding popped faster, like his hand was boiling the ginger ale. I held the gaze of his hazel eyes.

"Do you want to put on *Night Music,* Richard?"

My record was leaning against the wall under the window. A tree full of couples waiting to sing. I shook my head no.

"You want to hear it by yourself the first time," he said, reading my mind.

"How did . . ."

"I was a lot like you, Richard, when I was fifteen."

Ned set down my glass and uncrossed his legs. Then we were looking at pants. Eyeballing what he had there, I felt the volume knob in my ears zoom from three to ten. I heard an apartment door down the hall open. I heard a barking dog. I heard kids throwing stones in the parking lot and cars accelerating through a yellow light on Roosevelt. Then I thought I could hear the chunk of bowling balls at the Valley View Lanes next to Seven Dwarfs, where Del was listing syrup flavors over the psshht of the whipped cream canisters. I heard everything except what I said next.

"Can I see it?" I said.

"See what?" Ned replied carefully. There must be no mistaking the direct object.

"Your . . . uh . . . your."

Just past the bowling alley was the Hendries' chiropractic clinic, and at this point my superhuman hearing had picked up the sound of Mrs. Hendrie ripping white paper off the examining bed.

"Your *dick,*" I said, swiping a Steve attitude at the last second.

"You're sure about that," he said.

I swallowed. The effort pushed my eardrums out like hot glass beads.

"Yes. I am."

Ned stood up at the other end of the couch. I slit my eyes to keep faith with my ears. His belt buckle rapped the coffee table as his corduroys slid to the floor with a soft rustle.

The records, a miracle at the time, strike me now as a given, since their compact disc descendants rise in their own spire in my apartment, so really what I remember second when I look back to the time of Ned, after the soft fuzzy couch the brown of wet sand, is a pair of his bikini briefs.

Nobody at Wheaton-Warrenville wore anything but tightie whities. The briefs etched in my memory are the ones he wore that first Saturday. They had narrow bands of green, blue, and orange horizontal stripes. The waist and leg holes were edged in a ribbon of elastic so white that the golden hairs on his stomach showed dark against it. Sections of the elastic disappeared into the curves of his thighs, and with no fly to pucker the material, the stripes expanded or shrank as they strained or relaxed across his contours.

I liked to just look at him in them. I learned that if I looked long enough, the sweep hand of his erection would jerk counterclockwise—from five p.m. to noon—and the spongy, pebble-grained tip of his penis would arch up over the elastic, like the nose of a pink fish.

He had been a boy like me, so he knew that I wanted to see all of him that first time. He took off his sweater and his undershirt and waited. My gaze bing-banged from his body to the city of bottles on his lazy Susan. His chest and stomach weren't pulled as tight as on the jocks in gym class, and he was hairier than both my father and Carl. He crossed his arms. His crotch bumped forward, and his dick head poked up from the striped bikini. I swallowed again.

He kept going. He hooked the thumb of his right hand under the pouch of his briefs, then hooked the left thumb under the other side. He dragged them down. When his penis was fully released, greeting me with a forward dive from its ruff of fur, I fell back on the couch, not realizing that I had come in my pants.

"Are you all right?" he asked. He moved forward a step, and his dick bounced and held, bounced and held, like a live electric wire. Before another one of my senses could have a turn with it—touch, smell, *taste*—I felt what had happened to me and I balled up in the couch. I said I had to go home.

He drove a gray Pontiac Ventura. I made him drop me at the Briarcliffe entrance. The subdivision looked more pitiful from a stranger's car. One end of a string of colored plastic pennants had fallen off the garage door of the model Somerset and had gotten tangled in some holly bushes on the front walk. I asked him when I could see him again. He said that Glenbard West would be competing at the U. High overnight the following weekend.

He tried—and failed—to look serious. "I want you to think about all this, Richard," he said.

96

"I won't tell anyone," I said sarcastically, afraid that he didn't want to see me again.

"That's not what I mean," he replied. He burned his fingers into the back of my neck. "That's not what I mean at all."

I was hard again and made sure he saw that before I closed the passenger door. Through the window I saw the cleft of his tongue swell in his open mouth.

I walked up the Somerset driveway; the green Wax Trax bag swish-stroked my leg. I freed the pennants from the bushes and let them snap in the wind. If a sales rep opened the door, I was quite ready to introduce myself as a New Face of 1976.

∼✧∽

Heating her bottle in a pan, I balanced Lisa against my hip and whispered that I had been in the first shot of a pictorial, but she pulled off my glasses and I had to set her down. She fussed at having to give them back, then set off on a crawl for the dining room.

My mother thought it was funny how I kept revising Lisa's status. "She isn't really a person until she rolls over" turned into "She isn't really a person until she sits up," then "Not until she crawls." The current challenge was "Not until she can walk," but now that she was able to hoist herself up to chairs and end tables, her fat little knees jigging with excitement, I figured she was only a couple of weeks away.

Lisa's developmental hurdles stretched far into the future. Talking. Talking in sentences. Giving up her bottle. Using the toilet. Telling time. Reading, multiplication tables—all the way up to "Not until she has sex," which was my present and exact state of affairs. Dreaming about it that night, *A Little Night Music* spinning its adult rhymes and mind-blowing complications on my record player, the cover propped against the clock radio between my two speech trophies, I calculated that I had five days left before I cleared that final hurdle and became a complete person. On Friday Ned was going to find me in Bloomington, Illinois, and take me to his hotel room. The next shot in our layout would be me with *my* clothes off. The third would be both our dicks jutting like coat hooks over bubbling glasses of ginger ale. The fourth would be the kiss. By the seventh or eighth shot, we'd be folded together in the couch in soft-focus ecstasy.

Other than Lisa, I kept my word to Ned and didn't tell anyone what had happened, but that didn't mean I didn't want anyone to guess. For the longest time the only one to get close, and this was only two days after Wax Trax, was Hannelore Demetz.

Monday was a Teacher Institute day, so we had the afternoon off. Steve couldn't convince Carla to go with him to Martin Manor and play decoy. Black people were *fine,* but the elderly grossed her out. He followed her into the kitchen, where I was finishing lunch. Carla pulled a bottle of nail polish from behind a box of frozen waffles in the freezer door and handed it to him to open with his teeth. Nail polish in the freezer drove my mother crazy, but Carla's commanding gesture turned Steve to mush. He got an "Aren't chicks amazing?" expression on his face. I pictured his uncut dog dick dropping from its hood to wag along with his tail.

He caught me eyeing him and mashed his thumb into a package of hamburger buns. "Your mom making sloppy joes?" he asked.

"Looks like it," I said. The seasoning mix was under a green pepper on the counter.

"She does a good job with them."

"They were my favorite food when I was a kid," I said. Steve nodded like he remembered that. His favorite meal from when we were friends had been her sauerbraten.

"My dad's getting married again," I blurted out.

"Oh yeah?"

"Not to a stewardess though."

"That's too bad."

"Not to April Gladden," I said, trying to keep us going.

Steve laughed, a good sign. April Gladden, Miss January 1972 and a United Airlines stewardess, had been our absolute favorite and perfect centerfold. Steve worshiped the shape of her tits—"impeccable globes," he'd moan with rare eloquence at the sight of her unfolded along his arm. I secretly loved how the color of her nipples matched the purple of his eyelids. We agreed there was a God when April and her inch of heavenly blond bush made her Playmate of the Year.

Carla looked up from her nails. "Who is April Gladden?"

"Miss January 1972. She flies the friendly skies. Her hobbies are scuba diving, hang gliding, and bachelors," I snickered.

Steve had lost interest. "She's not as pretty as you," he said.

Carla and I gagged.

When I volunteered to visit Hannelore, Carla changed her mind. We waited in the front hall while she fixed her face. Steve abruptly asked me if I knew who R E G I was. He didn't find my answer—the guy on her stomach—funny. His eyes started to water, like he was trying to keep quiet about a nail that had been shot into his skull. Twice he declared he was going to make her forget Regi. "What do you think she wants, Rick, what do you think she wants," he mumbled, a question with no answer. I said he'd learned about what chicks wanted in the crawlspace, but the dope meant something bigger. I was about to say we were too young to know what we wanted, teachers and parents said that nonstop, but I knew what I wanted and it was coming in just four days.

A blast of sunlight through the little windows framing the front door changed his mood. "What it is is what I'm gonna get her," he announced, snapping his fingers. "What it is is what I'm gonna get her." By the time Carla came down, he'd turned his vow into a tune and was tapping it out on his belt buckle.

"Foxey Lady," he growled. Maybe he was high.

Martin Manor hadn't changed in the two years since I'd been there. Hannelore's door still opened to a smell of licorice and winter coats. She still shooed guests in with a quick flap of her apron, and grabbed the doorknob with both hands. Passing the bathroom I noticed a new metal bar near the shower, but the dark brown bottles with the handwritten labels were lined up on the toilet tank in the same old order.

Unlike the other farts at Martin Manor, Hannelore didn't try to look young. She wore high, laced shoes and black dresses with long sleeves. Her neck had disappeared, so her head seemed to screw into the middle of her chest like a Christmas bulb. Her hair collected in sticky white flaps around her head, and she had several gravity-defying bristles above her lip.

"So, taller now, Richard," she said, pronouncing my name the German way. Carla didn't like how her name—"Cow-luh"—sounded. Ducking behind me after the introductions, she muttered that this had better be quick.

Hannelore's furniture was black and carved. The chair legs twisted down into claws on balls, and the cushions were hard honeycombs of red velvet and gold studs. An ancient stuffed lion, with one cloudy glass eye and most of its fur rubbed off, dozed next to the sewing basket. Summer or winter, Hannelore never drew the sheers or opened the maroon curtains. It was like she lived inside a chocolate-covered cherry.

"Something to eat, my children?" she asked. She was tiny, but with her broad shoulders and thick, swollen knuckles she could have given Hansel and Gretel quite a shove, if it came to that.

Steve pushed me forward. "We can't stay long, grandma," he said. "We were just on our way to the store for Mom."

"Not fruit even?"

Instead of the fridge, where fruit belonged, Hannelore kept her weird stash of giant purple grapes and turdy figs and hard brown pears in a bowl on the table.

"We all ate a big lunch," said Steve. He gave me a look. The easiest pickings were in the tiny drawers of the massive walnut secretary.

I lured Hannelore away. "Was ist das?" I asked, pointing to the contraption next to the fruit bowl.

"Always you ask me this," she sighed. "Das ist die Käseglocke."

Fighting for air under a glass dome lay an oozy cream island, a veined, gray-green eraser, and a slab of orange stone dotted with tiny sweat beads. Frau Demetz was the queen of scary groceries.

"Kayzuh-glock-uh," I repeated. It hit me that I was happy to see her.

"Richtig," she said, and lifted the bell, as I knew she would.

Carla stepped around me for a look, and the gas blitzed her. "Eww," she cried, retreating from the stink with her hands cupped to her face. Hannelore's deep laughs pulled the shiny satin of her dress tight across her bosom.

I leaned over and inhaled. Carla gave a little scream.

"And now, a taste, Richard?" Hannelore asked.

"No thank you. I just like the smell. Ammonia."

"And feet, no? A little bit?"

"Ammonia and feet."

"Ja, das Ammoniak und die Füße Makes you strong."

We sat down, Hannelore facing me. I saw Steve's hand drift along the top of the secretary. To give him time, I agreed to eat a scaly pear, which she peeled with a small ivory-handled knife.

"So, you are in high school now, Richard, and taller. Are you taking German?"

"No," I said sheepishly, "Spanish."

She paused, letting the blade rest against her thumb knuckle. "Spanish—that is for babies. You promised to me German."

"I'm not very good at it."

"Americans do not work hard. German is for smart people. German is for being good at."

Setting down the pear, Hannelore opened a panel in a sideboard where she kept sweets. She pushed a box of sliced dates rolled in coconut at me. They looked like animal eyes. "What are you good at, Richard?"

"Speech, Frau Demetz," I said, shaking my head no. "I'm good at speech."

"I am glad for it. People who make good speeches become important later in life." She narrowed her lips as she inspected a date. "Soon is the holiday for the soldiers, ja?"

"Ja," I replied. "Veterans Day." Steve laughed and said, "Jawohl, mein commandant," which she ignored.

"Die Sprache, you make a speech about the veterans, the German veterans."

Her free hand fluttered to a picture behind me of her husband's military school class. I could point him out if she asked, second row, third from the right, big ears, killed at Stalingrad, Friedrich Klaus Demetz.

Carla had drifted over to Steve, who was shaking down the sewing basket. Next would be the brown jars on the toilet. There was a guaranteed twenty in the cotton balls.

"She is your sister?

"No, my stepsister."

"Stefan likes the girls," she said, but the endorsement was neutral. We both knew Carla should be making an effort.

"He likes *her*, at least," I said.

From some old lady place, Hannelore understood my need to maintain a claim on her grandson. She leaned over, and her rings grazed my knuckles as she dropped a hand onto mine. Her tongue went hunting for coconut shreds in her mustache.

"You do not like the girls," she said. To indicate what I did like, she tapped two fingers on a pair of the big grapes in the fruit bowl.

And they wonder why kids are scared of the elderly. I yanked my hand away. She freed another date slice from its crinkle cup and popped it in her mouth.

"Hey, Grandma, I never saw this before," said Steve, suddenly close. He had a knife in one hand, a leather sheath in the other. The swastika carved into the handle pulled me away from testicles and ammonia and feet.

"Where did you get?" she asked. "Das Messer," she added, to me.

"Das Messer," I said automatically.

Steve pulled it out of reach. "I was looking for a Kleenex. Can I have it?"

"Such a bad liar," she said, with a flicker of interest at the blade. "Wait until I am dead for things to come to you."

"Was this Grandpa's?" asked Steve, buttering her up.

Hannelore blinked her sharp blue eyes at the picture behind my head. "Your mother will not permit."

He tapped the glass bell with the point. "I won't tell her. I'll keep it in my room. Please, Grandma? It's so cool."

"This you won't need for cutting the cheese," she said sternly.

She didn't understand why we couldn't stop laughing, and we weren't about to explain. Steve made up some crap about wanting to learn how to hunt animals in the arboretum. He was always a great bullshitter, and soon he got her talking about the woodland creatures of the Black Forest and how best to skin them for a true German Hasenpfeffer.

∽∾

I loved my mother's sloppy joes, but her porcupine meatballs were another story. I was eyeing a platter of maggoty budget stretchers on Thursday night when she asked us all to hold hands and say grace.

We never held hands. We never said grace. We weren't even Christmas- and Easter-goers. Carl halted the plunge of his fork into a pile of succotash. Carla clicked her tongue. My mother hunched down, staked an elbow on each side of her plate, and let her palms drop open to Carl and me. Her boobs were almost in the meatballs. Nobody moved.

"What are you afraid of, boys?" she said, trying to joke.

Carl swallowed his cud. "I'm trying to eat here," he said.

"Take my hand, honey, I don't want dinner to get cold."

If he could, I could. We all looked to Carla, who scowled and shrugged the hair off her forehead. The brush of her fingertips on mine brought Ned back. While my mother said thanks, I watched the slow path of a drip on the gravy boat, surprised once again that whole hours could pass without Ned and his underwear invading my mind. All week at school I'd been stripping the male teachers, even the crusty bald ones. I imagined their erections diving out of their plaid polyesters and hydroplaning around the hallways on their cushy ball bags.

My mother was still talking, but she wasn't thanking God for the food anymore. She was reciting something. Strange words—"covenant," "verity," "endureth"—popped out like "sodomite" in my D.I., or "chinkle chankle" or "bone orchard." She stopped a couple of times to think, started the same line three times to find her place.

"There now, that didn't kill anybody, did it?" she asked, squeezing my hand before she dropped it.

"I think the food got cold," said Carl. My mother apologized and passed the plate of bread to Carla.

"What *was* that?" I asked.

"That was Psalm 111."

"From the Bible?"

"Of course, silly. It's a prayer about the Lord's care for His people," she said mildly.

"Why did you memorize it?" I asked.

She shrugged, took a sip of water. "A friend thought it was a good idea."

Her face said no more questions. Lisa dropped her baby spoon on the floor. Carl, hunched like an ape, was already eating. Carla was dissecting a porcupine meatball with her fork.

My mother came into my room later, while I was packing for the overnight. She smoothed the ties draped around the lapel of my suit hanging on the door. All my socks and underwear were out on the bed. I had decided that an old caramel-colored bag of my father's wouldn't look dorky, but I was agonizing about what to sleep in. I figured pajamas were babyish, but maybe High Knob boys wore them. Gym shorts? Cutoffs? Also, I wore socks to bed, because my feet froze no matter what. Would they make fun? *Who would I share a bed with?*

My mother began pulling the pins out of my new dress shirt, apologizing for not getting to it sooner.

"It doesn't matter, does it?" I said.

"It won't look so brand new if the creases get a chance to flatten out. If you remember to hang it up while you take a shower tomorrow night, the steam will get some of them out."

"But I'm keeping the jacket on."

"If you want, I can run the shower right now."

"He'll get mad, Mom." Carl timed my showers on the mornings I was allowed to take one. I washed my hair in the kitchen sink on the other days.

She offered to take *her* shower with my shirt, but that was creepy. I said no.

"Do you want to call your father?"

"Dad? What for?"

"To give him a chance to wish you luck. Tell him you're getting some use out of his old leather tote. He'd want to know, I'll bet." She plucked a pair of underpants out of the pile. "These are going in the ragbag, son. They're too holey to wear."

"He's probably out."

"I used to watch your father pack for business trips. I'd help him."

"Well, if you bring me a martini, Mom, I'll be happy to drink it."

"Funny funny."

Something was wrong. I turned and caught her wiping her eyes. I concentrated on the wings on my trophy and asked her why she was crying.

She sat down on the edge of the bed and thought about it. I flipped *A Little Night Music* to side B and set *Pippin* on deck. She told me that in the last year of their marriage she knew that Josephine was sometimes at the other end of my father's trips but there was nothing she could do to fight back, to try and keep him. She couldn't beg him not to go, it was his job. All she could do was slip love notes into his Dopp kit, notes in which she had to pretend that everything was okay and there was no Josephine. She never knew whether he read them or threw them away, because he never brought them up, not even once. Seeing my suit on the door and his tote on the bed had brought the old humiliations back.

Humiliation was not a word my mother had ever turned on herself. I marched in circles, balling and releasing my fists. I would refuse his calls, return his checks, skip his wedding. He left with love notes from my mother and came back with liquor bottles for me out of Josephine's cocktail-waitressing twat. I'd smash them all on the driveway. I'd mail the shards to New Jersey and make him cut his hands opening the box.

My attempt to cheer away her tears—"You don't have to worry now, because Carl doesn't take business trips"—was met with a sad swing of her head. I finally got her out of it by asking what a Dopp kit was.

She blew her nose in the holey underwear. "It's a bag men put their shaving cream and toothpaste and cologne in. They zip up. I'll get you one for Christmas."

"I don't want anything he has," I snarled. "I don't wear cologne."

She thought that was funny, but I wasn't going to be offended if it made her feel better. She stood to go, but I wanted her to stay. I gestured to the bed. "If you want to help, tell me what to sleep in tomorrow night."

She surveyed the jumble from on high. "Wait the other boys out, honey," she said, putting an arm around me.

"How do you mean?"

"Take a pair of pajamas with you just in case, but wait to see what the other boys in your room wear. Simple, huh?"

"Yep," I said, relieved.

"A Weekend in the Country" was playing as she put the socks and underwear back in my dresser drawers. On her way out, she picked up the blue *A Little Night Music* album cover and studied it. "There are naked ladies on this, Rick. Naked . . . couples."

"Yes," I replied smoothly, "that's because it's a musical about sex. It's based on an Ingmar Bergman movie called *Smiles of a Summer Night.* It's more musically sophisticated than *Company.*"

Her bewildered expression made me smile. Carla's birth control was easier to think through, I suppose.

❦

I still remember how cool it felt to stride through the front doors of Wheaton-Warrenville with a suit bag over my arm and my father's tote slapping my leg, how cool it felt to put *my luggage* in the pile growing just inside Wegner and Schuette's office door, how cool it felt to be released in the middle of Spanish class to catch a bus like the muscled ball-throwers did. I remember the bus driver telling us to pipe down as we neared railroad crossings in the middle of fields matted with dried cornstalks. Silence reigned until the back axle bumped the second rail, and then the roar of twenty-two Wolverines on overnight leave took my heart up with it.

Joe Bacino ended my private worries by announcing in the elevator, "I'm sharing with Rick, he's skinniest." He dumped his duffel on the far bed in Room 412, and I threw my tote against it. Below us, in the Motel 6 parking lot, girls slowly stepped out of buses like movie stars alighting from Hollywood limos. Joe mooned them while Brian and Ty scrambled into their suits for first round. My hand tucked in a dress shoe, I watched Joe's butt print on the window melt away to nothing.

After a group photo in the lobby, Wegner gave a pep talk. The tournament was an endurance test: five preliminary rounds and a final championship round. With sixty schools entered, U. High was the closest we'd come to statewide competition until the actual state meet in February. We were to behave like young gentlemen and ladies and be respectful of all our competitors. Miss Schuette echoed him on "all your competitors." What they meant, Eric Smola explained as we filed back into the bus, was, "Don't make fun of the hicks in your rounds." Parents and schools in the farm counties, which were four-fifths of Illinois, didn't have anything approaching the resources of the Chicago suburbs. They couldn't afford student teachers or nice suits or field trips to see plays. The code word for downstate kids was "Potasset," as in "I go to Potasset High School," said with a *Hee Haw* accent. Potassets did scenes from Neil Simon. Potassets read Carl Sandburg poems. Potasset orations denounced abortion and communism. You could tell a Potasset boy by the bowl cut and the Bicentennial tie. A Potasset girl might wear a hand-me-down prom dress and eye shadow like war paint.

There were no obvious Potassets in my Friday rounds, but Dina Demacopoulos, from Shepard High, was in my second round. She sat down in the chair in front of me and complimented me on my new tie. Not even Miss Schuette had noticed. I said I really liked her dress.

She plucked at a shiny striped sleeve, and the wrist rode up to reveal thick, dark arm hairs. "Oh, I wore this at Oak Lawn," she replied.

"I remember it, Dina. It goes with your eyes."

This dippy remark elicited a fake throaty laugh. Dina checked her schedule sheet. "Are you 11A today, Rick?"

I nodded. "And you're—"

"34A. You were B before."

"I guess I got promoted." Mr. Wegner had posted the roster on Wednesday. I was on the A team now, a distinction that actually made no difference in how school tallies were tabulated, but Stacy Granbur, 11B, hadn't even said hello on the bus ride downstate. Pretty un-Christian, I'd thought, for a major born-again like Stacy.

Dina took my critique sheet and smoothed it on top of hers on her desk. "I can give both of these to the judge when he gets here."

"Thanks," I said, not sure that this was such a favor.

"I placed second at Waubonsee East last week," Dina announced. "I had two firsts and a second going into final round. Fourteen points." She puffed her victory toward the competition. They rippled in silent alarm. On the wall behind us was a photo blowup of the moon. It was an astronomy moon, not an ecology moon.

"That is so great, Dina. Congratulations."

She flicked the air with her right hand and dipped her chin into the knuckles of her left. Then she slid her fingers up her neck to fluff out her hair. Her gestures were fascinatingly deliberate, out of a manual, or sent away for with box tops. "My parents promised me I could get my braces off in time for state."

"That would be cool," I said.

"If I even make it to state, I mean," she said, rapping the wooden back of my chair for luck. "Where is your team staying?"

"Motel 6."

"We're at the Best Western. That's right across the highway." Dina leaned in suggestively. Her hair was so black the skin of her part looked like a scar. "Do you guys have a pool?"

"I didn't look. Isn't it too cold to swim?"

"Best Western has an indoor pool."

The judge appeared in the doorway. Dina's face snapped front.

I joked later that the second round was my Death Row round, because the first three interps were Anne Boleyn going to get the ax in *Anne of the Thousand Days,* Thomas More going to get the ax in *A Man for All Seasons,* and Joan of Arc going to burn at the stake in *The Lark.* I drew skeletons beside their numbers on my schedule sheet, two with skirts.

Something happened in the middle of my D.I. Alan dialed Fran and freaked Michael out as usual, but during their argument before the phone call, something Michael said came out differently. Or I heard it differently, in a way that made me think that Alan *was* lying about Justin Stewart, and that Michael was right to accuse him of being a closet case. Except that I heard the difference before Alan did, and I was so startled I lost my place. The seconds dragged like minutes while I blinked at the surface of the moon, black and silver like Dina's dress. I clicked back in somehow for a shaky finish.

The judge dismissed us. Dina stretched her arms high, the better to capture her coat sleeves. Her folder flapped against the transom as she passed through the door. To the right of her rabbit collar, standing in the doorway of a classroom across the hall, was Ned. My legs turned to cement, and my palm began to sweat on my schedule sheet.

Lark girl and *Man for All Seasons* boy were easing around me before I could unfreeze and let them pass. I croaked out Dina's name. Way ahead, she turned, surprised by the distance between us. I babbled out a promise that Joe and Brian and Eric and Ty and I would come visit that night.

"I'll bet you can rent suits!" she exclaimed. "Be careful crossing the highway!"

I waved her off and lurched into the hall like I'd escaped from a human-sized cheese bell.

"Hello, Richard," he said.

I waited to hear "Lahrem Rhymes with Harem." Why wasn't he smiling? And why wasn't he wearing the toggle sweater?

"Hello Mr. . . . Mr. . . ." I blanked on his last name, like I'd blanked in the round.

"Ned. How did it go?"

I was so dumb I thought everything would be the same. I stared at the old-fashioned checkerboard tiles. Where were his desert boots?

"Second round, Richard, how did it go?"

"I lost my place. For like, hours."

Nothing was going to happen. My dick was rock hard, but

it wasn't going to boing out in the middle of the hallway, not without a fuzzy brown couch and glasses of ginger ale.

"You must be hungry."

If he was thinking about food, then he didn't *want* a pictorial. He didn't want me; I was too young for him. This was my punishment for not thinking about him every minute, for having fun on the bus ride, for flirting with Dina Demacopoulos, for sneaking a look at Joe Bacino's butt on the window, for not cutting N E D on my stomach to remind me every minute of the best thing that had ever happened to me.

"Mr. Wegner is taking your team to Jumer's."

I was so panicked, I looked up. "You talked to Mr. Wegner?" The light panel shining above his head made his face shadowy.

"It's okay, Richard, we know each other. We said hello in the tally room between rounds."

A door opened down the hall, and another session let out. The boys yanked their ties loose and raced right. The girls kept their red carpet walks going for a few more feet, then clicked full-speed after the boys. Dinnertime. Pool parties. Souvenirs.

"And you know what? You got a first in your first round. Mr. Wegner and I checked."

"Uh-huh."

"I suppose I shouldn't have told you that, Richard."

Enough of Saturday had crept into his tone for me to risk another peek. His features were still too dark to read, but one end of his mustache poked out like a twig in the moonlit *Night Music* tree.

"Why not?"

"Because I wouldn't want you to get too"—he reached over to pluck the schedule sheet out of my hand—"*cocky*."

We had twenty minutes before Wheaton-Warrenville went to Jumers's and Glenbard West went to Avanti's. There weren't any couches in the social studies wing, but Ned had scoped out a faculty john two turns around the corner from where we were standing.

I went in first. Ned pulled the door shut behind him. I smacked against him in the dark and cried out—just a little—when I felt his arms circle my back. Leaves shake, and rabbits, and hummingbirds, and I did too.

Horny. The seventh dwarf's name was Horny.

I was tucked in the throat of the soft brown couch. Ned's body blotted everything out except the turquoise starburst of the Seven Dwarfs sign blinking in his window. Beyond and below the cliff of his right hip were two heaps of clothing, the islands of our wickedness.

"It's getting dark," I said. My mother thought Mindy was giving me a ride home after coaching.

"Mmmm," he said, catching my mouth with his.

Okay, so no *Penthouse Forum* letter, no pictorial or photo or old Japanese print, *nothing* I had ever read or seen had made a case for kissing. After two hours, there was still no bottom to how incredible it was. It wasn't just first base on the way to better things, it was as good as the rest because it never had to stop; it had no beginning or end, it ran without rules and filled every in-between. It didn't think. It came and went, it was every piece of punctuation, and I was good at it right away.

Ned's arm shifted behind my head. "It is getting late," he murmured in the direction of his watch.

"I don't want to go," I said, pressing my whole self into him, as yet too shy to signal with individual parts.

I had read about being so happy you cried, but I hadn't believed it until the moment Ned whispered that he didn't want me to go either.

"Ten more minutes?" I whispered back. His neck smelled like cloves.

Ned had picked me up across the street from school. Before I opened his passenger door, I waved to imaginary friends so that things would look normal to the moms in cars. On the way to his apartment, as we headed east on Roosevelt Road, he asked, "So am I going to get to see it?" Without thinking, I unzipped my coat and my jeans and was about to free my boner at the stoplight in front of Aladdin Cleaners when he said, "Not that, Rick, the medal, the *medal*."

I couldn't stop laughing. I took the U. High prize out of my jacket pocket, a gold disc stamped with comedy and tragedy masks, attached to two inches of blue ribbon. It pinned on like an army medal. I'd only come in second this time, not that it bothered me so much. Considering that I couldn't remember anything from any of my rounds that day, I was surprised even to make finals. All I knew was those twenty minutes in the faculty bathroom.

"Put it on, Rick," he said.

"Why?" I asked, embarrassed. I'd already refused my mother's request. This time she'd made a victory cake.

"Just do it."

"Okay, okay."

I thought of Dina Demacopoulos, in her bedroom in Palos

Heights, twirling in front of a mirror with her first-place medal pinned to her bathing suit. I hadn't hopped on over to the Best Western for a pool party, so the only way to melt her frost had been to lose to her. Not on purpose; in a daze about Ned, I was happy she got first. She'd cried on my hair like Miss America.

"Ta-dah!" I said, flicking the medal on my coat.

Ned put his hand on my knee. The touch forked up my crotch like lightning. "I wanted you to bring the award, Rick, and put it on, because I don't want you to think—*ever*—that I gave you first place at the Central tournament just because—because."

"Because I had a boner."

"Because you were excited."

"I have one right now. Wait—" I'd thought of something funny. "Is that what you meant by 'outstanding'?"

Steering with one hand, he didn't even crack a smile. "You deserved that first I gave you, just like you did Saturday."

"I don't mind second place," I shrugged. "And Dina, the girl who won, is really good. *Desire under the Elms* by Eugene O'Neill." And after a few more stoplights we were going to have our first all-nude photo shoot, so nothing else could possibly matter.

"Here's the thing, though, Richard. Two of the three judges in your final round ranked you first. Out of seven finalists, *first*. You were the best in show for two of them, just like you were for me." He said this slowly, like he was reading out a word problem in math class.

"And the third judge gave me a fifth."

Ned took his hand back. I looked out my window like I didn't care. A little girl in the back seat of the car in the next lane was waving a stuffed turtle at me.

"I saw that on the score sheets. One, one, five. What did that third judge write on his critique sheet?"

That had been Miss Schuette's million-dollar question on the ride back from Bloomington. Wheaton-Warrenville had won big, six individual medalists, but we were too tired to celebrate much past the city limits. Eric Smola was droning on in the dark about his college application essay when Schuette called me up to the front of the bus, where she sat poring over a stack of mimeographed tallies. She pointed her pen flashlight at my wad of critique sheets, and I handed them to her. Mr. Wegner, across the aisle with his legs stretched over the whole seat, cocked open an eye. I watched the bus headlights catch ice crystals on the fence posts while she scrabbled through my papers.

"*Her* critique sheet," I said, correcting Ned. "The third judge was a lady, and she wrote that I was technically accomplished but she 'questioned the appropriateness of *The Boys in the Band* for a high school student.'"

"Is that her exact quote, Rick?" he asked severely, like a TV detective.

"It is. I'm not lying."

Ned smacked his turn signal lever with an open palm. "Jesus," he said.

"That's just what Miss Schuette said. 'Jesus.'"

"That last judge was a narrow-minded bitch."

"I know." I agreed just to agree, shocked to hear bad language from a teacher. "Miss Schuette checked her code number and said she taught at Rantoul High School."

"If she believed your D.I. was inappropriate, then she should have given you *last* place."

"Well, Rantoul is downstate, right?"

"It is. It's twenty miles from Streator, where I grew up."

That meant Ned had been a Potasset. I couldn't imagine it. His leg bulged inside his pants when he shifted gears. I wondered if it felt sweaty and prickly both at the same time, like mine.

"If that's how she really feels, she should have had the guts to rank you seventh out of seven. The stupid bitch was covering her butt, if you know what I mean."

I didn't know what he meant. I moved my knee closer to the gear shaft, hoping he'd put his hand back. We'd both feel better.

"She's full of—soybeans. You're the champion, Rick. Don't ever forget it."

At that moment, spotting the glass brick front of Ned's building, I did feel like a champion. I gripped the door handle and clamped my book bag between my feet. The lady judge from Rantoul *was* full of soybeans, I thought. Just how appropriate the material was for this high school student was half a block away and two flights up.

✎

Walking home that night from my drop-off in front of Briarcliffe was a nutty experience. The hall and kitchen lights on in the houses, the cobs of Indian corn wired to the door knockers, the dull gleam of the milk boxes on the porches, all the mothers hovering by the stoves, the kids setting tables, Mr. Hegna scraping his shoes on the mud mat, these ordinary things didn't go with the way my shadow on the sidewalk grew and shrunk, grew and shrunk under the street lamps. I was faster than any sidewalk, bigger than any version of my shadow. My cheeks and lips were swollen from cold air and hot kissing. I was Perfectly Richard, a complete person who had had sex, a person

119

who was going to keep on having it and having it and having it. I was coated and rolled and fried in Ned. Set me on your table. Pour me from a gravy boat. I was a bottle of milk in the box of him. Open the lid and find me. Open the lid and pour me out, pour me out in a river of kisses.

I had closed our front door and was sniffing out dinner when a woman in a dress of orange and rust swirls charged at me from the living room. "You're Rick!" she exclaimed, gripping my forearms. "The little man of the house. And look, your speech medal's on your ski jacket, praise His holy name! How we prayed over that!"

She had huge teeth and a bathing cap of icy black curls. She said her name was Patty Puller. "Mom?" I called out. "Mom?"

Now, over thirty years later, when my mother does everything but swallow poison in His holy name, it's difficult to remember what she was like before she met Jesus. If asked how she got over, she would maintain, as ever, that that year Carla moved in with us was so disruptive there had been nowhere else for her to turn. Her life had needed to change in a big way, and the Lord answered a desperate question she didn't know she was asking, answered it with an everlasting peace. She has no more distance or insight on the matter than she did the week it happened in 1976. Nor does she wish to. Jesus, the only insight, the only answer, negates distance, collapses all time and space.

Mindy Kendig's home visit had helped light the can of oil on the stove, as it were, but while she was out fabric shopping one morning during the same week I was counting down to Ned Bolang, my mother found herself with an overpowering need to turn into the lot of the Evangelical Free Church of Wheaton. She parked the car. Assuming the omen was mechanical, she was checking the tires for a flat when she thought she heard her name booming over a loudspeaker. She stood up straight. The voice was a man's, but a woman was motioning to her from the doorway of an office beside the entrance to the church. That was Patty Puller. Patty led her inside, took her coat, poured her a soft drink, gave her a Bible, and two nights later my mother was reciting the 111th Psalm over porcupine meatballs.

Patty's personal ministry was binding the wounds of the broken family, and her first meal on Kingston Drive was basic research. Her drawn-out "Amen" to end their two-hour freeform grace had a *Jubilee Showcase* throb to it, and in refusing the roast beef she quoted something about there being no blood in the meat. Whatever verse of Leviticus it was, never again would my mother serve, much less consume, rare meat. In the weeks and months to come she would cut out coffee and tea, renounce alcohol and beer and her beloved shellfish, and invite home more excitable ladies who gave full-body hugs if you didn't move fast enough.

Christians are starch fiends, so Patty more than made up for the roast beef with mounds of Spanish rice. Helping herself to a fourth serving, she brought up "the secular miracle of Thanksgiving" while I was stealing sniffs of Ned on my fingers. Her day of thanks, she declared, would be spent in praise and turkey service to the poor Mexicans of Aurora.

"There are Mexicans in Aurora?" my mother asked. Aurora was a big town in the southwest corner of DuPage County. You could say that Potassepotamia began just beyond its borders.

"In this very county, yes, immigrants of Mexico. Poor of means but strong of faith," said Patty.

"They've got processing plants out there," said Carl, head down, swilling.

"I did not know that, Carl," said my mother. Using his name was a show of company manners.

"They work so hard, Sister Marie. So very hard." Just like Carl, Patty had a bullet head and hard, segmented rolls of fat from shoulders to crotch.

"I'll bet the Mexicans of Aurora would like my corn pudding. I make it every Thanksgiving, and nobody eats it but me. It's a Southern recipe."

"Oh, they would indeed," Patty said. "Corn is very special to the Mexican peoples."

Carla, stoned and silent up to now, snorted at Patty's plural. "Peoples? Peoples?"

"We call it maize," I said, mocking the Mazola commercial.

"If I made my corn pudding, Patty, could you take it with you to Aurora?"

"Could you please?" I said. "It looks like Lisa's spit-up."

Lisa, hearing her name, waved her arms in the highchair. Patty brushed some rice grains from her bosom shelf.

"You could come with me, Sister Marie, and see for yourself."

"Oh, but I've got dinner to get ready here." My mother paused, then added a tentative "Sister Patty." Carla and I snuck a glance at each other—what was this sister stuff?

"Once your turkey's in, you come spend a couple of hours with me on the lunch shift. It'll do you a heap of good."

"She can't," grunted Carl. "We're going to Koontz Lake."

Carla and I groaned. Carl's face rose from his plate like a ham-colored moon.

"A Hoosier get-together?" asked Patty.

"My mother and my sisters live there," said Carl.

People hear the word "lake" and they think water-skiing, beaches, canoes, cabins. Koontz Lake, Indiana, was a scummy brown pond bracketed by freight yards. Koontz Lake, Indiana, was a three-hour drive to watch Carl and the Two-Ton Tessies sit around a metal kitchen table in a house that smelled like a wet dog. Koontz Lake, Indiana, was step-cousin Rochelle, called "Bucky" because of her teeth, gluing macaroni shells on cardboard to make frames for rock-star pictures she cut out of *Creem* magazine. Koontz Lake, Indiana was the Mook, Carl's father, so hateful he had been sent to live in a tarpaper shack at the edge of his own backyard, his meals ferried out in a pail by his wife. I met the Mook once. His face looked like a mashed-in armadillo. Carl hated the Mook the way I hated Carl, so, to quote my social studies teacher, the enemy of my enemy was my friend.

My mother pursed her lips. The Tessies called her "Princess." They made a show of reserving the white meat and the "nice" chair for her. Carla announced that no way was she going to Indiana.

Carl licked gravy off his dead-nail finger. "Why not?"

"Oh, but they're your family, dear," said Patty Puller. She and my mother exchanged a meaningful look. "A girl only gets one family."

"I don't give two shits," Carla said. "The last time you made me go there, Aunt Ronnie called me a fricking hosebag. What a joke."

Hosebag was so funny I spit out my milk. Turning over the image, as specialized as bone orchard—a vacuum cleaner with five nozzles, a purse full of sausages—I almost missed Carla's point: Aunt Ronnie was the real hosebag because she'd gotten herself knocked up with Bucky in high school.

"My oh my," clucked Patty. So much work lay ahead of her.

I put the puzzle together. "Does Rochelle know she's a—"

"Rick," warned my mother.

"If she doesn't, she's a moron. Or deaf, since the whole town calls her Bucky the Bastard," giggled Carla. "Her daddy left on the midnight train to Georgia. Her daddy left on the train they call the City of New Orleans."

"He left on the last train to Clarksville," I said.

"No, he left on the sooooul tra-ai-ain."

I cracked up at Carla's imitation of the *Soul Train* emcee, so she did it again, howling the *o* like a lovesick coyote. Lisa threw Spanish rice for backup.

"Clean up that milk, Rick," yelled Carl, breaking in.

I pushed back my chair to get a washrag. Patty Puller was beaming, but my mother's face was buried in her hands. Only for the time being, really. In a matter of months, personal embarrassment would go the way of coffee and oysters Rockefeller, another dramatic interpretation of the Book of Leviticus.

∽৽৽

My father the planner skipped ahead to the next holiday and asked me what I wanted for Christmas. My birthday was December 28, so I made it a double. "A car," I said, an outrageous request. I waited him out, counting the boxes of pudding mix and cans of frosting on the middle shelf of the pantry closet. A bib was soaking in a bowl of suds on the washing machine.

"Very funny," he finally said. My father liked to think my sense of humor came from him.

"I'm taking driver's ed next quarter."

"You know, Rick, I didn't get my first car until I was in college."

"Carl's not going to let me drive Mom's car, I know that much."

This put him on high alert. I rarely mentioned Carl by name.

"You don't need a car," he said.

"I don't know who's going to practice with me," I said, guilting him further. "You know how Mom is about driving."

"What do you need a car for?"

"To get out of the house. Speech practice. Stuff," I said blandly, wiggling the extension cord on the floor like a snake.

"How's that going, son?" he asked, happy to change the subject.

"I didn't win on Saturday, if that's what you mean."

"Oh. Better luck next time."

"It's no big deal," I lied.

Wegner, Schuette, and Ned were mystified that I'd been shut out of finals at the Hinsdale meet the Saturday before Thanksgiving. I'd gotten a third and two fourths—seven points total, the same as Stacy Granbur and a piss-poor showing for someone who'd placed in his first three tournaments. Champion that day, with a perfect score, was Veronica Satterwhite and *This Property Is Condemned*. Schuette poked me to make sure I watched how Veronica took hold of her trophy. She batted her eyes at the audience and mouthed, "Me?" but from the way she swung her hair back you could tell she wasn't surprised at all. It was nauseating.

"When you come out for the wedding, Julia and I want to hear your speech."

"It's not a speech, it's a dramatic interpretation."

"Fine, fine, we'd sure like to see it."

"You're getting married. You won't have time."

My mother knocked on the door and said she was expecting a call. No kidding. Every night was a new episode of the Patty Puller Phone Opera. They'd be in the den, Carl digesting in the booger chair, my mother cutting up the Pennysavers. The phone would ring on the dictionary cabinet in the hall. My

125

mother would swoop on it, utter, "Well praise be, it's you, Sister Patty!" and then shut herself into the laundry room. Baby Christians of all ages needed lots of attention, so it was forever before Sister Marie reemerged, wet-eyed and ravenous for wheat puffs, her hand a white peony of crumpled Kleenex.

"Give me a *minute*, Mom." I wondered what my father would think of her getting religion. I hated it when he made fun of her.

"Now, about Christmas," he said. "I don't think a car is appropriate yet—"

"I was joking, Dad."

"—so all I'm saying is maybe for graduation."

Now that I'd backed down, he could afford to be generous. He gave a tight cough, a sign something weird was on its way. "Your mother's been telling me you like Rodgers and Hammerstein records?"

"She said that?"

"She did."

"She's an idiot. She doesn't know what she's talking about."

"It's okay son. Hobbies are fun."

"It's not my hobby!"

To get him to stop yammering about how much he liked *The King and I,* a topic too alien to contemplate, I told him what I really wanted: contact lenses.

The lag here, even longer than for the car, gave me time to make a pyramid out of the cans of corn on the dryer, enough for a triple batch of pudding for the Mexican peoples of Aurora. Outside of models and movie actors, people didn't wear contacts back then, men especially, kids most of all. They cost over two hundred dollars.

"For your eyes?"

"Uh-huh," I said.

"What do you need contact lenses for?"

I closed my eyes to investigate. If I said, "So I can watch Ned's face when I lick his balls," I probably wouldn't get them. "Because my glasses fog up too much," was what I did say. My cruddy aviators would lie in the ashtray on Ned's coffee table next to the glasses of ginger ale, our beverage of choice. We'd watch each other pee it out later.

"I believe fogging is a standard hazard with glasses, son."

"And Miss Schuette—"

"Who's that?" he asked, suspicious, hand to wallet pocket.

"She's one of my coaches. She thinks I look better with my glasses off."

"People often do," he said.

"Miss Schuette says she wants me to have every competitive advantage."

"And does she want to pay for them?"

He could be cheap, my father, but it was hard to predict when. I grabbed a can from the corn pyramid and slammed it on the dryer.

"If I was on the track team, you'd get me track shoes, right? If I was playing football, you'd pay my equipment fee, wouldn't you? You'd buy me a trumpet if I was in the band, right? Right?"

"When you put it that way, Rick—"

"My coaches think I can go all the way to state, Dad. I want to go to state, Dad. Don't you want me to go to state, Dad? Don't you want to be proud of me for something?"

I slammed down another can of corn. Water sloshed out of Lisa's bib bowl. I wanted to go to state and leave Veronica Satterwhite, head shaved like Joan of Arc in *The Lark,* burning at the stake at sectionals. "Godammit!" I yelled, giddy with how good it felt. I heard the booger chair squeal in the den. My mother rushed the door and jiggled the handle. I was about to smack down the shelf of pudding boxes when my father caved in and said I could make an appointment with an eye doctor.

❧

It killed me to admit it, but Carl had been right. I had been jealous of Carla, jealous that everyone was getting it except me, but now I could relax. Carla and Steve did it more often, but Ned and I did it with more class. Late November was too cold for blankets in the arboretum or lunchtime quickies at Herrick's Lake, so they either steamed up Steve's sister's car or wore out the sofa bed in the basement room Carl was fixing up. The cement floor was covered with streaks from their cigarette butts, two for every fuck, I liked to think. A very deep window well provided twenty-four-hour access for Steve. They did it like animals in a burrow, while Ned and I, Broadway sophisticates, turned a key in a lock, hung up our coats, and appreciated the bustle of Roosevelt Road before drawing the curtains.

On the other hand, Carla could be casual. She could saunter out of the basement to pee or take the phone from my outstretched hand without so much as a blush, whereas my body, from the knees to the roots of my scalp, would stay blotched with excitement for hours after Ned. Steve would holler for her from the hall and Carla would pick that moment to redo her tiny side braid in the bathroom mirror, while I had trouble remembering my locker number on the days I knew Ned would be waiting in his car across Herrick Road. A shrugger at life, my mother called her, but a shrugger at *sex*? That was true

128

sophistication, or at least indisputable proof that girls matured faster than boys.

Steve couldn't be casual either. My stepsister's pussy had turned the Briarcliffe Wolf Man into a whipped dog. He got big with the gifts, trying to cover R E G I over with shiny baubles when a piece of duct tape would have done the job. He trailed me at school with a whiny monologue: "She like that opal necklace I got her, Rick? Did you see it? Nice, huh?" "Did she let you read the card? Is the card out on her dresser and stuff?" "I'm thinking, what do you think, a bracelet, not an ID bracelet, a solid gold bracelet, a *bangle,* man." "Maybe I'll take jewelry next quarter and give her something I made myself, what do you think?" "Does she like Emerson, Lake, and Palmer? They're coming to Arie Crown, I'm gonna get tickets, man, what's the nicest hotel in Chicago, we could stay over and eat room service." "I want to get her something, something nice, something real nice for Christmas, Rick, what do you think? She says she likes typing, you know, maybe a typewriter, an *electric* one, a serious gift, for the future, what do you think?"

And because she was a shrugger, Steve's big, essential question was, "What does she say about me, does she say anything about me, man?" He would press his left hand into the crook of his right arm when he asked this, as if the wrong answer might start a hemorrhage. But I had no answer. Other than a flat "He's coming over" or "He's waiting for me," Carla didn't mention Steve.

Then he tried to bribe me into bringing him up, which was embarrassing. *I'd* get tickets to Emerson, Lake, and Palmer, or a dime bag, or speed, or all three. The day before Thanksgiving he promised a fix-up with a slut from Lombard named Leanne if I'd just find out whether Carla loved him. To shut him up, I griped that I didn't need to get fixed up with any sluts from Slumbard, then made the mistake of blushing, the slow, guilty blush of a preteen caught dancing in her underwear with a microphone hairbrush.

"Got your own slut, huh?" he said, eyes narrowed. "Who is she? Do I know her?"

"Nobody. I'm not with anybody." To hide my face, I leaned over to yank at the sock bunched in my heel.

"Hey, that's great, Rick. We can go on a double date, or you know."

Hearing a boy suggest doubling—girls' business, like the words *bangle* and *love*—coupled with the photo flash of Ned and me with a roach clip and boners in the back seat of Marilyn Hendrie's Volkswagen, made me start laughing. I was still leaning over when I felt the heel of his shitkicker smash into my side. I fell down, and he gave me two more kicks with the steel toe.

I lay there fighting for air in front of the west entrance to the gym. For a split second I had this idea that Steve might apologize, but a forest of legs was sprouting around my scattered books. Steve growled that I'd ask her if I knew what was good for me. Above the grip of his fingers, clenched at his waist, I could make out the top half of a swastika. So that was why he'd been going around with his shirt untucked. He stomped away, hand still on his knife, and I heard Hannelore saying to me, "You do not like the girls."

Our one-sided fight couldn't have been that interesting, a random burnout whaling on a random play fag between periods, these things happened, even in District 200. Nobody knew but me that this time a real fag was crawling for his books, not a suspected sissy who brought artichokes to school. This time it was a first-class, true-blue, ball-licking boy in the band. The difference between pretend and real, stowed beneath my aching ribs, got me to my feet.

∽◡◡

And then, a miracle. Steve and Carla sprang from their grimy burrow in the middle of the night with two hundred dollars from Carl's bureau, and Koontz Lake Turkey Day was canceled. A state trooper picked them up Friday outside Macon, Georgia. They'd been headed to Florida. After thirty-six hours of listening to Carl ream the Hendries out for the loss of his spotless darling, it was a relief to have him catch a plane. To celebrate I took Lisa all around Briarcliffe in her stroller, then caught up with my records. Ned was in Streator for Thanksgiving, thinking of me because he had said he would.

My mother made bacon and egg sandwiches on Friday night, like she used to when my father went out of town. It was sad to see her free the can of silver polish from a tangle of pans in a bottom cabinet to get to the electric skillet. I used to help polish the silver before her bridge luncheons. Afterward I'd drink the cold dregs from the lipsticked cups before dipping them in the soapsuds. The gold rims on her apple-blossom china, we remarked every time, were too delicate for the dishwasher.

Handing me the egg carton and the wire boinger, she asked me to play one of my records while we cooked, so I brought down *A Little Night Music* and put it on the den console. Whisking the eggs, I sang loud on my favorite parts. I hoped she'd notice how amazing the songs were, but the rush of the tap or the sizzle of the bacon or Lisa crawling underfoot got

131

in the way. I didn't mind so much, because I was processing how strange it felt to hear my music on the first floor of the house. I decided that it was okay for the songs to have a life outside my room, but I was secretly relieved that she didn't ask for side B.

I kept my hands under the table while she said grace and prayed aloud for the safe return of prodigal Carla. Then she asked me if I wanted to go to the Adler Planetarium or maybe the Art Institute the next day. We hadn't been downtown in forever, and Carl and Carla wouldn't be back until late. It would be like old times.

"What about Lisa?"

"She can come in her stroller. Or if you want, I'll get a babysitter."

I visualized lunch at the Walnut Room in Marshall Field's, where we used to go when she was single. It was right near a store I'd been dying to visit.

"Mom, there's this place I found out about called Rose Records that's all show tunes and it's supposed to be right in the Loop."

"I can check the phone book."

"That's just DuPage County."

"I can call information." She smiled, pushing the plate of sandwiches in my direction. I reached for one and stopped. How could I have forgotten that I was supposed to see Ned, who'd be back from Streator?

"What is it, Rick?"

"I can't go. I have coaching tomorrow."

"Again? It's Saturday."

"But I just blew the Hinsdale meet."

"You didn't 'blow' it, honey. You let somebody else win for a change."

"Miss Schuette and Mr. Wegner are thinking of putting me into another event."

"Another event? Why?"

"They think maybe I should give D.I. a rest and do Verse Reading."

"Verse reading? You mean poetry? Poetry out loud?"

This part I wasn't making up. Wegner said boys had a major advantage with verse, big surprise, but I couldn't tell him I thought it was faggier to recite Robert Frost than it was to do a faggy D.I.

My mother picked up a blob of egg with shaking fingers.

"What's wrong, Mom?"

"I don't want you to run away. Rick . . ."

"Mom, it's just coaching!" I said, horrified that she was thinking I might.

"Some things are . . . are wrong here, I know that, son."

She reached over to muss my hair. I ducked.

"Mrs. Hendrie must be going out of her mind. You and Steve were such good friends."

"Not so much really."

"You're not . . . doing drugs, are you, Rick?"

"No! And I won't either, okay, so be quiet about it, okay?"

I trained my eyes on Lisa. Too bad she couldn't talk. I took a sandwich diagonal. It was our joke that bacon and egg sandwiches cut diagonally tasted better.

"I need you here," she said in an awful voice.

My face was getting hot. I knew I might lose it. "Where would I go anyway?"

"Your father's," she said, choking back a sob. She wiped her eyes with the back of her hand.

I had never thought of it, but it looked like she thought about it a lot.

"I'm not going to leave you, Mom. I swear. I promise."

It was true. I would never leave her with him. I coughed up a teenage reason and told her I would never switch high schools halfway through, that was insane.

"Things are wrong here," she repeated. "I'm praying over that, but you can't run away Rick."

"I said I wouldn't, okay?" I swigged some juice. "Why *are* you praying over it? What is all this God stuff about?"

"Oh, Rick, I feel the Lord working such change in my life. . . ."

That was when she first told me about driving the car into the parking lot, hearing the man's voice, meeting Patty, and finally getting baptized at her Wednesday night service. Her syrupy, Kendigy tone as she spoke coated my ears and held me dumbstruck. She wasn't just becoming religious. The Lord was bringing her a peace and a happiness she had never known before. Marie had been born again in the spirit, the way the freaks got religion at Wheaton-Warrenville.

"Was God the man talking to you?"

A tear slid from her right eye. "In a way, I suppose He was."

"If you're so happy, why are you crying all the time?" I asked defensively. Adults should keep their unhappiness private.

"Because I'm learning how to be with Him."

There He was again, Jesus the person, in a leisure suit and a short beard, like Mr. Watson, the sociology teacher all the ugly girls were nuts about.

Lisa held out her sippy cup for more orange juice and broke the spell. My mother laughed, and it was time for dessert. I couldn't take more of that talk.

It should have gone both ways. I should have asked her to promise not to leave me.

The next morning the drive to school was like *Mission: Impossible*. Everything had to seem ordinary. As I got out of the car I returned a Nerf ball to Lisa in her safety seat. I walked to the entrance and waved as my mother turned right on Herrick Road. The hallways were empty, but I heard music coming out of the band room. Then I crept to the dark performing arts office and started a count of fifty. The team picture from the overnight was taped inside the window. Joe Bacino had his arm around me, Mindy was leaning against my shoulder. The last picture of my innocence, three hours before Ned's hallway interception, I thought melodramatically.

I went out again and stood in the cold. November 27. 10:43 a.m. Was there a sniper behind the giant Spirit Turkey on the gym roof? I checked left and right as Ned's car glided down the turnaround. The passenger door clicked open at my approach.

Usually I'd charge the couch, shucking as I went, and arch up to catch him, but this time Ned didn't run after me. He stood by his bedroom door and said in a Mae West voice that he had something to show me.

I hadn't been in the bedroom. The living room was the zone of me and him and his records and ginger ale and the lazy Susan. Behind that door was all him. I took a deep breath, followed him in, and swooned at the show posters parading around the walls. *Two Gentlemen of Verona, No, No, Nannette, Coco, Purlie, Hair, Chicago, Grease, Mack and Mabel, Over Here!, Pippin, Dames at Sea, 1776, Seesaw, A Chorus Line, Sugar, Applause,* and finally, over his bed, *Company, Follies, A Little Night Music,* and *Pacific Overtures.* I spun in their magic until I was dizzy and fell onto his black velvet bedspread.

He goosed me with a plastic cylinder. His something to show me was a pair of bikini underwear, red with turquoise piping, no fly, featherweight on my fingers.

I scrambled into them and posed, waiting to hear how sexy I looked.

"What happened to you?" he said.

"Huh?"

"Those bruises, Rick. There! Do they hurt?"

Steve's shitkickers had left yellow and purple arrows on my side. The way Ned was stretching out his arms, his chin thrust forward, his knees bent—ready to catch me—made me scared of what we were doing for the first time.

"No," I said, my voice quavering.

"Come here, baby," he said, and I did, ball into glove, and he rolled us up onto the bed. While I told him the history and adventures of Steve Hendrie and me, he stroked my hair and rubbed my back and said uh-huh like a guidance counselor. The knife upset him most. He didn't find my Hannelore imitation funny, and said he was disappointed that I didn't know anything about the Nazis except from *Hogan's Heroes.* I talked him out of reporting the incident to our principal, I promised to stay out of Steve's way, and for the second time in two days I promised a grown-up I would never do drugs.

The conversation came to an abrupt end because he kept calling me "baby." I got so horny I jumped him and yanked down his pants and bikinis. It felt fantastic to start us up. Afterward we had time for a turkey sandwich picnic under the posters, which he called window cards. Best of all was taking a shower with him. Our afternoon had yielded enough raw experience to pen an amazing letter to *Penthouse Forum*.

When I got home *A Little Night Music* was on the hi-fi again, the last song on side A, "Liaisons."

"Get cleaned up, Rick," my mother yelled from the kitchen. "Dinner's almost on the table."

"I'm clean, believe me." I patted the tightie whities in my coat pocket.

"There's mail."

I headed for the phone table. Before I could open the plane ticket my father had sent, I noticed Carl studying the album cover in the booger chair. I froze. He had cracked it all the way open, and it lay nearly flat in his Neanderthal hands. His eyes flickered in my direction, then returned to the foldout. How could I have possibly left it in the den?

The song finished. My mother called us to dinner. I took my chair. When Carl came in I would run out, reunite the record and the jacket, and rush them to the hospital upstairs.

Carl lumbered into the kitchen. The cover was still in his hand. He caught me biting my lip. He looked inside the foldout again, then flipped it over to inspect the back. He was going to set it on the wet counter, or worse, spill gravy on it at the table.

He was a trained psychologist, however, capable of greater cruelties. Waiting until my mother had turned back to the stove, he pulled out his chair and set the cover down on it, tree side up. He paused with the tiniest smile at the corners of his lips. He dared me to say something, dared me to stop him. Then he sat down.

The Colonial chair seats bore shallow, scoopy depressions. *A Little Night Music* was being crushed into the pattern of an upside-down harp. While my mother and an unrepentant Carla silently ate pork chops and fried potatoes, the weight and stench of Carl's horrible ass was suffocating one of my dearest comrades. Every twist in his chair, every long reach for the vegetable bowl or meat platter, every forkful of food that sank into the pit of his stomach, killed another moonlit lover hiding in the logo. I shut my eyes. I would retaliate somehow. I would borrow Steve's knife and cut the skin tag on Carl's gut and ram it up his nose. Then I would cut off his nose.

He got up after fruit cocktail. I whisked up the cover, followed him into the den, where he had flipped on the news, and removed the record from the console. I waited until I got to the safety of my room to dress the wounds. Despite bearing his lard for twenty-three minutes, the cardboard only had two tiny wrinkles, near the northeast and northwest corners. I soothed them with my fingers the way Ned had soothed my bruises. Ned alone would understand this torture. Recalling his touch, and the gift of his underwear, I was about to lock my door when Carla walked in.

She claimed she needed notebook paper. Burnouts hate direct questions, so I let her release information on her own clock. The reason she'd persuaded Steve to run away with her was that Regi had passed word through his mother that he was breaking up with Carla. He had dumped her from juvie. I said I was really sorry about that, and she shrugged, saying she had gotten over Regi by Nashville. I said now she could focus on Steve, he was completely nuts about her. She thought about it. Carl was plenty pissed, but Mr. Hendrie had been breathing fire in Macon.

"What about his stash?" I murmured.

"I tossed the can out the window as soon as I saw the cop lights."

"Smart thinking," I said, proud to be her accomplice by proxy.

She doodled some flowers on a page in my geometry notebook, then added a tombstone with the letters R E G I R.I.P. She crosshatched a shadow behind it and some tufts of grass on either side.

"Hey, you can really draw," I said.

"You're such an idiot, Brother Rick," she said, and we both cracked up. She started a daisy wilting over Regi's tombstone.

"Why Florida, Sister Carla?"

I hadn't meant it philosophically—maybe she had cousins in Miami—but she took so long to respond I thought she might be drawing me the answer. Finally she said, "I'm in the wrong life. Do you know what I mean?"

I nodded.

"I mean, I tried to be good for as long as I could, studying and being polite and stuff, but—"

I tried to imagine a polite Carla with braids and a dress, like a little Von Trapp on the cover of *The Sound of Music* album. Even squinting, it was impossible. Her parents split up and she grew those tits and that was what happened to her.

She looked at my shelf of little liquor bottles and sucked her teeth because they were empty. "Well, fuck it, you know?"

I did know.

For Patty Puller, things didn't just come from the Devil; they were *sent straight from the pits of hell*. She loved saying this, and it often segued into her rapid-fire "Hell is hot, dontcha know?" Magazines and news stories and television shows gave her lots of ammunition. So did our Christmas decorations. God and Mammon, whatever that was, couldn't serve the same tree. Wreaths yes, candy canes no, garland yes, tinsel no, snowflakes yes, snowmen no. The Abominable Snowman ornament I'd made out of Styrofoam balls in the second grade hurt her spirit. He was a creature of the night, a relation to lizards, dragons, spiders, toads, dinosaurs, elves, and all the other demons sent straight from the pits of hell. I twisted his pipe cleaner arms and let him dangle from the chain pull of my bedroom lamp.

Patty was equally vehement in her praise of the Creator. Her "God is good, yes, He is so so good" generally signaled a launch into another box of doughnuts. I would have laughed harder, except our Christmas tree was half-naked and my mother had begun tying a length of rope around her waist by the middle of

December. I asked what for one morning, and she said, "So I know where I'm bound."

I'd always pictured hell as a one-pit cavern deep inside the earth, with stalactites and stalagmites, but Patty said the Devil was literally everywhere and I could think of hell as a gigantic ant farm, a network of cesspools connected, sin to sin, by thousands of narrow, flaming passageways. I should have said, "Just like the basement"—porn in one corner and Carla in the other planning fornication get-togethers under Patty's fat ankles.

Predictably, Carla was crazy for Steve now. A brush with the law had made them persecuted lovers, grounded and tonguing all the time at school. The bruises from his boots, which neither of us mentioned, were my initiation into their service. I took Hannelore on walks around Martin Manor while they screwed on the stiff red pads of her sofa. We'd pass the arc of wheelchairs facing the holiday decorations in the lobby, and the ancient, dozing ladies—whom Hannelore called "Die Pantzootsen"—would say I was a wonderful grandson. After a few wobbly circuits she'd suggest "Tee und Süsse," and I'd have to stall her in the reading room. Carla would eventually sneak in and pop her head over an armchair, and I'd maneuver Hannelore into the correct hallway for the trip back to her cage. She'd nod with satisfaction to hear the vacuum cleaner droning on the other side of the door, where Steve had just turned it on. Then, slick with sex and deception, we'd cross the parking lot to Shakey's Pizza. To look at us, Carla sitting in between, shrieking at the oil soak the pepperoni discs made on her napkin, Steve cracking "Sieg Heil" jokes, you'd think we were in a commercial for pimple pads.

I regarded walking Hannelore as easy money, ten from Steve's take and the tightly rolled cigarette of her five, but Eric Smola said "rehabilitating seniors" would look great on my college applications.

Eric had gotten into Princeton on early decision, so his parents threw a party for the speech team at the beginning of December. It was my first time in a High Knob house. To the left of the center hall was the living room, which had built-in bookshelves, intricately patterned rugs instead of carpeting, and furniture that went together without being part of a set. The dining room had wallpaper and curtains in a matching pattern; the silver urns and dishes threw wavy reflections on the polished oval table.

"Drinks are on the *island*," Eric kept announcing, kitchen islands being the latest thing for rich people. I copied the way he squirted a wedge of lime into a glass of tonic water. That was my version of the vodka stinger in "The Ladies Who Lunch." For food, they had chips and pizza rolls and other regular stuff, but also a plate of smoked fish no one touched and a big chocolate log dotted with meringue mushrooms. His mother had taken ten hours to craft "the booosh," Eric said, pushing out his lips like a chimp to pronounce it.

The Musical Kendigs were in South America on a holiday mission, so Mindy wasn't there to ease my social jitters. Joe Bacino was mauling Beth Cook in the coat pile, and Mr. and Mrs. Smola would force me to invent college plans if I wandered too close to their control tower in the family room. Finally, Stacy Granbur rescued me from three hours of petting the Smolas' stinky old Airedale. We said hello and I told her I liked her jingle bell pin. Sister Patty approved bells, but not holly. Holly was pagan.

Stacy pulled at a bunch in her plaid skirt. Her fingernails were chewed down like mine. "Rick," she said, "I am going to need to ask your forgiveness."

"What?" I saw that my glass had left a ring on a shelf full of college mementos, and I covered it with my arm. The wet seeping through the sleeve made me shiver. "What do you mean, Stacy?"

"I need your forgiveness, Rick. See, I prayed for you to lose at Maine West last week, and you did, and so I need you to forgive me for my bad actions."

I didn't know then what a huge deal evangelicals make of in-your-face atonement, and I had no idea what to say. Was forgiveness best granted as a yes or no, or were we going to have to discuss it? The tiger in a Princeton sweater kept his counsel.

I'd gotten two fourths and a fifth at Maine West, five points total. Stacy had scored seven with *David and Lisa,* her piece about retards in love. Miss Schuette was beside herself, and Dina Demacopoulos only waved to me in the lunchroom, and Carl hit me with a "No prize, huh?" when I came home empty-handed the second tournament in a row. My critique sheets weren't any help. If you sucked, the judges wrote things like "nice job" or "clear delivery" and ranked you fifth. It was suddenly conceivable that Stacy, a senior with three years on the team, could be Wheaton-Warrenville's D.I. entrant at the district meet in January.

"God answered your prayer, Stacy," I said sourly. "Maybe you should thank Him instead."

"Oh no, Rick. It was wrong for me to want that . . . even if . . ."

"Even if what?"

"Even if your piece goes against God." Evil, or thoughts of it, was making Stacy's eyes glisten.

The completely former champion had had enough. "I think you're full of shit, Stacy," I snarled. She fell back from my profanity, but God, who is good, who is so so good, had a leather armchair ready to receive her.

"Homosexuality is an abomination, Rick, and your interp, that play—"

"*The Boys in the Band.*"

"I won't say its name, cuz it gives power to the Evil One, but that play promotes sin. That play is sin."

I would learn the hard way that there is no comeback to righteousness and that trying to can kill you. In the meantime, I just wanted Stacy to disappear, so I could join Brian and Ty doing Monty Python routines.

"You have my forgiveness," I said, but her moist expressions of relief were lighter fluid to the flames in my heart. It was lucky we weren't by the food, because it would have been just as easy to slam her holy, twitching face into Mrs. Smola's booosh. "Eat the whole log, you diabetic bitch," I'd say. "You are not taking my spot at districts."

~⚬~

My wipeout at Maine West made Ned nuts too. Instead of sex one afternoon, I had to do my D.I. He sat on the couch with a notepad. His Christmas tree, decorated with silver and blue ornaments, glittered to my right. I got hard just standing in front of him and couldn't resist tilting my boner toward him with a clench of my butt cheeks.

"Stop that, Rick," he snapped, "and start over."

"Stop what?"

"You know what. Does that still happen every round?"

"I don't know," I said truthfully. "I just do the scene."

"Well," he sighed, "I suppose most of your judges aren't out looking for it. Concentrate this time."

I started over. I got halfway through my introduction, and he stopped me again. "What is that accent, Rick?"

"What accent?"

Ned imitated me. It was like Bugs Bunny when he wears a plumed hat. "You sound like Truman Capote."

"Who is that?"

He stretched his arms along the top edge of the couch. "A famous priss," he said, flipping a wrist.

I winced. "Like Paul Lynde?"

"Exactly!" he shouted, as if seeing his point would make me feel better.

I looked out the window, pressing my knuckles into my cheeks. Paul Lynde. Charles Nelson Reilly. Wally Cox. Tiny Tim. The first snow of the season was sticking, so the cars were inching up Roosevelt. Two men were clearing the apartment parking lot. I focused on the bite and drag of their shovels.

"Come here, Rick," I heard him say. I stared at a little painted crèche in the windowsill and didn't move.

"I don't want to sound like Paul Lynde."

Ned patted the couch. "Don't get me wrong. Paul Lynde is funny in context, but he can make guys like us nervous."

"Guys like us?" I said, pretending I needed an explanation, when I was melting inside to be considered a guy like Ned.

"Guys who like guys the way we do. Like Michael does in the D.I."

"Does Paul Lynde make you nervous?"

"No, he tends to make me laugh."

"Me too," I said. "Even when I don't get the joke."

"That's right, Rick—his attitude is his talent. Now come here."

I sat on the edge of the couch while Ned explained that the

attitude behind my voice was the problem. My introduction didn't sound like *me*. I wasn't the prissy center square on a game show. I was a boy from the west suburbs of Chicago. Sensitive, yes, but to start winning again, I had to be *real*.

I did the intro over and over. He kept interrupting. "Look at me, Rick." "No, no, talk to *me*, Rick to Ned." "*Talk* to me, talk *to* me, not *at* me." I tried it sitting down, I tried it pacing. "Okay," he said, "*don't* look at me," so I tried it while I studied the album cover of *The Apple Tree*, while I tied my shoe, while I poured a glass of juice from the refrigerator, while I looked in the Yellow Pages for the Valley View Lanes. Each time he'd stop me before I could get past the first sentence: "Homosexuals are sad and lonely young men." I couldn't be real for five seconds. I couldn't even fake being real for five seconds. The shovelers were halfway down the sidewalk before we gave up and he let me start and finish the actual scene.

His verdict was that Michael and Alan weren't listening to each other anymore. I was rattling the scene off, just going through the motions, and so the D.I. had gone stale. Because I was bored, I was boring.

I nodded, completely humiliated. The first thing I was good at was over. My two trophies and my medal, which I'd already stowed in my pants drawer, could migrate to the attic with Candy Land and Game of the States. I checked my pocket for a dime. I would walk to the Seven Dwarfs and call my mother for a ride.

Ned the coach clicked his pen and said everybody went stale sometimes, even Broadway stars. What was more, there was an easy technical solution that would get me over my plateau. All I had to do was switch voices, make Michael's low and Alan's high. The judges wouldn't expect Michael to be the masculine-sounding one.

"But Michael's got most of the lines," I said.

"So?"

"It'll be too hard to give him Alan's voice."

"No one said going to state was a walk in the park, Richard."

"Did you go to state?"

He smiled like he'd been waiting weeks to tell. "I did. I did Humorous Interp, a cutting from Joseph Heller's *Catch-22*. I just missed getting into finals. I finished eighth in the great state of Illinois."

I could have asked him what year and done the math later, but instead I asked him what he wore.

"I had a hand-me-down corduroy jacket. And a very skinny tie. And I wasn't anywhere near as handsome as you."

To outrun my blush, I agreed to change voices. The second thing I was good at would be over if I didn't. He pulled me into his arms, saying he *loved* my real voice and my real hair and my real lips.

"Is this how you coach the kids on your team?" I asked, hugging back as hard as I could. I had a vision of Miss Schuette lezzing it up with a Glenbard West prose reader. Or Wegner frenching an extemper.

"No, baby, it's only how I coach you. Now let's get you home."

He went for his keys. He loved my voice and hair and lips. It was the first time I had ever heard that verb in connection to me. My mother and grandmother didn't count. This is the point of snow, I thought, watching it fall on the world in soft splinters.

New Trier West was another humungous tournament. North Shore towns were even wealthier than the western suburbs, so besides Veronica Satterwhite, I had my first two Shakespeares in first round. A curly-haired boy sprayed his throat from a Chloraseptic bottle before and after doing *The Merchant of Venice.*

Veronica called him a dickhead, which was a bigger surprise than her deigning to speak to me in an overheated corridor crammed with kids. I had been walking behind her, trying not to trip over the food drive boxes. She suddenly turned around and used the socialite's trick of pretending that we had always been friendly. I almost slammed into her.

"Oh, Rick," she said, "I meant to wish you a Merry Christmas." To cover the drop of my jaw, she added, "I'm Veronica. Veronica Satterwhite. I go to Wheaton Central."

"I know who you are," I said.

She sailed right over that bump. "Gosh, what did you think of that round just now? All those strong D.I.'s. I'm worried."

"But you're always great, Veronica. I love your D.I. so much," I said, weirdly happy to tell her the truth. I wouldn't beat her by lying. "My Blue Heaven" had made me tear up again.

"Thanks," she said, swooping some hair behind her ear. She was even prettier, foxy even, now that she wasn't interping two twelve-year-olds. "How about the Shakespeare scenes?"

"I didn't get the first one." I checked my sheet for the name. "*Macbeth.*"

Veronica giggled. "I know, I know! I thought I'd die when she grabbed her boobs and screamed, 'Unsex me now!'"

"Those were the words?" I said. "I didn't hear them really."

I still didn't understand the line, but it didn't matter because Veronica had said the word "boobs," stuck out her own (on the small side), and then we both couldn't stop laughing.

"How about *The Merchant of Venice*?" I asked.

"Oh, Craig. I remember him from last year." And that was when she said it. "I think he's a stuck-up dickhead." She imitated the flourish of his Chloraseptic squirts. I crumpled against a wall and pointed to a jumbo can of Del Monte creamed corn in a box at our feet, and that made everything even more hilarious. I was in another teen commercial now, this time for breath mints, because suddenly we were face-to-face and the bob of her tiny gold crucifix against her cowl neck was hypnotizing me. I would ask her to the movies. Then we'd go see *The Nutcracker* at the College of DuPage, then to Rascal's for onion loaf and whiskey sours. We went to rival schools, so our love would be taboo, like Tony and Maria's in *West Side Story*.

"I wish you went to Wheaton-Warrenville," I gasped out. I'd tongue her against my locker. We'd double with Carla and Steve.

She touched my arm. It was time to be serious. Second round started in ten minutes, and we had bathroom checks. "I hope you won't start needing a Chloraseptic bottle," she said.

"Hey, what's that supposed to mean?" I gave her a playful nudge.

She smiled. "You changed voices in your D.I."

"You mean you noticed?"

"Of course I did. Michael's got the deep voice now."

"Was it bad?" I asked, fishing a little. Part of Veronica Satterwhite's power over me lay in never letting on whether she thought I was any good. I wasn't sure how "real" my intro had been, but my throat felt a little froggy from yelling in Michael's new register.

"Oh no, Rick," she replied. Her huge brown eyes stretched even wider. "Just—"

"Just what?"

"Strained. You know, scratchy. I would really hate for you to damage your vocal cords." She brushed my arm again.

"Thank you, Veronica," I said. "I'll be careful, I promise."

With so many schools in play, awards were in the gym. There hadn't been a final round, so everyone was a potential winner, which totally jacked up the tension. We sat way up top. What with the boundary and free-throw lines running underneath the trophy tables and the scoreboard and the winched-up basketball hoops and the stacks of wrestling mats and the old championship banners and the whistling and clapping, not to mention the thunder of twenty eight hundred feet on the wooden bleachers when somebody won, speech team felt like a blood sport. And maybe because Empress Veronica had let down the drawbridge long enough to feign concern about my vocal cords as a psych-out, I felt free to borrow a trick from her playbook. My hair wasn't long enough to flip, but I took miles of time stepping down the bleachers to collect my second-place trophy. Then I did her one better: I waited on the court to shake hands with the D.I. champion, a stocky black kid from Chicago Boy's Latin. Flashbulbs went off to record my magnificent interracial gesture.

"Very classy, Rick," said Miss Schuette. "Coaches remember things like that."

My diabolical red-and-turquoise underwear had trounced Veronica and her cross of gold. Ranking me first out of eight

(Chloraseptic Craig got second and Veronica fourth), my first round judge wrote, "You seem to be making up the dialogue as you go along." This, all three of my coaches agreed, was the highest possible compliment.

∽◡∾

Sister Patty rained Bibles down on Kingston Drive Christmas morning. I got the Young Man's Bible, Carla the Young Lady's Bible, Carl the Lord's Steward Bible, Lisa a New Testament picture book, and my mother a Concordance, whatever that was, which she slammed against her chest like a brick. I had bought her a twenty-five-dollar compact from Marshall Field's. Its silver cover was embossed in red and blue and green enamel, and it slipped into its own suede drawstring pouch. She said it was too pretty to use. I never saw it again.

Carla did an amazing thing: she got me the cast album to *Follies*. She wouldn't let on how she knew I coveted it, swore up and down that it was a hunch, until she finally admitted that she thought the cover was cool. Given Ned's opinion that *Follies* was "absolutely staggering," I had been afraid to buy it and disappoint his and my expectations. My scalp would tingle in Wax Trax even to look at the gorgeous stone goddess with the stars in her crown and the blue seaweed hair and the sad eyes and the perfect pillow lips and the crack splitting the right side of her face. I knew without knowing that the crack meant something wonderful was just about to end. It was possible I'd fall into that crack of *Follies* and never get out again, so I'd put the record back in the D-E-F's and purchase something safer.

I can still visualize the image of Carla stumbling her way to an unfamiliar corner of Wax Trax. She flips. Her right hand hovers, then picks up a record. The cover is the closest she's seen to a rock album. She turns it over to study the even larger face on the back, more mysterious, because the billing box is empty. What does it tell her? Too wasted to decode the goddess, wanting a cigarette, she shrugs, decides. She scuffs back to the counter, the frayed edges of her elephant bell bottoms tickling the floor. She crosses Rick off the list, and her life goes on.

My Wax Trax gift to her, Jefferson Starship's *Spitfire*, wasn't so loaded. She slapped me five and stuck the adhesive bow from my wrap job on top of Lisa's head. My mother caught the three of us with the Instamatic. *Follies* is cradled in my arms like the Christ child.

Ned had tipped a postcard of James Dean into the pages of his present. It said, "For Richard—to *bone* up on—Merry Christmas. XO N." It was two days before vacation, and he came out of the kitchen carrying a tray of cocoa and Toll House cookies, nude except for his socks, a holiday apron, and a Santa hat. Under the cookie plate was *The World of Musical Comedy* by Stanley Green. Suddenly ashamed of my gift, and plotting how to hustle it back into my coat pocket, I took some time over the book. Seeing pages of words attached to the names of my friends felt like school and made me anxious, so I skipped around looking at photos.

Ned's hand, warmed around a cup of cocoa, found the center of my back. "That book pretty much saved my life," he said.

"How do you mean?"

"It was a way out of Streator. One day I found it in the county bookmobile. After a while I was only allowed to check it out every other trip. The librarian was queer, I think. Anyway, he let me keep it when I graduated high school."

"I don't want to take it from you," I said, smoothing the cover.

"I have my own copy, kiddo." He flicked his arm at the shelf above the records.

He was somewhere else, somewhere sad. I crept up and put my arms around his waist. It was the first time I found myself making out for a reason other than how good it felt. Ned was saving my life, no "pretty much" about it, and I thanked him with kisses.

He loved my present. "It almost matches the tree," I said, trying to apologize for its dorkiness. "I made it in second grade. My teacher's name was Miss Nolan."

Ned put my Abominable Snowman on his all blue and silver tree, stretching its pipe cleaner arms out so it could reach the star on top, like King Kong on the Empire State Building.

All these gifts, Bible excepted, traveled to New Jersey. *The World of Musical Comedy* was in the seat pocket in front of me; *Follies*—to which I had surrendered completely—was swaddled in bubble wrap and lying in the manger of the overhead compartment; my father's contact lenses sat on my eyes like poker chips; under my suit coat and vest I wore a third shirt and tie from my mother.

Tucked in my breast pocket was a little black box Steve Hendrie had slipped me in our backyard on Christmas Eve. I opened it right there. He'd gotten me a pair of Playboy cufflinks, rabbit heads in profile, wearing tiny bow ties.

He shivered and crossed his arms even though it wasn't very cold out. "Uh . . . you can wear them at your meets, Rick. It's Bunny luck."

"Where did you get them?" I gushed, ready to sprint to the streetlight for a closer look.

He scuffed a heel on Lisa's slide, looking away. "A guy I know, Andy, he's been to the Playboy Club."

Andy was his dealer. "Cool," I said. Sex and drugs. "Thanks, Steve."

Back when we would snicker at a title like "It Came Upon a Midnight Clear," Steve and I made a pact to go to the Playboy Club on August 8, 1979, the night we were finally both eighteen. After parking the Camaro, we'd sink into a conversation pit by a roaring fire. April Gladden and her best friend Cheryl, tits sloshing like water balloons in their creamy satin suits, would bring us sloe gin fizzes, then sit in our laps and pull the hairs in our chopper sideburns.

"Andy gave them to me, but it's not like I'm gonna wear cufflinks."

"They are so great, Steve."

"They're not real silver or anything."

"I think they're great," I said. "I didn't get you anything."

"That's cool. You help me out, man. You're practically my brother and all now."

A shadow crept across the den sheer. Steve muttered, "Sieg Heil!" and stuck a smaller package in my coat pocket for Carla. He headed past the swing set. A sentry spruce swayed as he brushed against its branches, the fox gone out on a very dark night.

I pretended to one and all on the plane that I was a seasoned flyer. I ignored the stewardesses during the safety demonstration. As we lifted off, I trained my eyes on the aisle, not out the window. Until the meal, I was Benjamin Stone in *Follies,* a very big deal. I picked beef over chicken, and even though I knew I was supposed to think it was terrible, I ate the whole thing in a flash. The man on my right, a real Benjamin Stone reading the

Wall Street Journal, asked me if I wanted another piece of chocolate cake. I said yes.

His fingers crushed the ridges of frosting a little as he lifted his square and set it on the crumbs in my dessert compartment. He was already back in his paper when I said thank you. He didn't answer or speak again or look at me for the whole rest of the flight to Newark, not even to say goodbye when we landed or "Have a nice trip" or "Happy New Year." That second piece of cake was the best gift of 1976.

∾⋍∾

My stepmother brought three small children and two vans of heirlooms to the marriage. My father's chrome-and-glass bachelor-pad stuff was crammed into the guest room where Julia's parents, Bev and Cactus, were staying. The rest of the new house was coated with square and oval portraits, framed deeds and charters and family trees and horse pictures, needlepoint pillows and glass-knobbed dressers and bizarre knickknacks I had to ask the names of. "Sugar, your daddy married *up,*" cackled Bev when she surprised me in the dining room swinging a punch ladle the size of a Wiffle bat. Like "bone orchard" or "hosebag," "marrying up" was a gratifying metaphor, easy to attach to the wood stepstool set against the side of the canopy bed my father and Julia climbed aboard every night. My mother, picking a trail through the Schwobs' shit-filled dog run in Koontz Lake, Indiana, was a giant warning label against the hazards of marrying down.

Cactus and Bev were fun old people. They had matching tans and silver pompadours. They told dirty jokes and black jokes and Jew jokes and thought everything was funny. When Julia said "I do" in the civil ceremony, Bev smacked her butt

155

with the bouquet and wheezed, "Three times the charm." Afterward they all got sloppy drunk at the restaurant, and I scored points by lighting Bev's cigarettes the way my mother's Ginger Creek friends had taught me. By the time dessert arrived, Cactus, who had a habit of pressing the bottom of his stomach like he was testing a melon, was promising to get me into show business. He was the host of Louisville's longest-running children's program, and every last jack in bluegrass broadcasting owed him a favor. If I liked, I could gofer at the station and live at Mulberry that summer. Mulberry was the name of their house. My father, pulling at his bushy new Southern mustache, played along with the idea but said I'd have to bring my grades up, which was a definite first.

I did my D.I. for them the next night. Julia's kids were asleep, and the adults had poured themselves a round before settling into what Bev called settees. The backs curved up and out and down like roller coasters. In front of me, hanging above the middle swoop of the green settee, was a Confederate saber; above that was a portrait of its owner, General Edelen Custis MacCauley. One of his epaulets, its corkscrews faded to a dried mustard color, stood under a glass bell on the end table at Bev's right. The glass bell on her left housed the guts of a clock dating back before the Battle of New Orleans. Julia, sitting between her mother and my father, had drawn her legs under the circle of her skirt. The fingers of her ring hand were tucked in his fist. Cactus was belly-thumping in a matching swoopy armchair.

I shook my arms out in front of the living room mirror, like I thought I was a diver or a gymnast. The cashmere turtleneck from Julia made me feel taller, and lean instead of scrawny. The haircut she alone could talk me into—completely above the ears, risky for Illinois—suited the eldest son of the man she married. In my contact lenses I was more his likeness, and for a change that felt better than okay.

They loved my interp at New Trier West, two firsts and a second, but it was a different story in Ridgewood, New Jersey. I finished, and four hands reached for their glasses.

My father weighed in first. "Wow. That's . . . something. Son."

"That's something, all right," said Cactus.

"And you say you get prizes, sugar?" asked Bev after a swallow. "Prizes for saying all . . . just what you just said?"

The turtleneck was an electric blanket on high, and my ears were lit stove coils. I wanted to sit, but an antique doll with long red hair had taken the nearest empty seat. Picking up a doll, even to move her, would look suspicious.

"It wasn't very good this time," I said.

"Oh, Rick, don't speak false," Julia said quickly, too quickly, like she was afraid I'd ask for a do-over. "You were *very* good. It was a very professional presentation, and I thank you for it."

Cactus and Bev made vague agreeing noises as they hoisted up and out. Julia pushed on my father's knee to spring herself from the settee and keep him there to deal with me.

I dropped into Cactus's chair. I made a fake cough.

My father was desperate for a gesture. He wet a finger in his glass, trying to stir up a refill. He stuck out his chin, more deeply cleft than mine. He started to scratch his balls, then stopped. Finally he found a nickel wedged in a corner of the settee and zigzagged it under the lamp to read it.

"1967, Denver," he said.

I could have gone on offense. I was old enough now to begin blaming him for things, for having had to move seven times before I was eleven, for a different school every year because he wasn't climbing fast enough or couldn't get along with his bosses, but instead I just played along with our old game.

"I was seven," I replied. "Erdenheim, Pennsylvania, 404 Cedar Lane, phone number AD3-4835."

In the Erdenheim house, one of their early duplexes, the liquor was kept on a shelf in the broom closet, and the ice came out of the freezer in trays. Now Julia was rattling silver tongs in a crystal ice bucket at a freestanding bar in a game room, four more signs of marrying up.

"I was thirty-three," he said. "Philadelphia, Pennsylvania, 749 Locust Street. . . ." He faltered. I mouthed the word "twelve," but he didn't need it. "Twelfth floor, phone number . . . phone number . . ."

"I can't help you out there," I said, lying. My mother would let me dial the number if she needed to call his office. And I would charge his legs when he came through the front door, wait for the tap of his briefcase on the tile and then the giddy lift above his head. Once I began to talk, and finally got it through my head that my mother wasn't going to leave and never come back, it was funny how I began to seek contact with my father's body. From going stiff as a board in his arms, I looked for ways to get inside them. There was a period in grade school, until I was about nine, when I gave him back rubs on the den floor nearly every night. I perched on his tailbone, squeezed his arms and karate chopped his shoulders in front of the television while my mother ran my bath. I wondered if his stepkids would keep up the tradition.

He flipped the nickel and smacked it on his left hand. "WA6-2223," he said, tickled as hell to remember.

"Your boss?" I said, prompting.

"Hackie Vaughan. Sick bastard," he added, an improvisation. Because of Mr. Vaughan we only lasted seven months to the day at 404 Cedar Lane. After Erdenheim, I gave up trying to make friends.

We looked at each other, caught by the next question. Rather than risk a soppy scene by reminding him who *my* bosses were in 1967—"Mommy and Daddy"—I brought the hidden topic of our conversation to light and said that *The Boys in the Band* hadn't been my idea at all, but that I really loved competing.

"Good," he grunted, and flipped the nickel again, but to make sure, he took another cautious step. "So what happens in the play, Rick, isn't happening to you." Statement, not question, delivered hypercasually. I tilted my head and locked eyes with General Edelen Custis MacCauley. "Yankee cocksucker," he thundered in a cartoon accent. I told my father hell no, I was in love with a brown-haired girl from Wheaton Central. Who reminded me of Julia.

That whopper rated me my own bourbon. The five of us got really tanked on New Year's Eve too, Veronica Satterwhite the recipient of many elaborate Southern toasts.

❧

The Veronica dodge so relieved my father, I didn't need my backup plan to get into New York City on the third of January. I had intended to tell him that Eric Smola, incoming member of Princeton's Class of 1981, would be waiting for me with his mother at the far left pillar by the New Jersey Transit counter, but he didn't ask. Before he disappeared behind a line of people buying subway tokens, he made me show him my return ticket. "Now put your wallet in your front pocket, son," he said, "and stick close to your friends." He added two twenties to it, patted my shoulder, and that was that.

Eric Smola was Ned, of course, leaning on the pillar in white painter's pants, an exciting violation of the teacher dress code. His gold belt buckle had "After Dark" engraved on it. A magazine for guys like us, he told me with a wink.

We had been thirteen days apart, so everything felt like the first time. He closed around me on the third-floor landing of the crooked little building on Horatio Street, and I came in my pants. The apartment he was using belonged to an actress friend named Amy Conrad who was off on a national tour of *Grease,* a fact that blew my mind. Amy's apartment, like something on *Love, American Style,* was small, with weird angles, and was painted bright orange. A ceiling-high corn plant blocked her only window. Instead of a closet, there was a rolling rack of clothes in her hallway. On her fireplace mantel was a picture of Ned and Amy in costume from when they did summer stock. Their mouths were open midsong. She was Reno Sweeney and he was Billy Crocker. I didn't know *Anything Goes.*

I giggled at Ned's bangs. "You look funny with eye shadow on," I said.

"How about the tan blush number two?" He put his arms around my waist from behind, one of my favorite moves. "We were such kids. I had basically fallen off the turnip truck. That was the summer Amy talked me out of marrying her."

I scrunched in my shoulders and slid my arms together.

"You mean married married? Did you . . . you know . . . did you and Amy do stuff?"

"Sure, but it didn't feel right, Rick. And Amy, God bless her, knew it before I did."

"Why 'God bless her'?"

"It was a confusing time. What's wrong, Rick?"

I'd only been in the city two hours. I didn't have the words to say that New York was not a place for confused people, and that I didn't really want to dial Veronica Satterwhite's phone number and make good on my whoppers when I got back to Wheaton. My parents were confused enough to get married twice apiece, and here was Ned confused about something as simple as dick or pussy. The world was blowing up again.

"I don't want to like girls too!" I cried.

"Do you?" Ned asked calmly, like it was no big deal if I did, which scared me even more.

"I know I'm supposed to. When I was around Steve, I pretended to. It was something to talk about. Some are sexy sometimes."

"They are."

"And sometimes . . ."

"Sometimes?"

I explained the Veronica Satterwhite thing. Ned said that didn't sound like the hots to him, it was probably that I just had a crush on Veronica's talent, like the kind he'd had for Amy back in stock.

"How old were you in that picture?" I asked, wondering if sex confusion could be plotted like a graph, or marked on a timeline, like B.C. and A.D.

He pushed up his sweater sleeves. "Twenty-two. Amy was a year older."

"Are you thirty-three?" I blurted out. The age of Jesus on the cross, another Sister Patty fact.

Now he was surprised. As he turned me around, a knife of sunlight through the corn plant hurt my eyes. I covered them with a hand.

"No, Rick, I'm not."

He took my hand and held it against his heart. I counted along with the beats. Twelve, thirteen, fourteen, fifteen, sixteen. I had a crazy thought that his heart would tell me his age by stopping.

"Do you want me to tell you how old I am?"

I looked at the kidney beans of his nostrils, the double creases in his lower eyelids, the scar under his lip. Behind him was a poster of *A Star Is Born*. He was positioned almost exactly in Kris Kristofferson's spot. He belonged to Barbra Streisand, not me.

"No," I said. "I don't want to know. I don't care."

He took a step backward. My hand slipped from under his. The blood was rushing to my head.

"Do you want to stop what we're doing, Rick?"

"Are you crazy?" I reached for him, and he stepped back again, putting more space between us. He was asking for a divorce. "I don't want it to stop, ever ever ever," I said, shaking my head like a dust mop.

Ned kept still, brushed down his mustache. To get him back, to get him to move to me, I said what needed to be said. From a corner of what scientists have since designated the lizard brain came forth what I knew he had wanted to hear ever since we'd started things at Wax Trax.

I said, "Come here, Daddy."

The sex—sex after a fight—was, to use a *Penthouse Forum* cliché, mind-blowing. To ice the cake, I refused the rarefied company Ned tempted me with at Footlights Records, *110 in the Shade* or *The Happy Time* or *New Girl in Town*, in favor of *Anything Goes*. *Anything Goes* wasn't worth the trip, he said, when I could get it in Lombard, but I told him I wanted to hear "You're the Top," his duet with Amy. I wasn't jealous of her anymore.

"With all the places to go in New York, the kid picks Footlights," Ned sniffed to his friend Reed at lunch, but I knew he was proud of me, proud to show me off.

"Show Queen Central," said Reed.

The one woman lunching at Uncle Charlie's Restaurant on Third Avenue at 36th Street (I took a matchbook) was a man. I leaned into my daddy and took a fry from his plate. "I can come back to see the Empire State Building any old time."

"How about this summer?" Ned said.

"That would be great." More than anything, I wanted to spend a whole night with him.

Dark and compact, Reed Goodkin reminded me of Mr. Malchus, the wrestling coach at Wheaton-Warrenville. His hair was going on top, but he had black sworls of it on his knuckles. His nose flared when he talked, and he talked very fast. Reed and Ned had done musicals together too, but now Reed was in advertising. His job was casting people in television commercials. Eighty-five college-age kids had come in that morning to pretend to be surprised for the camera when they found out that the gum they were chewing was sugarless.

"Why do they pretend?" I asked.

"Because they already know the product is sugarless."

"Isn't that like cheating?"

Ned and Reed both thought that was a riot. The red leather started to fart under their shaking backs. A couple of men in plaid shirts and painter's pants looked over at us across the aisle. I ducked my chin a tiny bit to the right and pointed my right forefinger and thumb like a gun in the direction of my mouth.

"You mean, this is sugarless?" I asked.

Ned shook harder on the banquette, but Reed stopped laughing.

"Do that again," he said.

I repeated the line, this time inserting a crucial pause, the pause of a dramatic interp champion: "You mean, this is"—wonder, surprise, joy—"sugarless?"

The gun went off.

"Do you think you can come in this afternoon?" Reed asked.

"I have to meet my dad at the train station."

"I can call him, arrange to put you on a later train. Can you come back tomorrow?"

"Come on, Reed," said Ned.

"Come on, Ned. With that look? Why save all that talent for the speech team?"

Something awful passed between them. "Because he's still in high school, that's why," Ned hissed over the table.

His neck went as red as the leather. Ned was angry, a first. I don't know why *I* apologized, but I did. Eventually they pulled back and fought to get the waiter's attention. That brought up old actor-waiter stories. I looked around, amazed at all the queers, Paul Lyndes and lumberjacks, eating in broad daylight under the hanging ferns. After a bite of banana cream pie, I said, "This is sugarless?" and made a joke of the whole thing.

I sat between them in the cab. A crime, Reed said, that I hadn't come in on a matinee day, since he could have gotten me into any show I wanted, even *A Chorus Line*. He knew the assistant general manager. "Stay with me next time," he said, brushing my cheek with his lips as I got out of the cab. Then, just like at the restaurant, he wouldn't accept Ned's money, and that set off another mini-fight.

"Is he rich?" I asked later.

"He's done well for himself, but he's lonely," said Ned.

"But the city is full of boys."

"Not so many boys like you."

For my last two hours in New York, Ned and I had an amazing time just walking through the West Forties. The cold wind and the skyscrapers put a bounce in his walk that I tried to imitate. We couldn't hold hands, but I slipped in a "Daddy" when things felt perfect, which was like every two minutes. He kept telling me how cute I looked, the contacts and the haircut and the turtleneck I guess. He took a picture of me holding my nose by a cart selling roasted chestnuts. The famous Triton Gallery was closed on Mondays, but we looked at the show posters in the window. Ned took me into the lobbies of the theaters where *Chicago, Grease, Shenandoah, Pippin,* and *The Wiz* were playing. I stared at the cast boards, hardly believing that the magic in my room happened live behind the locked gold doors. I said I felt like I was visiting my friends' apartments, and Ned didn't make fun or tell me that was dumb. Instead he played landlord. *Company* used to rent *Shenandoah's* apartment, *Pippin* had taken over *Fiddler on the Roof*'s lease, things like that. My daddy really had been a boy like me.

We saved the Shubert—*A Chorus Line*—for last. We took Polaroids of each other standing in front of the door panels covered in silver mirrors, and got a lady in a white fur hat to snap the two of us together. I let him buy me a T-shirt in the lobby, and then we went to have hot chocolate at the Howard Johnson's in Times Square.

"*Anything Goes,* huh?" said my father, looking at the record in the train car, another all-male situation, but so unlike Uncle Charlie's that I couldn't stop giggling at the comparison. "I think your mother and I saw *Anything Goes* in Philadelphia. When you were a baby."

I didn't believe him.

"What's so funny, kiddo?" he asked. He was in a good mood too. I guessed we both got laid that day.

"Another show biz offer," I said. I'd found a business card in my coat pocket, Mr. Reed Goodkin, Creative Supervisor, Grey Advertising. He must have slipped it in during the cab ride.

"Huh?" he said, already into his paper.

I wondered, when Julia stripped off his undershirt during sex, did his chest glow a hot cherry red like mine?

Mindy Kendig came back from Peru with a cockroach
the size of a change purse pinned to her sweater.
Repulsive to begin with, it was *alive*. When Mindy
blew down onto its head, as if into a flute, it buzzed and slowly
flicked its wings, one at a time, shiny veined windows reflecting
light as they cut the air.

All day nobody could talk about anything except the green-
black bug on Mindy's left tit. After a first look I kept away; my
scalp tingled even to contemplate the thing, but Carla was so
beside herself she stopped me in the hall to say that while they
were changing for gym, Mindy had unpinned it for Carla to
hold. Its legs scratched her palm like toothpicks.

"So it's not mechanical," I said. That rumor had started
third period.

Carla shook her hair. Steve had left a fresh trail of grape
marks on her neck. She repeated something Mindy had obviously told her. "The exoskeleton is durable enough to glue the
pin mechanism to its abdomen."

"What does it eat?"

"Plants. Lettuce. I'll find out."

"How?"

"I'm going over to Mindy's to help her feed it."

"You're what?" This was unbelievable, like me fishing for muskies with Carl.

"Tell Marie I'm getting a ride home from Mindy," she exhaled, suddenly mature.

"Don't steal it, klepto," I said, fuming that she'd see Mindy's house before I did. I had envisioned the Kendigs' as a Jesus version of a *Playboy* vodka ad, decorated in polar bear fur, white leather, ivory crucifixes, and sleigh bells. Carla and the roach would be dark magnets for each other in the blond Scandinavian splendor. She'd steal it, and she and Steve would screw in our basement with it buzzing between her jugs. Then it would come after me.

"As if Mindy didn't already get enough attention," said Miss Schuette after school. I was learning that she liked to get her digs in at our Doomsday preacher.

Districts were a couple of weeks away, and Schuette and Wegner were picking the team. Stacy Granbur had seniority and diabetes, but I was fifty-three points ahead in cumulative scoring. I peeked in through the side window to watch a little of Stacy's D.I. *The Boys in the Band* might give me boners, but *David and Lisa* made Stacy's hips twitch like she was doing the hula on a full bladder. When she was finished she shot across the hall into a herd of born-agains. She garbled out a shaky good luck through a wet, pebbly mouthful of Baby Ruth.

I walked to the spot in the front of Room 100 where I'd first read "The Scarlet Ibis" back in Oral Com II. The A on my report card was a first. Schuette noted and approved of my contact lenses. Wegner crossed his arms when she observed that my shorter hair would let the judges see my face better. Then he leaned across the aisle and she drew a line on another pad in her folder. They were like scientists in a Tang commercial. To break the tension, I said I weighed 136, and my shirt size was 14$\frac{1}{2}$, 34.

"Just do your piece," barked Wegner.

Schuette ate her knuckles through the whole thing. I could tell she loved the voice change. When it was over, Wegner jabbed the eraser end of a pencil up the desk. "Do you think your voice will hold up?" he asked me.

"Of course it—"

A flick of his pencil cut Miss Schuette off. I suddenly understood that Mr. Wegner didn't like me, not really. I didn't know when or how that had happened. I jingled the change in my pocket to camouflage a boner check, then walked to the podium and flopped my arms over it. "I made it through three rounds at New Trier," I said.

"Your voice is strained, Rick. It's not natural to you."

"You never said that when I used it for Alan's character."

"So we'll keep working on the voice," said Schuette. "I have exercises."

Wegner shut her up with a cough. "I'm thinking like a judge at the state finals, and I'm saying I'm not convinced."

"But you gave me this piece, Mr. Wegner," I countered. "I didn't have to be on speech team, but you asked me to do it, and I love doing it!"

Cheryl Ito and Ellen Bintz, on deck for the face-off in Prose Reading, were peering in the glass window. It wasn't supposed to take this long.

"Why did you change your introduction, Rick?" Wegner asked.

169

"He didn't. It's the same as it's always been," said Schuette.

"Quiet, Jill," he said, looking at me. "Rick added a word to the first sentence of his introduction. In fact, it's the very first word out of his mouth. The very first word you said was 'some.' Instead of 'Homosexuals are sad and lonely young men,' you said, '*Some* homosexuals are sad and lonely young men.' Did you say that, Rick? Or did I mishear?"

His voice was buzzing like Mindy's cockroach. Schuette began to fold the cuff of her shirtsleeve.

"Did you say 'some' homosexuals in your intro at New Trier?"

I nodded yes.

"Why did you change it?"

Ned was happy. I was happy. It was my interpretation.

"Because it's probably not true," I replied. "They can't all be sad and lonely, I mean. And besides that, some homosexuals are female lesbians, and some homosexuals are old. Like Paul Lynde. So the intro doesn't make sense. It's an unfair *stereotype* is what I think."

Angry as he was, Wegner nearly cracked a smile. Like my father, he had his doubts, which I shot down, not with Veronica Satterwhite and her perky tits but with one of the magic high school words teachers cream to hear. Gerund, bicameral, photosynthesis, integer, assonance, totalitarian. Stereotype was definitely on that list.

Wegner wasn't finished. "This material is controversial, Rick, it pushes buttons. Remember that judge at U. High who questioned its suitability?"

"That judge was full of soybeans," I said. Schuette snorted behind her hand.

"She's entitled to her opinion," he said, buzzing again. "And remember, 'state' means just that, the whole *state,* and once you get past Joliet, Illinois is part of the Bible Belt."

"Is it made out of rope?" I said, thinking of my mother.

He rubbed his oatmealy neck and sighed. "It could be a noose to swing from if we're not careful."

Miss Schuette applauded. I was on the team.

"So you're going back to your original introduction, aren't you? The one I wrote for you."

I sniffed an advantage. "It's one little word, Mr. Wegner, but if it makes you feel better—"

The chair squealed. Ellen and Cheryl ran from the door.

"It's not to make *me* feel better, Rick!" he shouted. "It's to cover our behinds. We can't risk the charge that the Wheaton-Warrenville forensics team promotes homosexuality."

Too late for that, I thought, checking over his head. The clock stood at 4:42. My pederast—I'd looked up the word over Christmas—was waiting in his car about eighty yards from my present position, waiting for my back handspring onto his lap.

We shook hands, and Miss Schuette said I had to buy and break in a pair of black leather lace-ups, no desert boots or Hush Puppies.

∽∾

It was the wrong week to need shoes. Carl announced after dinner that same night that I owed him three hundred dollars.

"What? How do you figure that?" It was my night to clear, and I was wiping down the highchair. Carl was hunkered over his plate, so I couldn't get at it. A recent haircut made his black roots and his scaly red ears stick out more. My mother, over by the refrigerator, was leaning on her hands against the dining

171

room archway. Something was coming to get me, and she was sticking by the border in case it got rough.

"To pay me for the missing items in the basement is how I figure it," he said.

"What missing items?" I didn't know what he was talking about.

"Those six collector's items you stole."

"Collector's items? Me?"

"From the crawlspace."

I remembered rock dust on Steve Hendrie's blue jeans. "You mean your *Playboys*?" The idea that I'd taken them was so absurd that I named them. My mother flinched.

"That's right, Rick. The first six issues of *Playboy*, from 1954, aren't in the crawlspace anymore."

"Well, I sure as hell didn't take them."

"Don't fool with me, kid, they're worth real money."

I scooted some Jell-O down the disposal with the spray attachment. "Honest, Carl, I didn't take them, you can search my room."

"I did search your room."

"Mom!"

The table rumbled and his fork fell to the floor. His neck had already started blotching. The ridged ring of his lips looked like a dog's butthole.

"Mommy's not going to bail you out of this one, little Ricky. Not this time."

"Did you find them in my room?"

"No."

"You see? I didn't take them."

"You're either going to return my personal property, or I want three hundred dollars to cover my loss."

172

The open dishwasher and extended cup rack cut off my only exit. On the other side of the wall, changing Lisa on top of the washing machine, was the likelier thief. "What about Carla, did you think of asking her? She stole from you at Thanksgiving."

He loomed closer. His upper lip peeled back toward his snout. I saw gray teeth and spiky nose hairs.

"I didn't take them," I heard her yell from the laundry room. She'd spent a happy dinner babbling about Esmeralda, the newly christened cockroach.

"No, she didn't take them," he said.

"And you believe her. Just like that you believe her!" I yelled, dropping the spray hose into the sink. The water shot up and began misting the toaster. "Did you search *her* room, huh? Did you check behind the hash pipe? Or the bottle of Boone's Farm? Or the birth control? Or the letters from her boyfriend in juvie? Jesus fucking Christ! I didn't take your stupid porn. Maybe you need *Playboy*s to jack off to, but I don't."

Though expert at psychological torture, Carl chose a quick backhand that sent me into the dishwasher. The glasses toppled from their hooks in the rack. Off-balance, I stumbled into Lisa's highchair; its metal tray slipped and sent her plate and sippy cup flying.

I crouched, so as to escape under the table if he tried more, but he crouched down with me, a move so surprising I sat back on Lisa's plate. His chest heaving with angry breaths, he waggled his dead-nail forefinger in my face and snarled that I should remember he could put me through a wall whenever he liked. I could smell the gaggy fermenting leaves of his breath.

He stood and stomped the floor hard enough to rattle his plate on the table.

The hose kept up its hiss in the sink. My mouth was stinging, and green bean juice soaked into the seat of my pants as I stared up at the counter next to the oven and read the cursive script on the wedding present I gave them: Flour, Sugar, Coffee, Tea, Flour, Sugar, Coffee, Tea, Flour, Sugar, Coffee, Tea. I was always a sucker for sets.

I waited for my mother to say something.

"You need guidance, son," said the bacon grease can.

"I didn't take the magazines. I swear."

I tasted blood in my mouth, but before I got up to turn off the tap, I told Lisa, who was clutching my mother's skirt, that I was okay.

Later that night, my mother came into my room. She said that she believed me, but that the magazines *were* missing, they were Carl's property, worth real money, and he was upset, the way the man of the house should be. I mustn't defy him. She was learning from Sister Patty how a Christian woman must cleave to her husband. She must obey his every decision, or the marriage wouldn't bind. And if I didn't respect Carl as the man of the house, I was jeopardizing the unity of the family. While she spewed I watched the white plastic numbers fall inside the face of my clock radio. Minutes, hours, days, years.

❧

"Three hundred dollars?" Steve was outraged. "Those issues didn't even show muff."

Of course he'd taken them. I'd figured that out under the kitchen table, but I wasn't going to rat him out.

"Why did you do it?"

"I didn't think he'd notice the old ones."

"The first centerfold was Marilyn Monroe, you idiot." That was Carl's most major point.

"Shit. She's got famous tits, right?"

"That's right. Like Raquel Welch."

"You're saying I should have held out for more?"

The stoner logic made me smile despite myself. I could never stay pissed at Steve. He was growing his hair rock-guitarist length for Carla. It was a glossy shag now. I missed the Wolf Man's widow's peak.

Carl's collector's items weren't the only situation we were trying to address in the Hendries' garage that Saturday morning. Steve was sorry for my fat lip, but the *Playboys* had been sold through Andy back in November. He couldn't spare more than the forty-five he fished out of the tennis ball can behind the bicycle pump, because he was my stepsister's slave and girls always wanted that one next impossible thing. Without yet knowing how or where to buy one, he was planning on getting Carla her own Esmeralda. With diamond and ruby wings. It didn't bug him that Carla was hanging out with a Jesus freak. Better than flirting with other boys.

"Why don't you just steal Mindy's?" I suggested.

"There's an idea," said Steve. "But they'd trace it."

He climbed up on the hood of his father's Seville to reach for an octagon basketball box. I watched the curve of his ass push out the pocket of his jeans. Our old pup tent headquarters, its rusted pole strung with cobwebs, was hooked on the wallboard above his head. I thought about what the Andover Boys might have done in the pup tent on those summer nights if I hadn't been so chicken. There were things Ned had taught me that Carla couldn't know about.

"Here's what I can do, Rick," he said. "You can take some of this crap off my hands and sell it." He placed the basketball box on the hood, then hopped off the car. He didn't have a boner.

As he handled the souvenirs, his breath clouds rolled over them like mist in a horror movie. Besides a bunch of rusty bullets at the bottom, the box contained two felt armbands, one of them with black stripes around the edges of the swastika; a purse-shaped black banner with a white eagle perched on a red diamond trimmed with thick gold braid; a pear-shaped pincushion bristling with little black tank pins; a bigger blue pin with a painted zeppelin; a silver cross with "Stalingrad" written on it; a yellow medal with the words "Waffen-SS"; and finally, a dagger. It had a spread-eagle hilt and was longer than the one Steve took to school.

These were horrible, terrible things, but World History was junior year, so I didn't know why. "Does she know?" I asked.

"She won't miss them," he sneered. "But I can't hock this stuff while I'm grounded. Andy doesn't like coming here. He says subdivisions make him nervous."

I touched the silver cross. Wiggling rays like lizard feet projected from its four right angles. I pointed to the "Stalingrad" written in the jagged letters they used on Schlitz beer cans. "Your grandfather died there."

"He was a Nazi, Rick. They were bad guys."

"These are keepsakes."

"I'm doing my family a favor."

I pointed to the scoop of bullets in his hand. "Why isn't there a gun?"

"Now you're talking."

"Alles für Deutschland" was stamped on the blade of the dagger. I willed myself to pick it up. The feel of freezing metal made my hand close around the eagle. The beak pecked between my third and fourth fingers.

"Ve hav vays of makink you tock," I said, in my best *Hogan's Heroes.*

"Velly intellesting," he answered, doing Arte Johnson from *Laugh-In.*

I rested the blade against the back of my skull and posed.

"Suicide king," I said.

Steve shook the hair from his eyes. "Diamonds?"

"No, hearts. The king of diamonds has an ax. Like this," I said, arranging space between the dagger and my scarf. The cock of my arm reminded me of something. I ran my tongue over the knot on my lip. We looked at each other. My mother used to say, to my secret delight, that it was a good thing Steve wasn't my older brother, since he could make me do anything he wanted.

"You know what?" I said. "Carl."

Steve blew on his fingers and motioned for my hand. He knew the feeling. We had something in common still. He switched my grip from overhand to underhand. "If you're serious about killing somebody, you have to hold the thing like this. You want to shove it *up* his guts, not down, see? Going up guarantees you get under the ribs to the heart and lungs. Stabbing down isn't a sure thing, 'cause the ribs get in the way."

I watched my moves in the reflection of one of the Seville's passenger windows.

"If you've got the time after it's in, jerk it hard back and forth. That'll fuck *everything* up in there."

With a burst of linguistic inspiration, I corrected him. "No, it'll *messer* everything up. Das Messer, remember? It'll messer him up."

177

We couldn't stop laughing. Recalling Hannelore's vocabulary lesson gave us permission to confiscate her treasures. We Sieg-Heiled, clicked our boot heels, and pushed the box back up on the shelf between two lawn chairs. I slipped the dagger into my sleeve. That was all I was going to take. I could feel the point resting in the pad of my bent palm as we ran into the house. Mrs. Hendrie, waiting for her husband to drive them to their clinic, was so surprised to see me come through the blast of cold from the garage that she put her right glove on her left hand.

∽∽

Steve and I had a second thing in common, a good thing. He said that morning in the garage that when he was having sex with Carla, he forgot who he was. I had to pretend this was news. I couldn't tell him how I melted in the hot envelope of Ned, how I felt my edges go, like I was a drop of ink racing across a paper towel. With my body talking, my speech smeared into growls and mumbles and high echoes of my daddy's words. Lisa was groping toward language while I was backing away from it. Ned's place had become this weird science fiction zone of total comprehension where I didn't have a name or eyes or parents or clothes. Being with Ned made me feel like nothing bad was ever going to happen.

Our last time together before districts I made him take me into Briarcliffe. He had been refusing to see the goldenrod Andover unless I told him why. I was afraid to say, "I want to see my whole life in one picture." I could only say, "Because. Just because, that's why," and then I pushed my door open while we were doing forty-five down Butterfield Road. I leaned out the tiniest bit, trying to hit a snow dump with a gob of spit, and he reached for my arm with a terrified shout.

178

"Get a grip," I said, yanking the door shut. "I wasn't going to jump."

He turned into the far corner of the Dominick's parking lot to calm down. This was the strip mall next to Martin Manor. I checked for Hannelore's head in the row of fuzzy white bolls lined up along the front window like used Q-Tips.

"Tell me what's wrong, Rick."

Lots of things were wrong, but I had one immediate worry. "I want to make it out of districts on Saturday." The tournament loomed as the first pavement square on the road out of Briarcliffe. If I failed, I had a dagger for self-defense, and that was it.

"You will. You only have to get third place to advance."

"I want a first again," I pouted, sinking against the door. There was a Foto-Mat booth twenty yards away. The Foto-Mate was inside, bent in profile, the lonely mistress of the parking lot.

"But if I lose . . ."

"If you lose?"

"Can we still get together?"

The shame of my need made me mumble, but Ned heard. He pulled me close, kissed my eyelids, sucked my breath out with his lips. His stomach rumbled. I twisted a hand up his sweater to pet it, tugging at his shirt. I gave that up and dug into his crotch.

He groaned no, aimed his lolling head at the Foto-Mat booth.

"She's reading," I said.

"Or she's doing homework. Don't you have homework?"

"It's dark out. She can't see us." I tensed my hand. He groaned again.

179

"You're depraved."

Uh-huh, I thought, digging, listening to his body. Whose fault is that? I wondered again if Ned was thirty-three, like Jesus. Jesus was a definite enemy now, along with Carl and Veronica Satterwhite. Thirty-three was more than double my age. Half my age was eight. Eight was third grade. Addition, subtraction, and trying to color inside the lines. Would I have sex with a third grader? The thought grossed me out. Would Ned? If Ned met a third grader in the Broadway section at Wax Trax, would he go up and show him his boner?

I took my hand away. He pulled it back, thinking I was teasing.

My depravity forced him onto Kingston, but he wouldn't come up the driveway. I got to point out my bedroom windows, some sort of victory. "I am you," I said to the milk box before I took the taste of him inside the rest of my life. "Moo."

❧

Then came the underwear event. Maybe my timing was poor, but no given day would have been ideal for a nonentity to make a sexualized fashion statement at my high school. If a jock had been the first to sling his nuts in bikinis, it would have been a different story; within a week, his hotshot teammates would have followed suit and Wheaton-Warrenville would have been underwear-integrated without police dogs and fire hoses. But I was someone who sat in the middle of the school bus, head to the window.

It was speech team tradition to videotape the district entries the day before the tournament. I wore the bikinis for the permanent archival record. I'd stopped hand washing them. My mother thought they were another Christmas challenge from Julia that she would have to endure, like the very short haircut.

I had thought about the taping, but not about second period. My jeans were halfway down my legs in the locker room before I realized that I should have cut class. Mark Garrow, a second-tier soccer jock aiming to move up the ladder, followed the toss of my blue-piped vermilion scanties onto the shelf in my locker with wide eyes. "Scanties" was my name for them, from a *Follies* song, a record I'd placed on restricted rotation, once every other day.

January was circuit training. Coach Carnahan blew his whistle after six minutes, and we'd switch exercise stations, from barbells to dumbbells to squat-thrusts to jump rope to sit-ups, etc., solo endeavors designed to get us bored enough for the group horror of February basketball. I was hanging thirty feet in the air, pausing up a rope, when I noticed Mark below, pointing me out with an Indian club. I twisted as he talked to Jay Stack. The custodians were hauling the wood bleachers out of the east wall of the gym, and the screech of the steel casters drowned out Mark's words. I shinnied down, expecting the worst, but nothing happened. Mark's arms whirred like windmills in my direction all period, but nothing happened. If I was without friends, I was also without enemies.

To verify Mark's claim, a few boys plugged the ends of my row after showers, leaving me to dry and dress in a boxcar of steam. Some teeth were sucked when I pulled out my scanties and put a leg in, but the "sissy" and "weirdo" I heard were random and unsupported, like the first drops before a rain skips over you. In the grand scheme of gym class humiliations, my underwear wasn't like the tiny, third nipple underneath Derek

Wingerter's left tit or the famous boner Stan Burdette popped in the shower freshman year.

Mark Garrow, however, had made an investment, and there was still a pep rally to weather at the end of the day. It began routinely: the winter teams, boys' and girls' basketball, wrestling, girls' volleyball, processed to the school fight song, followed by the gymnasts of both sexes. Their shiny green and gold warmup suits caught the lights as they strutted past Principal Dahlbeck's podium to assume positions on a small portable bleacher on the gym floor. They high-fived, totally used to having the cheerleaders kiss the floor with their twats in their honor. Then the Wolverettes stomped in opposing concentric circles and shook their poms to The Bay City Rollers' "Saturday Night." We stomped along on the bleachers. Even the burnouts loved that part.

Dahlbeck handed the microphone to Vice Principal Havertine, better known as Miss Foodstains. His scurry from the podium clued us to a bad moon on the rise. Havertine, a do-gooder second only to the school librarian in overall fruitiness, began her guest spot with a cackle so hearty it set her corsage flapping. Then she screamed into the mic, "Rook knight bishop, king queen pawn, hooray! Rook knight bishop, king queen pawn, hooray!"

Sixteen hundred minds wondered, "What the fuck was that?" Havertine answered by announcing that this rally was a celebration for *all* the winter athletes and would the chess team come down to grab its glory. "Stand up, ye mighty Wolverines!" she cheered to blistering reverb. "Chess team chess team rah rah rah!"

The athletes on the floor started to whistle as rocks were turned over in the hunt for the bespectacled creatures who met after school in the calculus classroom. Arms beckoning them toward her green and gold carnations, Havertine began calling them by name—"Daniel Boykin, Come on down!" It took a while, but at last five boys and Yvette Engelman, the only self-identified Jew in the entire school, had slunk onto the floor and were drooping into one another at the free-throw line like day lilies on day five. The nastier cheerleaders were doubled over with laughter.

Miss Schuette darted over to the podium with a piece of paper, and it stopped being so hilarious. Before I knew it, Havertine was hooting, "Comedy, drama, prose, and verse. We know that speech will come in first!"

No need to name names. Joe Bacino was the lead in all the plays, Mindy Kendig lived in the spotlight, Eric Smola would one day run for Congress, and the rest of the team did musicals, plays, or swing choir. They all ran down and applauded each other. Havertine started gassing about the challenges of public speaking and the excitement of districts, and I thought I was safe, but Joe had picked me out in the bleachers, and the rest of the team had started chanting "Rick, Rick, Rick," so to avoid being even more conspicuous, I shot out of the stands and sprinted behind Mindy. Robin Baver shook her poms at me from the platoon of Wolverettes. I peeked over Mindy's shoulder and found myself locking eyes with Esmeralda. Her nap disturbed by the whoosh of my entrance, she popped one sparkly wing like a car hood and wiggled her pincers. I practically fainted into Brian Tadder.

Havertine couldn't resist getting personal. "In Humorous Duet Acting . . . are seniors Cindy Spinner and Dahlia Svolos." Cindy and Dahlia stepped out of the group for a second. "In Original Comedy, we have junior . . . Joseph Bacino." Joe's elaborate bow and kisses to the crowd got some laughs. On Havertine went, Schuette whooping like an idiot by the foul line. I had decided that on my turn I would just wave my arm over Brian's head.

"In Dramatic Interpretation is sophomore . . . Richard—"

"Cocksucker," someone with great timing shouted from the jocks' pen.

"—Lahrem."

"Cocksucker!" repeated the voice, full exclamation point.

Havertine heard, but didn't believe. She repeated my name, and "Cocksucker!" rang out a third time. Her mic banged the podium. The reverb was earsplitting, like a bomb had gone off. Joe Bacino, big and fearless, charged the portable bleacher and hauled Mark Garrow off the end of the third row. The stands went wild with Wolverine spirit. Joe had just started a chokehold when Carnahan and Dahlbeck pushed through the hive of jocks and screaming cheerleaders.

I hadn't sucked any school cock, so when I was summoned by Principal Dahlbeck after the rally broke up, I said I couldn't understand why Mark had used that offensive slur. Gravely nodding toward the U.S. and Illinois flags in the corners of his office, Dahlbeck began a speech about how our nation was made great by all the different sorts of people who pitched in and got along. It was the same thing with Wheaton-Warrenville. We were a *microcosm* of American *democracy*, did I realize that? I should think of the athletes and the thespians and the musicians and the honor students as a *federation* of states that had to respect one another, get along the way Illinois and Indiana and Iowa got along.

It was time to agree contritely, but throughout his canned lecture my mind had been working a parallel groove of a certain box social that started a certain second act. Instead of "yes sir," I drew an analogy, probably the first of my entire life, and said that the farmers and the cowmen should be friends.

He showed me teeth as shiny as his desk. In a principal, a smile could cut either way, but just like Sister Patty at a teen reach-out, Principal Dahlbeck preferred to encourage rather than rebuke. And it turned out he knew the show.

"You're doing fine Richard Lahrem, Richard Lahrem, okay," he finished. "That's right, Mr. Lahrem. You're doing okay. Good luck at your meet tomorrow. Send in Mr. Bacino."

Rodgers and Hammerstein saved us from getting expelled. Miss Foodstains probably got the worst of it.

∽⌣↩

I ate my bowl of cereal at the sink, rather than sit down with her. Trying any way she could to get me talking, my mother even reminded me on the drive to school that if she and my father hadn't divorced, I would have attended Downers North, the high school where our district meet was being held. As soon as I saw our bus in the turnaround, I slid Lisa off my lap and set her between us. My mother reached out, but half of me was through the door. "Take your lunch, honey," she said, tears in her eyes. I snatched it up. "Cleave to him," I muttered to myself, "Cleave to his back like a clove in a ham, you stupid Christian cow."

It was a quiet ride to Downers Grove. I showed Mindy, sitting in front of me, the left turn to my old elementary school. I'd had at most one friend in any given grade, usually none, but now I had ten, a squadron who would walk through fire or rumble at a pep rally on my behalf.

The video session in the home ec lab had been the absolute best thing. While Wegner set up the camera, the girls, tethered to a row of electrical outlets with their curling irons, steamed their wings higher off their foreheads and Schuette worked the boys over with a lint brush. We wore paper towel bibs to catch crumbs from the cake and chips the Booster Club had donated for the taping.

It was exciting to do our events for each other. Katie Casco's Humorous Interp was the Mad Hatter's tea party in *Alice in Wonderland,* four characters instead of my two. Her Dormouse was hilarious. Cindy and Dahlia's Humorous Duet from *The Importance of Being Earnest* took place at another tea party. Their classy accents impressed me, but I wasn't sure what was funny. Then Sue Behm read a long poem called "Little Word, Little White Bird," her vocal swoops reminiscent of Miss Havertine. I was relieved I hadn't been switched to Verse Reading.

I went next. With "some" out of the intro, the first word my teammates heard from me was "homosexuals." I felt Mark Garrow's version of me leaking like poison gas out of the home ec ovens, but when I finished the team gave me a standing ovation. Not so much because I was great, I think, as to make me feel better about the pep rally disaster.

Then came the body count. There was the *Zoo Story* scene I saw back in October. Ty Vandenhoop held the knife overhand, the wrong way, to kill Brian on the park bench. Cheryl Ito's Prose Reading, a story about an escaped criminal who shoots an entire family at the side of a highway, added five to the pile. "Holy Christ," Joe whispered in the awed silence. Eric Smola's extemp about fuel consumption predicted more highway deaths if we didn't urge Congress to lower the national speed limit to fifty-five.

Then Mindy *really* scared us with "The Doomsday Clock." The opposite of plastic, she dinged each one of us with real eye contact and a horrible fact, as if she blamed us personally for that slice of the destruction pie. She finished with a description of human flesh melting under radiation. Because Wegner had forced Jesus out of her equation, Mindy's message was basically "Get ready to die, everybody, in ten seconds."

Joe Bacino went last. We clapped with relief just to see him slide off the counter, but his Original Comedy, set at a wake, was about death too. He imitated his parents, his airhead sister Anna, a religious aunt, a wino uncle, a stupid priest, and Mamma Mia Rita, who screamed at his grandfather's corpse in Italian. His finale was a sped-up dirge to the tune of "Funiculì, Funiculà." At the very end, his grandfather sat up in the coffin and said to his wife, "Not so loud, Rita, you're giving me a headache!" We laughed until the soda came out of our noses.

The frost on the Downers North lawn sparkled under the bus headlights, and the cold air made our eyes water. The team unloading ahead of us wore matching hats and did a cheer as they stepped in formation up the walk. We chose stealth.

I felt ready. I had made up a ritual before going to bed the night before. First, I put on my *A Chorus Line* T-shirt and tucked it into my lucky bikinis. To keep from freezing, I put on a second pair of socks. I cleared my nightstand of the clock radio, lamp, and contact lens case, and arranged my three trophies and one medal in four compass points. I took the Polaroid of Ned and me on Broadway out of my nightstand drawer and placed it in the center of the compass. My very first focal points, Madison and Taft, I placed at opposite corners of the stand. In each of the other two corners I put a Playboy cufflink. Then I drew a folded paper slip from a bowl of nineteen and selected one song to play from the musical named on the slip. As

I listened, I wrote the titles on a sheet of notebook paper in my most careful script. "Ya Got Trouble" from *The Music Man* was first; I finished with "Beauty School Dropout" from *Grease*. I thought about Ned but didn't jerk off, because I'd read in a magazine that the best American athletes stayed pure the night before a big game.

District tournaments fielded twelve schools. First-, second-, and third-place winners advanced to sectionals, so I only had to beat nine other entries. Miss Schuette, bunkered at the end of a cafeteria table behind our coat pile, gave me some last-minute advice. "If you can, Rick, I want you to enter your room last," she said. "Hang back and let your opponents go in before you do."

"Huh? How?"

Miss Schuette pointed to my mimeographed map of Downers North. "D.I. is here. Stand at the other end of the hallway, here, and watch them go in, one by one. Wait them all out."

"What if the judge comes?"

"He'll be last, I promise. Then I want you to stand in the doorway. Look at each of your opponents and slowly count to ten. Then take a seat in the middle of the room."

"Do I talk?"

"Chitchat only. Friendly but impersonal. And don't mumble."

She took my hands in hers. Her fingernails made a scarlet bracelet around my wrists. "Kill the people," she said.

"Yes, Miss Schuette." Ned had said the exact same thing. His team was competing in Villa Park.

From my sniper's position I did as she said. When Veronica Satterwhite, a paisley scarf tented over her glossy hair, clicked up the hall to Room 221, I cocked a fist on my hip to display my vest and gun. "Pow." I smiled to myself. I'd shoot the stars out of her blue heaven. The wall clock read 7:56.

Schuette sent us into the fray, Wegner took us out. Sue Behm, the only Wolverine who didn't make finals, wept on his shoulder in a hallway off the gym. He turned her away from the patchwork of finals sheets and pointed to something through the window to distract her.

The girls rushed the bathrooms for touch-ups. Before heading to the driver's ed room to begin my third stakeout of the day, I went into the cafeteria and made peace with my mother by eating the lunch she'd packed. I skimmed her note.

"He who loves a pure heart and whose speech is gracious will have the king for his friend." This is from Proverbs 22. Good luck. I love you, Mom.

It wouldn't kill me to accept her prayers.

Joe Bacino came up to me and took a bite of my scooter pie. Chewing, he motioned for me to follow him. Before I knew what was happening, he had pulled me into a stall in the boy's bathroom. Two in a toilet was tight. I knew Joe smoked weed, but I couldn't believe he'd toke before finals. I was already stammering out that I didn't partake when he pulled his pants to his knees.

"Look what I got, Rick," he said.

"What?" I remembered his thighs, scaly with follicle bumps, from our room at the Motel 6 downstate.

He looked down too. "Oh." He yanked up his shirttails, and his stomach lipped out between his undershirt and waistband like dough in a can of pull-apart oven rolls. Joe's bikini underwear was yellow with green piping.

189

"I got them for Christmas," he said, "but this is my first time wearing them."

"They're cool, Joe."

His eyes were at my waist. "Are they like yours?"

"I don't have them on," I said. "I changed this morning."

"Oh." The tiny edge of disappointment I thought I heard in his voice started my boner.

"Mine are blue and red," I said. I casually dropped a hand to cover myself. "I think they're the same brand, though."

"Cool. I'm glad my mom bought me yellow. I'm a dribbler."

"I'm not," I said, stepping back. The coat hook jabbed behind my ear. Joe pulled up his trousers. Right before his knuckles brushed over his crotch, I thought I saw something of his own move down there.

I fell out of the stall, gushing about his stupendous Original Comedy. We washed our hands at the sink, even though we hadn't peed, and checked for scooter pie in our teeth.

"Comedy, drama, prose, and verse," he said, turning off his faucet.

"We know that speech will come in first," I said, turning off mine.

We marched out of the john chanting Havertine's battle cry.

A trio of leisure suits was planted in the living room. A man waved the wet mouth of a pipe at me, the wood crucifix over his turtleneck swaying with his reach. A bossa nova record was playing. Had I walked into the wrong house?

"Howdja do, Rick?" asked Carl with a grotty chortle in his voice. A surge of winter culottes bearing down the hallway cut me off from an escape up the stairs. Before I knew it, my step-father's fat hand was steering me from the front door to the love seat in the living room.

There was a notched border of napkins around a punch bowl. Set evenly among the cheese balls and the chafing dish of cocktail franks and the onion dip and chunky bayberry candles were small pads of paper. Bridge pencils stood in an eggcup and a glass toothpick holder at either end of the credenza. One windowsill was stacked with Bibles, thick and floppy as telephone books.

My mother came through the arch with a tray of ham fingers and gutted pineapple. A bow topped a frosted pillow of hair in her upsweep, and she'd pressed her red ruffled hostess apron. It still fit, I thought idiotically.

"How did you get home, honey?" she cried with pleasure, having found her men in a nonviolent hold.

"The Bacinos drove me. What's going on?"

"It's Marriage Encounter," throbbed a familiar voice.

I exhaled as I ducked away from Carl and forked Patty Puller's hand before she could suck me into one of her grinding hugs. Tonight's miracle was Roy Puller: tall, stooped, pumpkin teeth, a goiter, a wandering left eye. No wonder she was always at our house.

"What's with the pads and pencils?" I asked.

"Those are for later," said Mr. Puller. I looked at his feet. Sad aqua socks drooped at his ankles above white leather pontoons with silver side buckles. "For our feelings."

"That's right, honeybunch," said Patty, patting his arm. "HDIF."

"HDIF," he wheezed, his eye strafing me on a pass-through.

Carl, with more of an audience now, asked again how I'd done. My mother was moving in. I dipped into a vest pocket. She had penciled in the beauty mark on her cheek, a first since the divorce. It shouldn't have mattered, but she was the prettiest mother there. I held out a three-inch brass state of Illinois dangling from a bar stamped IHSA Forensics.

"Praise Jesus," said my mother and Patty.

Carl lifted the medal from my palm, turned it over. "Dramatic Interpretation. First Place," he read from the back.

"Oh, God is . . . so so good," gurgled Patty as I let my mother gather me up.

She had used some of the last drops of her real perfume. Christmas mornings once included a bottle of Chanel No. 5 from my father. The scent carried me back to the parties she threw with him, the rhinestone clips she slipped onto the mouths of her black high heels, the sound of his cufflinks dinging the ice bucket as he twisted orange slices into Manhattans, the ring of bathing beauty shrimp hanging just over the pool of cocktail sauce, the blankets of spinach over the oysters Rockefeller.

"Marie and I prayed for this victory," I heard Carl say. The moms fluttered and the dads coughed approval.

My back stiffened. It's a sin to tell a lie, and this one was probably the worst I'd ever heard. My hands clenched, then fell from my mother's waist. "Please," she whispered into my ear, and let me go.

The dyed straw sprouting from Carl's flushed forehead made him look like a scalded beet. With my tongue I probed the last of the bump from my split lip. I pulled the medal from his fingers. "I get to go to sectionals now," I said. I took off my boiling parka and tried to ball it up.

"How about the Wheaton Central girl?" he asked, another surprise attack. "That's his rival," he explained to everyone. He had his arm around my mother, was leaning in, interested and innocent, but his eyes were still tiny and cold. I wanted to board the pineapple crown bobbing in the punch bowl and float away. On the dining room table was a white frosted sheet cake decorated with a red icing heart growing out of a cross. The names Carl and Marie were inside the heart. My mother was holding her breath, but the hair bow, the beauty mark, the perfume, the pulse of the music underneath, all spelled h-o-p-e.

"She got second place, but I skunked her in finals," I said. "Three firsts."

"That is just terrific, Rick," Carl enthused.

"The glory is His," Patty reminded the room.

"I'm sure Rick won't forget that," said Carl, with a trace of a smirk at Sister Patty's expense. I couldn't help but smirk back, a traitor to my own cause. Before he could say or do something to make me puke, like chuck my shoulder, I went to hang up my five-thousand-pound parka. I slumped against the closet door, down for the count. He had been listening all along.

While I waited for my mother to fix me a plate to take upstairs, I called New Jersey. My father came through without my having to poke him in the eye with a stick. He'd send money, another suit for sectionals, a blazer for state, I'd be going to state all right, no doubt about that, I was a champion, *his* champion. His excitement was more evidence that I'd been a complete flop to him my first sixteen years. Julia got on, wanting advice about what Broadway musical to see first. "*A Chorus Line*—" I said, biting "you idiot" off the tip of my tongue. If she didn't know that, she didn't deserve a ticket.

I hung up my suit and put on pajamas. I set the districts medal with the others, sat on my bed with dinner, and listened to the congress of album covers arranged around the room. Downstairs there was the bossa nova and laughter from the Christian invaders, but up here, for the first time, I knew that a party with my records wasn't going to make me feel better. I decided to jerk off. They could turn away or not, I didn't care.

I'd only had to kill off nine dramatic interps to stay alive that day, but I'd slain eleven. Now the sniper had a fresh hit list. Joe Bacino for showing me his underwear. Beth Cook for rubbing Joe's leg in the back seat of the Bacinos' car. Ned Bolang for not being in the school parking lot. Mindy Kendig for inviting Carla over to her house to watch television. Carla for going. My father for buying me off. My stepmother for seeing *A Chorus Line*. Patty Puller for brainwashing my mother. Roy Puller for his pathetic aqua socks. Carl for being a brutal, hypocritical fuck. My mother for believing him. Me for believing, even for an instant, that he who loves a pure heart and whose speech is gracious will have the king for his friend.

My speech was gracious, but I had no friends, none at all.

I let go of my dick, got up, and reached into the pit of my closet. I gingerly lifted out an old poster tube and tipped it. The hilt of the Stalingrad dagger stamped the heel of my palm. I swiped the air above my head. I switched from overhand to underhand again and again, until the gesture was comfortable and the knife was warm. I looked at the party ranged around the room, deathly silent now. Which guest was a mistake? Which would take a mortal blow? I went to them one by one.

Shenandoah. Too many ballads. *Carousel.* No really fast songs. *Camelot.* Too many ballads. *Oliver.* Screeching good-time orphans. *The Wiz.* Fake funky. *Oliver.* British accents. *Oliver.* The dopey lime-green cover of a boy's smeary charcoal face. *Oliver,* the pathetic orphan, the angelic boy soprano, the opposite of Sondheim.

I picked him up. I wouldn't have to kill. It could be a simple bloodletting, a slash of warning across his back. Or instead, a deep, precise cut, an amputation of the three songs I hated on side B: "My Name," "As Long as He Needs Me," and "Reviewing the Situation."

I wouldn't have to use Hannelore's heirloom either. On the nightstand was my districts medal. With just the southern tip of Illinois, its baby toe, side B would be feeling no pain. I could turn my back to the others, or do it in the closet, no witnesses.

There was a knock at the door. I dropped the dagger and kicked it under the bed, killing my foot. I covered my crotch with *Oliver*.

"What?" I asked.

"There's a phone call for you, Rick." Carl's voice was still friendly.

"Who is it?"

"Somebody named Ned."

No friend of mine. That he had figured out my phone number—when it was listed under Schwob—increased my spite. "I'm too tired to talk. Say I'm asleep."

Carl didn't answer. It was suddenly a sin to tell a lie, I suppose.

"If he wants to know, tell him I got first place."

I set *Oliver* back down against the beanbag chair, between *Can-Can* and *Kiss Me, Kate*. Next to Illinois on my nightstand was my piece of chocolate Marriage Encounter cake. A stretch of Carl and Marie's piped icing heart ran through its middle.

I sheared off the frosting with my right hand and clamped it around my dick. It took a couple of strokes to get stiff. The grit of the sugar scratched a little at first, but not unpleasantly. The blood-red squiggle of the heart quickly creamed into pink.

❦

The week between districts and sectionals was bizarre. Monday in gym class, two jocks had bikini underwear on, solid with piping, like mine and Joe's. Tuesday, Paul Hicks, varsity basketball and boyfriend to Robin Baver, whose tears in speech class had started absolutely everything, broke the pattern barrier with zebra stripes. Wednesday night, I placed six fifties under Carl's fork from the money my father had wired. He sat down to eat. After his grunted amen, I snuck a look at his reaction.

He picked up the bills, curved them once around his middle finger, reached over, and tucked them in my shirt pocket, ignoring my flinch.

"That's for your suit, Rick," he said.

Four sets of eyes bugged. Lisa's mouth was a cherry Lifesaver.

"There isn't time to get one before Saturday," I mumbled.

"Well then, for state. Would you pass the mashed potatoes, please?"

By now, the horns of plenty and the coffee grinders on the Polish wallpaper were spinning like rust tornadoes. "It won't cost that much," I stuttered, extending the potatoes with a shaky hand. "I'll give you whatever's left over from it."

"Fair enough," he said, palming the dish. "It's only money."

My mother explained that HDIF was Marriage Encounter shorthand for "How Do I Feel?" It was a writing and sharing exercise couples used to unblock their channels of communication. HDIF when you don't support my disciplining of the children? HDIF when you resist my romantic advances? HDIF when you belittle my faith?

As for "Kill the people," Schuette snapped that it was a showbiz line meaning wow your audience to death. She and Wegner were in lab-coat and bad-mood mode again. She'd phoned coaches from other districts to sniff out my sectionals competition, and I was going to be up against two lesbian pieces: *The Children's Hour* and *The Killing of Sister George.*

"Cool," I said, snickering at this information.

"Do you find that funny, Rick?" asked Wegner.

"No." I was flashing on all the nipple-pinching lesbo pictorials I pretended were hot for Steve's benefit.

"Because it's not funny," he said. "You could cancel each other out."

"What do you mean?" I asked.

Wegner sighed. "Let's suppose a judge gets all three of you in the same round—gay, lesbian, lesbian, boom, boom, boom—and gets tired of the theme. Believe me, you won't all make it into finals."

"Maybe the other two aren't so good."

"This isn't the time to get cocky, Rick," he said.

I'd heard that one before, from my cock-cock-cocky cock-sucking coach. Wegner's sense of humor was wearing thin because Wheaton-Warrenville was sending only six events to sectionals. *Zoo Story* had missed third place by one point in Dramatic Duet, and Katie Casco had "choked"—Schuette's grim verdict—in the Humorous Interp final. And then God, making His demands all over Wheaton, had personally requested of Mindy that she put Him back in her oratory at sectionals. She'd withdraw if He couldn't be her Doomsday solution, and her parents were backing her up.

Since both our teams were competing in the same sectionals tournament, I asked Ned if he'd scoped the faculty bathrooms at Libertyville High. It was a joke, but Ned was as cranky as Wegner and Schuette.

"You shouldn't be focusing on that," he frowned. Something was wrong with the heat in his bedroom, so we were rolled in an afghan on the brown couch. "Focus on winning. Focus on that Veronica Satterwhite girl."

"You know I'm better than she is," I said, fishing. Ned didn't say anything. "You gave me first and her third in October. Daddy?"

His dick chugged against my stomach, but instead of using it, he slid his feet to the floor. "I have to watch the weather report," he said, hoisting himself out of our cocoon. "It's supposed to storm this weekend."

"You ranked me first," I persisted, alarmed, "and the black girl doing *Raisin in the Sun* second, and then *This Property Is Condemned*. You said so later, in your car—you said I was the best D.I. and not because I had a boner."

Ned wouldn't look at me. He inspected the sky while he waited for the TV to get a picture. He picked at a skid of dried semen on his hip. Finally he said that the Veronicas of the world get what they want.

The afghan was suddenly thin as tracing paper. I felt myself go cold all over. "But not the black kids and the . . . and the . . ."

I heard Mark Garrow yell, "Cocksucker!" I scratched the cocoa ring out of my mug and onto the cushions, slitting my eyes to keep the tears from splashing. It wasn't that I wanted special minority treatment. Ned had already hurt me by saying that "Kill the people" was from a movie called *All About Eve*. Knowing famous lines from it, he said, was a major merit badge. It was a movie I must see every chance I got. Whenever it was on TV, even at two a.m., or if it was playing at a college film society or a revival house downtown, I must watch and learn the lines. He was stirring our cocoa at the stove while he told me this and every whap of the whisk felt like a stab in my heart. Where would *he* be all these times I'd watch *All About Eve*? I didn't know what a film society or a revival house was, and I wasn't college material. I was his material. I wasn't holding my breath anymore. He was what I breathed, he was what had happened to me. When I graduated, I wanted to live on Roosevelt Road with my daddy who walked nude in his apartment and didn't listen to God.

I dried my eyes with a corner of the afghan. I blew the cocoa dust in his direction, fairy dust to turn him around. "What happens after state?"

"Nationals," he said to the window.

That wasn't what I meant.

"Don't count your chickens, Rick. Let's get you to Peoria first."

"So you do think I can win?"

HDIF when you won't look at me? HDIF when I can't tell you how I feel? HDIF when future isn't a word or a tense we use?

"Homosexuals are sad and lonely young men," I simpered in my best Paul Lynde.

That got him back to the couch. I kicked the afghan over his goosebumpy legs, unaware that my retort had just earned me another major merit badge—the one for self-mockery.

Cartoon snowflakes were falling on the screen as the weatherman gleefully streaked a marker across a map. Wyoming was snowed in, the storm was blanketing western Nebraska, and it was headed our way. Ten to fourteen inches were predicted for Chicagoland.

"Dammit to hell," Ned muttered again and again at the footage of buried cars and stranded cattle. Mr. Wegner had planned ahead, reserving rooms at the Libertyville Best Western back in December to make sure we were fresh at sectionals.

We were leaving the next day, right after school. Carl was going to have to clear the driveway himself. Heart attack, I hoped, face down, his tongue frozen to the metal scoop of the shovel.

"Maybe you can find a motel," I suggested, plotting a room service pictorial.

"We would still have to get there, Rick."

"Our bus won't be full. You could call Mr. Wegner."

WGN took a station break. Ned got up and stomped around. On the third kid who said, "This is sugarless?" I made the connection.

"That's Reed's commercial!" I didn't know they got made that fast.

"Reed?" he said.

"Your friend Reed, in New York." A girl was chewing on screen. Flowers popped around her head.

"That's not Reed."

"Duh. But that's his commercial. That is so cool."

Ned, looking straight at me, stated that Reed had the Trident account.

"No, it was Carefee," I said. A boy was pointing to his cheek, the same way I had at Uncle Charlie's restaurant. Maybe Reed passed on my interpretation. "It was that gum there. Carefree sugarless gum."

"*Trident* sugarless gum."

"He told me it was Carefree."

"Told *you*? We were both there, Rick. Reed has the Trident account."

"Carefree."

We argued through commercials for Piper's Carpet Warehouse and Sport Mart and Parkay margarine. Finally I proposed that we bet on it and call New York. I could see a set of hairy knuckles reaching for a black phone surrounded by blinking skyscrapers. Was the boy in the commercial in bed next to him?

"He's at work," Ned said.

"So?

"I'm not betting on something as juvenile as a gum commercial."

∽⌀⌂

The wind was so strong off Lake Michigan that the snow blew sideways against the neon sign at the Best Western restaurant. On the ride to Libertyville, Eric had revved us up by explaining the traditions of the medieval tournaments, how the knights and damsels and their retinues would ride for days to a castle and be welcomed by the King and Queen in the Great Hall, how the knights donned their ladies' favors before entering the lists. I felt favored just to step off the elevator and give the name of my party to the Wagon Wheel hostess. Through the windows I saw pedestrians tipping side to side like penguins as they picked their way over the icy sidewalks, but my feet were dry, my armor was hanging on the closet bar, and the TV in our room got good reception. Wegner let us order whatever we wanted. Nobody made fun of my scrambled egg and bacon sandwich.

After dinner Joe laughed at Eric's matching robe and pajamas and left to hang out with Cindy and Dahlia. Alone with Eric, I felt stupider than usual. While I cooked my contact lenses in the bathroom, I listened to him on the phone with his father discussing Libya, wherever that was. Now Eveready Eric had the TV news on to take notes in case President Carter had done something that day that would affect his extemp topic.

The wind kept up, whipping flakes against our window like handfuls of sugar. Drifts were piling against the slatted corners of the fence surrounding the outdoor pool. Men in blocky orange nylon coats were clearing the sidewalk over and over. The serfs are shoveling for their liege, I wanted to say, to prove my grasp of the medieval world. What I knew about olden times came from *Camelot* and Saturday cartoons. I visualized my competitors, their caravans converging from every direction on Libertyville, a walled suburban hamlet with battlements and a drawbridge over the moat. The velvet cone fixed on Veronica Satterwhite's head was fitted with a streaming veil and a flashlight to guide her retinue. The girls with the lezzie scenes had short double-coned hats. The *Children's Hour* lezzie from the north twirled a spiked ball over her head. The *Sister George* lezzie from the south smacked her lance against her horse.

"Eric, what's that word again?"

"What word?"

"The word for a medieval lady's horse."

"Palfrey," he said through the toothpaste foam on his lips.

"Right. Cool. Palfrey."

I could list the presidents, because I'd collected them, one a week, from the Jewel grocery store. I knew that Irene Ryan from *The Beverly Hillbillies* had been in *Pippin,* that Lily Munster had been in *Follies,* and that Dean Jones, from *The Love Bug,* was the leading man in *Company*. If the right gum commercial aired during Johnny Carson, I would know who produced it. In other words, what I knew was basically nothing.

Johnny Carson came on. I dialed ten random digits, let the phone ring eight times, and told Eric that my father must have gone away on business. Before turning in, I improvised a ritual in the bathroom. I took Taft, Madison, the Playboy cufflinks, and the Polaroid out of my Dopp kit and spaced them evenly along the mirror ledge. With the districts medal pinned to my *A Chorus Line* T-shirt, I recited the titles of my albums under the sound of running water in the sink.

Hours later, Joe's foot on my calf nudged me awake. I hadn't felt him getting into bed. A yellowish light from the parking lot leaked around the edges of the window shade.

"Is it time to get up?" I asked groggily.

"No. I have some vodka," he whispered. "Want some?"

"The ironing board is out," I informed him. Eric had set it up at the foot of his double bed right before lights-out. He'd tipped the housekeeper two quarters when she brought it in, another impressive feat of Smola derring-do.

Joe goosed me with a cold flask. I said no thanks. The flask fell away, but his fingers stayed on my arm.

I listened to four things at once. The light, steady whistle of Eric's breathing on the other side of the nightstand. The heavy whistle of the wind. The scraping rhythm of the snow shovels. The low, dry drone of the heating panel.

"You are, aren't you?" he whispered. The sweet vodka smell on his breath curled into my nose.

"Are what?"

"You know."

I rubbed my eyes to gain time. His hand fell off my arm. "No, I don't know."

"What Mark Garrow said."

I studied the ceiling. Slowly I lifted my hands and curled them on top of my thighs so that the covers would hide what I imagined was a gigantic telltale boner. I began to list the presidents under my breath. I had gotten to Zachary Taylor when Joe shifted onto his side and said, "It's okay, Rick. I'll let you."

The sheet and bedspread lifted higher with his left elbow and knee. I had room to burrow. The quiet inside his tent was amazing. The lady bestowed her favor upon the knight, thanking him with all she knew for defending her at the pep rally.

On the morning of February 5, 1977, in the foyer of Libertyville High School, Mr. Wegner handed each of us an IHSA Sectionals Program. This was my page:

Dramatic Interpretation
Round One 9:30 am.

Room 214:

Charles Palia, *I Never Sang for My Father.*
Lester Schomas, *The Subject Was Roses.*
Andrea Rennhak, *And Miss Reardon Drinks a Little.*
Merle Kulinski, *The Lion in Winter.*
Richard Lahrem, *The Boys in the Band.*
Kim Woodman, *All the King's Men.*

Room 218:

Robin Moons, *The Children's Hour.*
Dawn Luebbers, *Two for the Seesaw.*
Veronica Satterwhite, *This Property Is Condemned.*
Danielle Scheie, *The Killing of Sister George.*
Jeanne Williams, *Anastasia.*
Craig Miller, *The Merchant of Venice.*

Palia, Schomas, Rennhak et al. are as deeply etched into my memory as Washington, Adams, Jefferson, Madison for the simple reason that my name had never been in print before. Eric's history lesson had come at just the right moment; it made me recognize this stapled program as the first effort in my life that would survive me. Centuries after my death, a pair of unknown hands could flip to page four in a copy of this very same program lying in a folder in a drawer in a cabinet in the Great Hall of Illinois High School Records. It was the future and the past at the same time.

I tore myself away from page four and found the names of my teammates, who seemed blasé about their immortality. I returned to D.I. and read the twelve names again and again. Three of them—of us—would travel to Peoria in two weeks. I began to hyperventilate. I tiptoed over to Miss Schuette, keeping my trouser cuffs out of the dirty puddles of melted snow.

"What's up, Rick?"

I looked at the program balanced on my palm. She understood without my having to say anything. She brushed fuzz from the shoulder of my suit and said, "The state program is even nicer, Rick. You'll see. It's not mimeographed. They have two weeks to print it."

Print was all the pep talk I needed.

Before we left the motel room, Joe Bacino had brought up Beth Cook five hundred times while I tried out the feeling that I was in love with him, and not Ned, who I'd decided was pretty much an old perv. The soft bag of Joe's belly was sexy. He was funny and popular. He was my age. So I went looking for him, instead of Ned, during the break after first round.

His butt was pushed out on one of the pancake stools attached to our cafeteria table. I asked him how Original Comedy had gone. He looked everywhere but at me, his face as red as the roof of Eric Smola's retainer.

Cheryl Ito slapped her binder on the table. We both jumped. "Holy fuck, that was hard," she said. Heads popped all around us. Asian girls didn't swear. There had been not just one but *two* other girls in her round with Flannery O'Connor stories. Joe tore open a bag of corn curls and interrupted by asking her if she was going to Turnabout.

"Turnabout? The dance?" said Cheryl, confused. "That's in March."

"Yeah, the dance. Ask me. You can make Beth jealous."

"You'd like that."

They teased each other, Beth's name banging like a gong. Speech team was going to be over in two weeks. The rest of the team would keep living while I set the table at the Briarcliffe Jesus Ranch. My mother's note for sectionals, which I'd found in my suit pocket, was a set of batshit instructions to take on the full armor of God: the belt of truth, the shield of faith, the breastplate of righteousness, the helmet of salvation.

"I have to go drain my lizard," I said, borrowing a Joe line. He got laughs with it, but Cheryl said, "Gross." I turned around at the boy's room door and waited. Joe sat spinning on the stool. Cheryl was dressing her fingers with corn curls.

During second round I made one last discovery about my piece. I was slotted first: Lahrem, Scheie, Luebbers, Kulinski, Rennhak, and Palia. On the back wall was a map of World War II. Red and black arrows churned across Europe like licorice whirlpools. For focal points I picked England and—for Hannelore—guessed at where Stalingrad was on the right border of the map.

I had gotten about halfway through *Boys in the Band,* at the point where Michael begins haranguing Alan about Justin Stuart, when it clicked in my head like a stupid cartoon light bulb that Michael *loves* Alan. Michael has always loved Alan. Michael still loves Alan. He was jealous of the attention Alan paid Justin in college, he hates that Alan is married, and that's why he's such a horrible person. I switched to Alan and kept thinking. Does Alan suspect, has he ever suspected, that Michael loves him? Is he going to call Fran because he loves her or because he's guessed about Michael and he's freaking out?

These questions surged through my divided brain, along with flashes of Beth Cook's long black hair and the feeling of Joe's fingers dragging my scalp and the lunch meat smell of the sweaty crease between his nut sac and his thigh and the push of his dick in my mouth like the heel of Italy's boot in the middle of the map on the wall.

The last two minutes of my interp were like my very own drug movie. At the end, when Alan heard his wife's voice on the phone, I felt tears coming on, but I stifled them. And when Michael heard Fran's voice, he staggered back and howled out her name instead of simply saying it like he—or I—usually did. Listening to Fran at the other end, Michael stared at Alan and gulped a wad of snot in his throat. They both wanted to cry. Michael handed over the receiver. All three of us were struck dumb with fear. I bowed my head.

Because I had scared myself, I wasn't surprised, ninety minutes later, to read on a sheet of butcher paper:

Dramatic Interpretation
Final Round.

Room 304:

R. Moons
V. Satterwhite
C. Miller
R. Lahrem

J. Williams

M. Kulinski

I repeated my discovery final round, and it didn't feel fake.
Neither Veronica Satterwhite, her eyes popped with wonder,
nor Craig Miller, Shakespeare's Chloraseptic dickhead, seemed
pleased with my progress. While I watched icicles drip holes
into the snow on the windowsill, judge number one was writing, "Your ending is almost too painful to watch, Mr. Lahrem."
Judge number two was writing, "Michael is very subtly
drunk—excellent." Both of them ranked me ahead of Veronica
and Craig and the not very lezzie *Children's Hour* and the black
girl playing the Grand Duchess of Imperial Russia in *Anastasia*
and a strange love scene between The Queen of France and the
King of England in *The Lion in Winter*.

Judge number three, however, was writing, "This piece is
entirely inappropriate for high school forensics." Unlike the
soybean gal from Rantoul, he had the courage of his convic-
tions and ranked me last. I had two firsts and a sixth, enough
for third place and another Illinois medal for my vest pocket,
but Miss Schuette was beside herself. On the crawl home
through giant piles of dirty snow, she composed an appeal to
the IHSA on a manila envelope, muttering furious phrases
until Wegner told her to be quiet. At least I was advancing to
state, along with Mindy and God, first place in Oratory, and
Eric, first place in Extemp. Joe, Cheryl, and Cindy and Dahlia
had been eliminated.

We trooped back into school. My feet were so cold I couldn't
feel them. Wegner stopped me just inside the vestibule.

"What's that in your hand?" he asked.

"My suitcase."

"*That* hand."

I looked down. Our shadows stretched yards down the hall, away from the phones, where the rest of the team was calling for rides.

"A couple of programs," I said. I'd tucked one inside the other, so it would stay in mint condition; the outer one I'd send to my father.

"What's the white thing sticking out?"

"Oh. The D.I. finals sheet." R. Moons, V. Satterwhite, C. Miller, R. Lahrem, J. Williams, M. Kulinski. Folded three times.

"How did you come by that?" he asked, very quietly. Kids who made finals tended to take them as souvenirs, but it wasn't a Wheaton-Warrenville thing to do.

Eleven inches of snow, plus two days of heavy drama, had wiped me out, but I remembered how, with terrible clarity, in the middle of a yawn. Awards were over. Coats were going on. Ned, flat to the wall on the auditorium stairs, was letting kids pass. Early in the morning, when I was in love with Joe Bacino, I'd spotted him and shouted "Kill the people" as I walked on by.

Wegner spoke again. "Did I see somebody give you that sheet?"

"Uh . . ."

"A coach from another school, maybe?"

"Uh . . ."

"Mr. Bolang from Glenbard West. Did he give you the sheet?"

He had, but I couldn't remember how I had thanked him. Had I fallen into him? Hitched my legs up around his waist? Unzipped his fly? Only his prose reader had made it to state. There'd be a motel room, I thought, my mind drifting to a total all-night sleepover.

"Is that his name?" I finally said.

Mr. Wegner crossed his arms. He shook his head a little, then tilted it, the better to read "Daddy" in the thought bubble over my ski hat. Miss Schuette, who'd been heading our way, stopped at the edge of the tension.

"It is," he said.

We left it at that.

◦◡◦

The next morning, my mother, dressed for church, set a plate of homemade doughnuts on the table. The front door opened. Carl had been warming up the car. "Another couple of minutes, honey," he said.

"Right there."

As he came up behind me, my mother stopped humming. His gloved hand dropped an oblong box on the comics section. "Here, Rick," he said. "This is for state."

The only gift he'd ever given me was a fishing reel the year they dated. This was a tie, wide and amber, with stripes and a pattern of tiny yellow horses. I wouldn't touch it. "I don't want to mess it up," I said, displaying greasy fingertips.

"They're Capricorns."

"Yeah."

"Your sign."

"Yeah."

"I knew you'd get to state." He unzipped his coat. Yellow fish were swimming under his chins.

"Pisces," I muttered.

He was actually going to church, actually taking my mother to church. He held Lisa in the crook of his arm while my mother applied a last swipe of lipstick in the hall mirror. Lisa's squeals made it clear that she wanted to practice walking to the

211

car, but Carl cooed that the porch was too slippery. I heard his spinal cord snap like a corn cob. His blood would soak the ice under his head like cherry syrup in a Bomb Pop.

Carla slunk down eventually. I told her where they'd gone.

"Jesus for pussy," she said, disgusted.

"Huh?"

"My dad is only doing this Marriage Encounter crap to get in Marie's pants."

I sat up straight. What was she talking about? "How would you know?" I said, trying to cover my confusion.

"I have ears, Rick," said the shrugger at life.

"Then why did he get me a tie, for Christ's sake?" I flicked the hateful box and watched it capsize over the table.

"Maybe she'll do something extra for that."

"Like what?" I demanded.

Foot up on her chair, she was patiently reaming out her toes with her middle finger. "Like leave the light on."

"What?"

"Rick," she said, not unkindly, "you should know that Marie is colder than a witch's tit."

What kept me from lunging then and there was that Carla had no reason to lie. I felt like I was suffocating. My mother, trading her favors? For what? For kindness? Decent treatment? Family healing? Was this why my parents split up? Had my father been forced into the arms of Josephine the cocktail waitress? Was that the only way he could get what he needed? Was that why I had no brothers and sisters?

I put my head down on the edge of the table. My bathrobe had fallen open. I saw the pale blue veins in my thighs, carrying blood to my crotch, and I hated them, hated it, hated that the true answer to every question lived between somebody's legs.

"How long does church last?" Carla asked, oblivious.

I tried to pull myself together. "Hours. There's a social after."

Carla took the time to finish cleaning her feet before she picked up the phone. Steve, on the other hand, ran up to her room like he had explosive diarrhea. After the first round, twelve minutes by the oven timer, they came down to rub it in.

"Keep an eye out," Steve smirked. He tilted his head to chug some orange juice. A strand of Carla's hair was twisted in the stubble on his neck, and I spied more of his sleepy purple color in the fold behind his ear. I looked for the outline of his dog dick panting under her thin makeup robe.

The phone rang. I made Carla get it.

It wasn't Ned, like I hoped. The Kendigs were having a celebration that night for Mindy. The sugar sprinkles in Carla's voice made Steve squirm. She swatted the hand he put on her waist and took the receiver into the powder room. My mother had bought a longer cord for Patty Puller Phonathons.

"What's with the socks?" I asked Steve. One of his big toes had escaped.

"It's freezing out, dickwad."

Carla announced that she was going to the Kendigs' with me. Worse, she wouldn't let Steve crash the party. He demanded her early departure and a hookup after at their spot. They had been screwing at Martin Manor, but Carla had developed scruples about locking the old farts out of the recreation lounge. The argument got more intense. Steve went a little out of control, punched the refrigerator, tore up the newspaper, whipped some doughnuts at the wall, not that I gave a shit. Girls like Carla sent guys like Steve to prison. It was all between the legs.

The Kendigs didn't live in a fantasy fur-lined igloo. The track lighting would have melted the ice. "Keeps the darkness out, darlin'," Mr. Kendig kept saying.

The lights were brightest in what they called the "Glory Chamber." Mrs. Kendig had wheeled a cake cart under a five-foot stained-glass Jesus with a lamb across His arm. A lamp cast its concentrated beam on Mindy's two Oratory medals, which lay like royal earrings on a tasseled cushion next to the cake knife. Brass sconces lit the photos and plaques that coated the other walls of the Glory Chamber. There were Kendigs standing with Jimmy Carter and his mother Lillian, with Jim Nabors, with Zsa Zsa Gabor, with Johnny Cash, with Chuck Berry, with Mayor Daley, with black men in suits and leopard-skin hats, with nuns every color of the rainbow.

Millie, Margie, Monty, and Madeleine passed out cake and punch while Mr. and Mrs. Kendig, each holding one of Mindy's hands, sang a specially composed duet of thanksgiving. The refrain, which the guests were encouraged to warble, went, "Blessed Mindy, held in the palm of His hand. Blessed Mindy, saved by the blood of the Lamb."

The track lights picked out the jewels in Mrs. Kendig's holiday-bread hair, and as the whole family swayed with praise, the hem of her chiffon gown swirled like sea foam over the sparkly tips of her golden shoes. Carla's bell bottoms swayed along. Her eyes were shut and her palms were out.

I set down my plate and started to back away.

"Hey, watch it," said Joe.

"Sorry," I said. Our party policy had been to ignore each other. I'd overheard him telling Millie Kendig that his final-round judges were prejudiced against Italians.

"What are you sorry for"—he leaned over and breathed into my neck—"cocksucker?"

It wasn't a threat. It was a suggestion. My mouth went dry. On the other side of the room, Beth Cook, her face tie-dyed by the light of the stained-glass Jesus, was chewing a nail. Mrs. Kendig's voice was pole-vaulting higher on the phrase "Oh the rose of Sharon has no thorns." Her bouffant blinked like a pinball machine while Mr. Kendig's free arm traced fruity scallops in the air. Mindy, a dreamy smile plastered on her lips, was the opposite of embarrassed.

I slipped out of the Glory Chamber, Joe close behind. We snuck into a solarium dark and humid and stinky with plants. Floodlights trained on the house from the pool patio magnified the webs of water pearling down the glass walls.

"Do it again," Joe said.

"Now?"

"No, not here."

"What makes you think I want to?" I said.

"Because you like it."

The light glowed behind the frizz in his hair. I wanted to tell him he'd be going to state too if he'd only kissed me back. Instead I said, "What about Beth?"

"She doesn't have to know," he said.

Down the hall, the refrain had come round again on "Blessed Mindy."

"No, I meant what about Beth doing it?"

His voice went cold. "She's not going to do that."

"She's your girlfriend."

"She's a *girl*, Rick. Girls don't do that."

They do it for Jesus, I thought in the dark. Jesus for pussy. Poor, desperate Marie.

I took an encouraging step. The white iron arms of the patio chair behind Joe glowed brighter to receive him. For once I didn't have a boner. I unzipped my fly.

"What are you doing?"

"You blow me first," I said.

It was the only way to drive him away. Another merit badge.

I stayed in the hot rankness for quite a while, watching and listening. I gathered strength from the certainty that the plants and I were breathing together. It wasn't until later, when Mindy was driving Carla and me home on Herrick Road, that I realized I'd been listening in the solarium for the magical buzz of Esmeralda—surely she lived there. I was hoping she'd show herself, so I could hurl her like a grenade through the glass and watch her guts sizzle like a chemical spill on the frozen patio.

Something wasn't right. Something didn't add up. Wouldn't Esmeralda want to challenge any invader of her jungle? How could a giant tropical cockroach survive an Illinois winter? And Carla never had told me what it was that Esmeralda ate.

"Hey," I said from the back seat. "Is Esmeralda fake?"

In the silence, I heard the tires crunching the snow.

"What do you mean?" asked Mindy sweetly.

"You know what I mean. She's a gizmo, right? Mechanical."

Carla's head swiveled toward Mindy. "Oh no, she's real all right, Rick," she said.

"No, she's got to be a fake. It's too cold for her up here."

Whispering. Then snickers broke out.

"She's always been a cockroach—"

"Just not always alive—"

"So you've been lying to me—"

"Don't be a baby, Rick." Carla was holding in her laughter.

"You've been lying all this time, Mindy? Why?"

"It's just a little fib."

"It's not a little fib, it's . . . it's . . . Esmeralda!" I shouted.

"Poor baby," cackled Carla.

"But I believed you!"

"Rick believes in the Easter Bunny. And Santa Claus."

"Does he believe in the Tooth Fairy?" shrieked Mindy.

"Fairy" was their last intelligible word. Then they were laughing so hard that Mindy lost control of the wheel. Carla and I slammed against our doors. Attempting to recover, Mindy wove into the other lane as we were heading down a long stretch of Herrick that led onto Butterfield Road. Then we were fishtailing on the ice into the path of an oncoming truck, just like in a driver's ed movie. Our screams, as wide and round as the truck's headlights, were drowned out by horns.

Then—nothing. Nothing of the earth, that is. I can offer no rational explanation for what happened. As Mindy would testify to one and all, it was as if a giant hand reached from the sky, took up the car, and gently set us down, intact, unharmed, aglow, facing the other direction along the left side of the road.

Over the whoosh of passing cars, I heard Mindy praise God. Her voice pealed in counterpoint to my chant of "Are you okay are you hurt is anybody hurt I'm okay I'm okay I'm okay I'm okay," although nothing came out of my mouth. Then I heard Carla accept Jesus Christ as her personal Lord and Savior.

They were still shouting and sobbing, wrapped in each other, as I opened the car door with the last of my adrenaline and hurled myself into a snow bank.

$\sim$ 10 $\sim$

My third at sectionals was included in morning announcements, but Carla Schwob's blacktop conversion was the true sensation. At lunch, Wheaton-Warrenville's most glamorous Magdalene to date sat with Mindy at the play fag table, the two of them baptizing tater tots in each other's ketchup and witnessing to the faithful. Stacy Granbur and a bubbly trio of Campus Lifers were first in line for hugs. They shuddered as Carla's huge boobs shamelessly buzzed their sockets, she had been so total a sinner. Carla's promise to witness at their Bible study launched a chorus of "God is always in the driver's seat"s and "You're so cute"s.

"Bring Esmeralda with you," I said under my breath, certain that the junior Pattys would enjoy hearing how Mindy's falsehood about Satan's pinwheel had sent us spinning across the ice.

"Congratulations, Rick," Stacy said warily, warding off paganism with rapid flutters of her white eyelashes.

218

I set down my chili dog. "Yeah. I'll be promoting sin downstate."

"Mindy said you were in the car too."

"Uh-huh," I drawled. "It wasn't my time to die." Or get saved. In the back seat, beyond God's reach. I'd only pissed myself with fright.

I tipped my empty carton of milk to my mouth and noisily swallowed air. The sight of Carla's trusting, gentle smile punched me in the gut. Was that what beatific looked like? To keep from going under, I babbled out, "In the words of Conrad Birdie, 'I've got a lot a livin' to do.'"

There was a fresh volley of Campus Life squeals. Wegner had posted sign-up sheets for the spring musical that morning: *Bye Bye Birdie*. Auditions were in two weeks, the Monday after the state meet. By third period the sheets were half-filled, Joe's and Mindy's names near the top. Having revealed at lunch that both Dick Van Dyke and Paul Lynde had been in the original cast, I'd become the resident expert. Would Joe and Mindy play Albert and Rose? Or Conrad and Kim? Was Joe too fat for Conrad? Did I think it was fair that they always got the leads?

The Campus Life squad was going to try out for the teenage chorus and convert from within. They asked Carla if she was going to audition.

"You mean audition to be in the play?" Carla's astonishment would have made me laugh any other time, except the clotted, cottage-cheese sound in her voice had disappeared overnight.

"Do you sing, Carla?"

I saw her dirty hair oil-slicking the pillows on the love seat as she croaked along to her Aerosmith records. On the other hand, after The Miracle on Herrick Road, maybe she sang higher than Minnie Riperton.

"Not like Mindy," she protested.

Mindy dabbed ketchup from her lips. "Don't receive that!"

"You're a lamb of God now, Carla," Lisa Halsey gurgled.

"Sing for joy to God our strength; shout aloud to the God of Jacob!" cried Stacy.

"Oooh, what was that?" asked Carla.

"Psalm 81. You're gonna love Psalms and Proverbs!"

"Begin the music, strike the tambourine, play the melodious harp and lyre . . ." Mindy was continuing the verse when she stopped with another idea. "If you don't sing, maybe you could be in the orchestra. Do you play any instruments, Carla?"

"Steve's skin flute," I muttered. "Uncut."

"I'm not musical in any way—"

"Don't receive that, Carla!"

"Only take in the good!"

"Let go and let God!"

"He moves mountains!"

I wished I knew how to barf on cue.

"Well, I guess I can think about the chorus," Carla said shyly. Then, eager to give back to her brand-new best friends, she suggested that they get a jump on auditions and learn the lyrics by listening to her brother's record.

"You have a brother?" said Ty Vandenhoop, still under Mindy's sway.

She turned to me. "You have *Bye Bye Birdie,* don't you Rick?"

"Rick is your *brother*?" asked Stacy over more girl squeals.

"He is. He is definitely my brother," said Carla, proud of the fact, and not faking it, a second kick in the stomach. "Praise God," she added, blushing as she tried the phrase out for the very first time.

I picked up my tray and fled, leaving it to her to explain the step-connection. Everything was so instantly perfect for her. Was that what God was? I ran down the math department stairwell, outracing the question.

At school Carla became another Zombie for Jesus, part of the pack, insulated from Steve and the burnouts by Mindy and her heavenly choir. Home was more frightening. Her voice continued to unclog with Marie's help. I would eavesdrop after dinner from halfway up the stairs, my outlaw's elbows pinned into my clenched knees, listening to them trade Psalms and Proverbs from the Young Lady's Bible. Carl, drowsing in the booger chair, was a poor watchdog in case the Devil spiraled up through the heat duct from the basement. Discovering kindness everywhere, Carla became kind. The more she confessed and confided and praised and asked forgiveness, the less I had to say. We were trading places.

∽✺

"Come here, little man," said Patty Puller, too quick for me as I tried to duck upstairs. She was lying sideways on the sofa, feet warming under a gap in the cushions.

"I have homework," I said.

She crooked a forefinger, and her Bible tilted on her segmented lap. "Now, don't make me come after you," she softly crooned, as if keeping secrets from Marie, who was rustling up a bowl of starches in the kitchen.

"Homework."

"Come here," she repeated, rubbing a pillow. "Patty's tired."

I took a step, worried about her foot smell, her breath smell, worried she'd pull me down and crush me like a piglet against the cushions.

"Do you know the story of the Prodigal Son?"

221

I stopped. "Yes," I lied.

"Good." She set her Bible on the end table and cracked her knuckles. "Then you need to know that you too will have your fatted calf, Rick."

"Sure."

"And if there's one thing I know, it's teenagers, so I'll bet, while Sister Carla is feasting on the roasted succulence of her fatted calf and all its delicious trimmings, I'll bet Brother Rick is wondering when's he gonna get his, where's his succulent feast, am I right, little man?"

Nearer to the lamp now, I saw the gray-green strip of her gums, like a paste of dried peas, above the glistening Chiclets of her teeth.

"Let's ask the Lord for your succulent fatted calf, Rick. He wants to meet every need, He does, He does, He does, He listens, oh ask and ye shall receive. . . ." Her feet were digging, twisting, picking up strength under the cushions. "Do you know what you want, sugar?"

"I guess so." I'd have said anything to get her to stop saying "succulent."

Her feet popped out of the couch. "Okay, let's pray for your fatted calf then, shall we?" she said, all business. "Tell Sister Patty what you want and we'll pray for it."

Asking for a brand-new life would be jackknifing into her snare, so I said all I wanted was to make final rounds at state.

"Ooooh yes yes yessss," she hissed, shuddering, as if the answer was boiling in her bosom and her mouth was a spout.

She grabbed my hand and pushed her thumb hard into the center of my palm. I fell to my knees in pain. From somewhere, just where I hated to think, she produced a tiny cold cream jar and unscrewed the lid with one hand.

She wiggled her free thumb in the jar. "Thou hast loved righteousness and hated iniquity, therefore God, even thy God, hath anointed thee with the oil of gladness above thy fellows."

She crossed the middle of my forehead and let her greasy thumb rest in my hairline. "Lord, we ask You to bless Your servant and anointed steward Richard Lahrem, for he is of You in Your image, bless him in Your holy name and see fit in Your wisdom to guide him to glorify You, Lord Jesus, at state, at the state meet, at the state meet in . . . in . . ." Here Patty dug harder in my palm.

"In Peoria," I said.

"In Peoria—yes, yesss, march Your humble servant to Peoria to glorify You at the state speech meet, You have shown him his gift in speech through districts and sectionals, Lord, we ask You to take him to the mighty final round—" She paused and switched to her regular voice. "Just the final round, sugar? Don't you want to win it all? God is there for the asking."

"Um, no, just the finals," I stuttered.

Like an interper switching characters, she flipped back to prayer voice. "In the final round at state, in Peoria, bless him and put him into finals, for Your faithful servant Richard is deserving, his gift is Yours, put him into finals O Lord, put him into finals O Lord put him into finals O Lord . . ."

Patty was stuck. I was about to say, "On February nineteenth," when she gave a long, low burp, and then out rushed a torrent of syllables—"Abba elekelaba keleballalah laba laba ha shondelah lashondalasha abababababah kelalaba . . ."

Her hand was a vise. I cracked open my left eye. Her head was moving in tiny side-to-side jerks, like a snake's, and froth was gathering at the corners of her lips. I was too stupefied to scream.

I felt my mother take my other hand, but instead of rescuing me from Sister Patty's fire, she began pouring her own crazy oil on it, quieter, softer, and shaped around the short u sound: "Gluhluh gluhluh luhluh baluhluh pusuhsuhsuhsuh guhluhluh . . ."

I shut my eyes tight, tried to cram my body into them, so I could ship out in these twin walnuts, ship out on these vowel streams and wash up on a brown velveteen couch, dry and whole and unharmed.

One last time, Patty Puller switched channels from the Laba Laba Land of her tongue language back to Jesus English. "You will march him to Peoria, and he will be in those finals, we ask this O Lord in Your Holy Name, Amen."

"Amen," said my mother. "Are you hungry, honey?"

I ran up the stairs. My right hand felt punched clean through by Patty's thumb.

Lisa was awake in her crib. "Up," she cried, holding out her arms, lifelines back to sanity. After a long hug and lots of raspberries in her neck, I stood her on the rug and chased her into my room.

She headed for the bookcase. Lisa had a thing for my presidents. Ours was a serious game. She would point to the one she wanted, and I would lift him from his Styrofoam slot, saying his name. She'd study him carefully, and either hand him back or carry him over to my bed and drop him in the pile of his friends. She had her favorites, like I did, and couldn't be influenced. If she was pointing to Chester Arthur, I'd better not try to give her Grover Cleveland.

She wanted Franklin Delano Roosevelt, who wore a short black Dracula cape. "FDR."

"Effeerrrruh."

"Very good, Lisa. Here you go."

From the back row I picked up Kennedy and waggled him in front of her. "FDRJFK."

"Effeerrruhjaykay."

I laughed, so she laughed. "FDRJFKHDIF," I said in a rush. Lisa dropped Roosevelt on the bed and clapped for Kennedy. I handed him over and repeated "HDIF" in the goopiest possible Christian voice.

"Ayshfuh."

"HDIFJFK."

"Ayshfuhjaykay."

I started shaking my hips and singing "HDIFJKF" in an awful falsetto. John F. Kennedy, killed by the people, even I knew that.

Lisa, spooked I guess, didn't join in. She ran over to the beanbag chair and pointed at the collection of miniature liquor bottles on the shelf above the presidents. I hesitated, remembering the glass bowl accident as if it had happened years ago, instead of three months. The October Carla and Marie Schwob were gone to God, and now maybe Carl was too. Only Lisa and I were left.

I took down a brown heart-shaped bottle of Paul Masson Rare Tawny Port and rubbed the dust off its shoulders. My father had brought it back from a trip to Jamaica. The bottle had a jagged, handmade-looking label and antique lettering, so I used to pretend it was booty hauled up from a sunken pirate ship. Now it occurred to me that Josephine had probably gone on that Jamaica trip with him, one more nasty, between-the-legs adventure.

"Be careful, Lisa, it's glass," I said.

She looked back at me, eyes wide. "Glaaa . . ." she said.

225

"Sssss . . ."

"Zzzzz . . ."

"Gulaaassss," I said, lowering the heart. I let her take it. She bounced with happiness.

Downstairs the front door opened. Fresh cries, fresh delights. Carla had come home from school with Mindy Kendig. Two cows and two calves, rubbing Jesus udders against each other, squirting God streams into each other's mouths. Had I found words to describe what had just happened with Patty and my mother, my father would still never believe me.

"Sazerac Sling," I said abruptly, studying the rows of bottles. "Sazzzzerac Slingggh."

Lisa laughed and buzzed. "Zzzzzzzz zak. Zzzzzzz zak!"

"Sugarless Sazerac Sling."

"Zzzzzzzz Zak!"

"Jesus is for lezzies."

"Zzzzzzzz ZAK!"

"Do you want some mustard for your sandwich?"

She caught my serious tone. She nodded.

"Please."

"Peezzzzzz."

She patted my hand. I traded her a Gilbey's Gin for the Paul Masson Port.

"Drink up, little lady."

⌒⌒

Veronica Satterwhite put her arm against mine. "Look! Butterscotch in our sweaters. We match!" The flash went off.

"Butterscotch?" I blinked, a beat behind, as usual. Miss Schuette asked the photographer for a do-over because I wasn't facing the camera.

The Great Wheaton Dramatic Interp rivalry was going public. A reporter and photographer from the *Daily Journal* had posed Veronica and me on a big table at the town library. Piled around us were plays and drama anthologies. Miss Schuette and Veronica's coaches, Mr. and Mrs. McCracken, kept to the sides. Mr. Wegner wasn't there, Schuette explained fifteen hundred times, because the choral books for *Bye Bye Birdie* hadn't arrived and he had important calls to place to New York.

Miss Schuette had instructed me to praise Veronica nonstop. I guess the McCrackens told Veronica the same thing, because each of us predicted the other would win state, each of us hoped for a tie, both of us loved our schools, and neither of us thought of the other as competition. We posed with the books — reading over one another's shoulders, pointing at passages, having a tug-of-war with the Shakespeare, holding the titles upside down, so cornball we might have been Donny and Marie launching a medley. Patrons began to cluster at the edges of our butterscotchy goodness. Veronica and I, at the same time, put our fingers to our lips and said, "Shhhh." That was a big hit, worth six shots.

Preening for this crowd of geezers and crazoids who lived at the library, I felt the return of my talent crush for my sexy and ruthless rival. Maybe God had lifted Mindy's car off the road so I could date Veronica. Maybe Veronica was the succulent feast Patty promised. My father would cream when he got his copy of the article. I could circle our photo and write, "This is Veronica. Doesn't she look like Julia? Send a thousand bucks for prom. Ha Ha."

The reporter, fat with bushy sideburns, helped my fantasy along by asking whether we had sweethearts. Valentine's Day was coming up, after all. Veronica and I looked at each other, shrugged, and burst out laughing. Flash.

"Gosh no, I'm too busy," said Veronica.

"I'm available," I said, deepening my voice.

Flash. Schuette and the McCrackens beamed.

Veronica held up a book titled *The Last of the Red Hot Lovers* and announced she wanted to do comedy next year. On the cover was a naked lady in a seashell. Flash. Mrs. McCracken replaced it with *Butterflies Are Free,* and Miss Schuette cracked up. She came over to pull my collar out of my sweater.

"Why comedy, Veronica?" asked the reporter.

She thoughtfully rested her chin in her hand. "Oh . . . the dramatic events are so difficult. Screaming and killing and dying. Sometimes it just . . . makes me so . . . sad, all that pain." She patted my forearm. "Don't you think so, Rick?"

"I do think so," I said, clearing my throat.

"I mean, I can come home from a tournament all upset, and it's not because I won or lost. I get so depressed I don't even feel like doing my homework." Veronica had slipped into Willie's voice from her interp. "Next season I want to laugh. I want to make people happy. I want to be happy too."

"How about you, Richard?" asked the reporter.

I tried to recall the last time I'd done my homework. "I have to say . . . honestly . . . that it doesn't faze me."

"Well, Rick, you're a boy. His D.I. is so amazing," said Veronica, batting her eyelashes at the reporter. "You should see him do it."

Schuette shook her head from the sidelines. I was not to reveal or discuss the nature of my piece. Stimulated by Veronica's reference to my gender, I had an inspired change of subject. "I

wish that next year Veronica and I could do an acting duet together," I said. "Humorous, dramatic, it doesn't matter."

"Central and Warrenville bury the hatchet!" Veronica cried,
inviting applause with a backward toss of her hair. Flash flash
flash. "Could we, oh could we?" she pleaded to the McCrackens.
Schuette was rolling her eyes, but I liked the idea. Even if we
couldn't compete for trophies, we could perform our duets in
the library, tour them to rec centers and old folks' homes. Hannelore would applaud our man-woman act at Martin Manor.
This, I thought, was God's work. He had spared my life so I
could go straight. I couldn't wait to unhook Veronica's bra.

I swept my arm over the piles of books. "There are a lot of
plays here."

"You can pick, Rick. Just don't make me *sing*."

"Sing?" asked the reporter. "Do you sing?"

And that was all Veronica needed to cut to *This Property Is
Condemned*. Sucked in, the photographer slowly lowered his
camera, the reporter his pad. I headed for the bathroom, not
needing Schuette's prompt to be out of the frame if they asked
for a taste of *The Boys in the Band*. No moral controversy for
the papers or anybody. Why that third finals judge at sectionals
had ranked me last was top-secret.

I went into the men's stall to blot my pits. Thoughts of
burying the hatchet *into* Veronica flew out of my skull as I deciphered a message right above the toilet paper roll: *"For blow
job call 393-1676 Ask for Jay."*

The first astonishment: 393 was a local exchange. There
were other band members in my town, a roomful, maybe a restaurant full of mustached men wearing *After Dark* belt buckles.
I had to find them.

The second astonishment: Jay's need was so fresh, the letters blurred under the touch of my fingertip. I groaned with lust—the tongue language Ned had given me—and pulled down my pants. *Here* was where I belonged, not out playing Donny and Marie with the Satterwhite android. I flopped onto the seat and jerked off. The swastikas and peace symbols decorating the stall circled my head like cartoon stars after a knockout punch. While Veronica warbled "My Blue Heaven," I dried my hands and opened the door on wild applause.

The third astonishment: The reporter asked me what my hobbies were. I said show tunes and Nazi souvenirs.

❧

Things could get worse, so they did. The next day Ned said on the phone that we couldn't be together again until after state. In between three hundred "Why nots?" I told him I missed him, I threatened to walk to his apartment, I threatened to drop out of state, I suggested the arboretum, the Seven Dwarfs, Rascal's, Yorktown, Wax Trax, Glenbard West, *anywhere*. He kept saying it was only ten days, couldn't I wait, until I was shouting, "I can't! I can't! I can't!"

Marie knocked on the other side of the laundry room door. "Can't what, honey?"

"Go away!" I yelled.

"Don't hurt your voice," she said. "You've got state coming up."

I watched a blackbird chip at a suet cage in our neighbor's backyard. The window cooled my hand. At the other end, I heard Ned swallow.

"I want some of your ginger ale, Daddy," I whispered.

"Rick, please listen to me—"

"Why don't you want to see me?

"I do want to see you."

"It's been so long, Daddy."

"Oh baby, I know. You know how much I want to be with you."

"Then why aren't you?"

He swallowed again. "Because I got a warning from Mr. Wegner."

The blackbird, sharing my shock, tore off to the top of the McClellans' swing set. "Mr. Wegner? What do you mean? When?"

"He left a message for me yesterday."

"What did it say?"

"It said to call him."

"What did he say when you called him?"

"I haven't called him."

"Why not?"

"I don't need to call him," he said, impatient again.

"Why not?" I was shivering, so I stepped into the basket of clean, unfolded laundry. The day before, Carla had separated lights from darks for the very first time. Much was made of it at the dinner table.

"It was warning enough."

"A warning what?" I put my other foot in the basket. Soon she'd be taking cookbooks down, stirring boxes of pudding mix into bowls, draining bacon grease, hand-washing china with my mother. She'd sprout hair wings and prairie skirts, squirrels would gather around her feet, robins and starlings and sparrows would land on her outstretched arms, but not my blackbird. My blackbird was mine.

"A warning to keep away from you."

231

"All you did was give me the finals sheet after awards. That's all he saw. That's all, right?"

"That's quite enough, Rick."

"I don't understand."

"Well, right, you're too young to understand."

"But not too young to molest." The blackbird cocked its head.

It was a desperate verb. I hardly knew I knew it. After an electric pause, Ned said he'd pick me up in front of Briarcliffe on Sunday at two. I said no, pick me up in front of Martin Manor Senior Center at ten. My mother and Carl would be away all weekend with Marriage Encounter, and I needed hours and hours for him to make me feel better.

I'd gotten my way, but I didn't like how. I was too upset to stay inside. The house was dangerous. There was my room and the laundry room. Everywhere else was Jesus. I went out to find my ally. Chickadees bickered inside the spruce hedges, and I spotted a lady cardinal, but my blackbird had disappeared. I sat in one of the swings, kicking snow until my butt felt frozen to the rubber disc and lights began coming on up and down the gulch of backyards. I ignored the spatula waves from Marie, who was stirring chow mein in the electric skillet.

Eventually an orange tabby sidling through the dried stalks in the Florians' vegetable garden reminded me that there was one person in Briarcliffe even more pissed off than me. I twisted two last times in the swing and went to share a plate of misery with Steve. He probably wouldn't agree, but life was easier when sex was just me reading letters and checking for his boner in the crawlspace.

❧

Some things you never forget. Jay's *393-1676* was already stamped in my brain when I found *665-8520* next to "*Matt 8 inches*," and then a number for the anonymous "*Fuck & Suck Fridays 12-1*" in the toilet stall at Mark Shale.

"What took you?" asked Carla. She and Marie were leaning against the alterations desk with shirt and tie combinations to go with a cashmere sport coat for state. It was already more expensive than my three-piece Cerruti from Madigan's.

"665-8520," I said, having decided that Matt 8 Inches was more my type. Blow Job Jay and Mr. Fuck & Suck Fridays were too specific with their needs. Ned had been teaching me to be "versatile," like him.

"Is that a phone number?" asked my mother. Distracted by mix and match, they weren't really listening, but the salesman flashed me another semi-secret look. I'd felt him studying me in the fitting room mirror as he tugged the chalked-up sleeves off my arms.

Matt 8 Inches was on the swim team, so he wasn't fat like Joe. He was circumcised, so he wasn't like Steve. He wanted to kiss me, so he wasn't like Joe or Steve. He was a sophomore at Downers North, so he wasn't against the law like Ned. And since he shopped at Mark Shale, he lived in a swanky subdivision and was a good dresser. We could meet every afternoon in his bedroom once I got my driver's license.

"That's 'Bali H'ai,'" I said.

The salesman, sitting out the selection committee's deliberations, looked up at the speaker in the ceiling. We all stopped to listen.

"*South Pacific,*" he replied.

Four ties around her neck, Marie waved her hands at her waist and hulaed to the Muzak strings. She was in a fantastic mood. Carla had let her braid her hair after dinner. They were going to shop for blouses together.

"Which side?" I asked.

"A."

That was definitely worth a smile back.

Ten minutes later, Marie had cheerfully written a check for $175 and we were on our way to Casual Corner. Collecting other names from other Yorktown toilets would be cheating on Matt 8 Inches, so I sat down in front of the store to wait. The mall was deserted at night; the screaming red Valentine's Sale signs were the only noise. Bali H'ai still whispered, so I pitched a nickel into the wishing well and wished for the total tropical transformation of my life. Matt 8 Inches would teach me to snorkel where the sky meets the sea. We'd spearfish, drink out of coconut shells, live in a hut more luxurious than the Howells had on *Gilligan's Island*. Thinking about him, the latest draw from my deck of fatted-calf cards, settled my stomach some. Since Ned's phone call, I'd been walking around wanting to throw up.

Carla leaned her shopping bag against mine.

"Mom's gone to the pattern store." We both made a face. That could take hours. "She gave me money in case we want ice cream or something."

"I'm not so hungry."

She sat down. "Okay."

"Find stuff?"

"Yeah."

Two teenage boys drifted by. A woman slowed, then stopped in front of a freestanding candy cart. The man with her was two stores ahead before he realized he was walking by himself. He turned around. They kept signaling each other to come, slicing the air with their arms.

"Bet you want a cigarette," I said.

Carla shook her head.

"So you're going to call her Mom now?"

"She said it was okay."

"I'll bet."

"Is it okay with you?"

I shrugged. Carla tossed a penny and knitted her hands together. I wanted to pry them apart. Wishing wells were for wishes, not prayers. She swung her legs up and pointed her toes. Shoes with heels. The sneakers scrawled with Steve's name in puffy, Day-Glo letters had vanished. Things were disappearing every single day.

"What are you going to do about Steve?" I said. The woman in front of the candy cart was in the "Oh yeah?" pose now, chin out, hands on hips. The man tore off his hat and finally trudged back.

"You better talk to him," I warned. "This is making him nuts, I can tell you that."

"I know," she said softly.

"He loves you, Carla. He told me yesterday he'd marry you if it were legal."

She rubbed the top of her nose. Also gone missing was the cakey blue eye shadow. "I've been praying to be shown the right words to say."

"The right words to say what?" I had a terrible thought. "No, Carla. You *can't* break up with Steve, are you mental? It's February. Valentine's Day is Monday." He had shown me a diamond and sapphire bracelet he bought for her at Zale's with two months of drug profits.

"Oh no, Rick," she said. "I'm going to try to bring him to Christ."

I had never heard anything so insanely wrong, at least not

since Monday, when Patty and my mother squirted "elekella-bah puhsuhsuhsuh" milk all over me, or Wednesday, when Ned told me I couldn't see him.

"Knock it off, Carla. You've been a Christian for four whole days."

"God loves Steve. He loves you too."

It was too much. Far from loving me, God was fucking me over from every direction. "Why are you doing this to me?" I snarled.

"Doing what?"

"Jesus. God. Everything. Is this just for attention?"

"I have found the Lord. He has my attention now."

"A week ago you were a burnout, stoned all day long—and now—look at you!"

"God works miracles, that's what God is, praise His holy name," she said rapidly, now so fluent in Jesus double-talk it was scary.

"If you were sick of being a burnout and a slut, you know you could have just stopped. You don't have to fake this Jesus shit for attention."

"Oh, Rick," she said calmly, "His love is real. 'For God so loved the world that he gave his only Son, that whoever believes in him shall not perish but have eternal life.' John 3:16."

"You sound like a fucking robot, Carla! I mean, anyone can memorize the Bible."

She reached for my wrist. "It's okay, brother."

I slapped her arm away, picked up her bag, and whipped it as hard as I could at the candy cart. "You can't do this to me!"

I was screaming, but she didn't raise her voice as she explained that she had been a sinner for a long, long time, for her whole life, and now she would sin no more. She had Jesus now, instead of everything she'd ever known. She had Jesus love instead of Valentine love, Steve love, Regi love. Jesus' real love was filling her up. If it could happen to Marie, and Ty Vandenhoop, it could happen to her.

I wasn't there, so I could only imagine she used words to that effect on Steve the next day. At the mall I had buried my face in my hands to ward off the blows in her message of higher love, but Steve, having ambushed her in the lockers by Industrial Arts between fourth and fifth periods, gave as good as he got. They said she dodged his fists pretty well but eventually he was able to slam her head against her locker and bash her in the left eye. Yet he was the one crying, they said, when Mr. Zarcone pulled the knife out of his hands. They said she forgave him in a voice thrilling to hear.

∞∞

I bounced off the glass walls of the Martin Manor vestibule at the sight of the Pontiac nosing around the entrance hedge.

He idled from a distance, waiting for me to come to him. Nothing doing, I said to the sky. To pop him out of the car, I cupped my hands around my crotch and squeezed. His plumes of breath as he approached were like a warning from a volcano. Goodbye, Matt 8 Inches, Daddy has helicoptered onto the island.

I fell into him, whimpering. He let me rest there the tiniest moment. "Two of clubs," I said in standard greeting, pressing mine into his.

"Two of hearts," he said. I tilted my head for the kiss, but he said, "Not here, Rick."

"Oh right," I replied, pretending I'd forgotten where we were.

Penthouse Forum writers often testified that the risk of exposure intensified any encounter, so public sex was still one of my major goals. My own non-solo sex life had begun on a bedspread in the arboretum with Carol and Kim and Steve. Two weeks previous I had blown Ned within partial view of a Foto-Mate, and in the meantime I'd done Joe Bacino one bed over from the sleeping Eric Smola and discovered that there were men advertising their need in toilets all over DuPage County. The Seventh Dwarf was Bashful. That wasn't me anymore.

So, saying I had to pee, I tricked Ned into the Martin Manor rec room. The residents used it for crafts, but on weekends they vegged in the TV room, which got the most sun. I pushed him onto the couch that Steve and Carla used and jiggled the doorknob, only pretending to lock it. Ideally, Hannelore would find us and count our four big grapes. Ned wouldn't let us get naked, so I couldn't vanquish Steve and Carla's smell with ours. I had to make do with flinging Ned's cum strings onto a dorky painting of a sunflower.

We did it again at his apartment, with *Jubilee Showcase* on the TV. The Musical Kendigs had returned with a special guest. I raised the volume when I saw Carla clap her way to the altar for the finale. The song, dedicated to her by Mr. Kendig, was "How I Got Over." She found a spot in line and oooga-boogied with her black eye between chicken-winging church ladies. Maybe she could change her name to Marla and become the eighth musical Kendig.

"His love is real," I said, getting up to switch off the program. I thought it would be a hoot, but it made me feel sick again. I was sick to be jealous of Carla's joy, jealous that she didn't care who knew of a passion that couldn't be shamed.

"Whose love is real?" said Ned, sliding up the headboard.

Glenbard West didn't have Jesus freaks the way Wheaton-Warrenville did. I crossed my hands into my pits and explained my week, what had happened with Carla and Mindy, and my mother and Patty Puller talking in tongues, and Veronica Satterwhite's treachery, and the toilet messages, and missing him so bad, and Steve getting taken away from school in a cop car. By the time I cried it all out, naked and shivering in the middle of his shag carpeting, I had even told him about what I'd done for Joe Bacino.

Ned Bolang, pastor of the heat-seeking Church of Come Here Now, took me in and softly preached of how much he had truly been a boy like me, shy and pained in the crowd of his family, afraid of the loud, angry farm machines, happiest counting out the plates for Sunday dinner, fretful when his mother was late getting home, coming alive when the *Ed Sullivan Show* broadcast fifteen minutes of *Do Re Mi,* coming alive in the Broadway section of the Streator Record Shop, coming alive in speech team and plays, and of how he finally got over when his Uncle Zak, short for Zachariah, found him alone in a hay wagon one August afternoon. They kept it up all through high school, finding time to conduct their special business whenever either farm needed extra hands. Winters were slow, and too cold for visits. Planting and harvest, and summer picnics, were the busy times.

"Where is he now?" I breathed into Ned's side, hardly believing that such an uncle could exist.

"Farming. Soybeans and a few hogs. My cousin Rand will take over in about ten years, God help him."

Nor was I prepared for a family. "He's *married*? You have *cousins*?"

The question seemed to puzzle Ned. "My aunt Greta is a

mother of eight, a grandmother of twenty-three, and a home canner of statewide distinction. Eldress of her church. Zak's a deacon."

"At a *church*?" I lifted my head. His eyes were so kind. I started crying again.

"First Lutheran. You have to be religious down there, but he's not spiritual. Greta is the spiritual one, like your mother, but quiet about it." He brushed my tears with his fingertips. "Oh, baby, don't feel bad. We all lose our mothers, one way or another."

I wasn't crying about Marie specifically. I was having a hard time grasping how it was that Ned's "down there"—Potassepotamia—could be as fucked-up and hypocritical as the suburbs.

We lay breathing in unison. Ned scratched the small of my back. No geographical place could be so safe. I calmed down enough to ask him what might have happened if Aunt Greta had never existed. Ned held me tighter and called me a romantic and said he didn't think he'd been particularly special to Uncle Zak. Sex didn't mean as much on a farm. A man got it where he could find it. After Zak died, Ned figured he might ask his male cousins if they'd been diddled too.

"Will you be sorry when he dies?"

Ned took a very long time to answer.

"I don't know, Rick. "

Then, because he was my pastor, he read my mind. He said that he was a city boy now and that sex meant everything to him and I was extremely special, exceedingly so, one in a million, the needle in his haystack. To prove it, he took a little envelope out of his nightstand. "Happy Valentine's Day," he said. I opened it and swooned. Two light green pasteboard tickets for the tour of *A Chorus Line,* coming in July to the Blackstone Theatre.

July. He wanted to be with me after school let out. I thought I couldn't be happier than I was at that moment, lying naked under the covers, staring up at the show cards, the stained-glass windows of our church, but then I managed to talk him into coming to my house.

Carl and Marie were in Rockford; Sister Patty and Brother Roy had Lisa for the weekend; the Kendigs were dropping Carla off at her mother's on the South Side; and my dream of having sex in my own room was going to come true.

Ned made no objection, because talking about state in the car, I remembered to ask him about my discovery at sectionals. Did he think that maybe Michael has always loved Alan? And that Alan figures it out before he makes the phone call?

The minute the words left my lips, Ned smacked the steering wheel. "Oh my god, of course, of course, of *course!*" He rocked his bucket seat at every stoplight. He had never guessed, never considered, never imagined my interpretation, he was going to have to call every faggot in America. He would track Mart Crowley down in Hollywood, if it came to that. He practically shoved me through the Andover's front door.

"Show me," he barked, "show me now." We ran up the stairs. I kissed him in front of the mirror behind the door, eyes open, to capture how he and I looked with my bookcase, my beanbag chair, and my beer mug trash can in the frame. He didn't want to neck, he wanted to see the D.I. We shucked our coats, and when he stretched out full-length on my bed, the second shot in my Valentine's pictorial came true.

It was my last coaching session. Ned said if there was a God in heaven, I would win state. He sighed deeply, then patted the bed. He wasn't going anywhere. My presidents, my liquor bottles, my trophies, my albums, would root for us. And when we were done, we would face the windows. *I* would cradle *him,* he would spoon inside me, in my room, in my life. My left hand would lightly cup his right breast as his breathing slowed. I would keep watch while he slept. The time would come to wake him. He would open his eyes, check the numbers on the clock radio, and see the world I woke to. Once granted this perfect understanding of me, he would never leave.

I unzipped my pants. He smoothed his mustache with the heels of his hands. I freed my boner. He kicked off his shoes. Ten minutes later his dick was in my mouth when Carla, not in Calumet City, not in Calumet City at all, walked into the room.

❦ 11 ❦

The week before Peoria was agony. Carla, getting unbelievable mileage out of the black eye Steve gave her, was coming down to state and rooming with Mindy. The two of them were talking about doing a Dramatic Duet the following year, and she wanted to see what speech team was like. It was her ultimate larceny. Baby Christians point and get whatever they want.

I begged Wegner and Schuette not to let it happen. Alluding to troubles at home, I argued that having my stepsister along might wreck my concentration. I couldn't tell them that I was Carla's hostage, that I was studying the Young Man's Bible to buy her silence. Wegner, who had stopped meeting my eyes, said I should show some sympathy, and he shut Schuette up when she tried to take my side.

After Ned threw on his clothes and left at Road Runner speed that Sunday, Carla and I conducted an exhausting exchange. The oxygen in the room would get used up by the alien, adult concepts we were throwing around—redemption, sexual identity, sin, the Holy Spirit, children of the righteous, weak or absent father, forgiveness, bisexuality. Carla, more and more horrified, would run to the next room, and I'd follow, more and more terrified. Finally there was a concept we both understood. Carla asked how it all started, and I said Steve Hendrie.

She touched her eye socket, a crescent of bruised pear, and rolled her hands under the bottom of her sweater. I told her the story of how he'd forced me to blow him while we babysat Janey and Joey Hegna. I didn't tell her that, except for the forcing part, I had wanted it to happen.

It was her only moment of hesitation. A week before, Steve had been standing in the kitchen in her makeup robe, scratching his balls, and now he was expelled from Wheaton-Warrenville and was on his way to military school. Mindy had counseled her that Steve wasn't T & R (Teachable and Reachable), but Carla, having accepted her share of the fornication blame, refused to press charges. Carl was beyond furious.

Carla's anxiety about Steve being cast into the fiery pit for love of her gave me an advantage. With a trembling voice, I said that Steve, my only friend in the whole world at the time, had made me confused about my feelings. As for that dirty old queer in my room, I had never seen him before; he had given me a ride home from Wax Trax and tricked his way inside. Since I didn't know his name, how could I possibly ever see him again? I was a loser. I was a sinner. I was pathetically in love with Veronica Satterwhite, but she was out of my league. I would go to Bible Study with Carla after state. I agreed that God would be my new father figure. Trusting me the way Jesus trusted her, she promised not to tell. Down in Peoria she would ask Veronica if she'd go out with me.

We made egg salad and heated a can of tomato soup, taking care to use vitamin-fortified milk instead of water. We were excessively polite to one another, almost as if we were on a first date. We stayed clear of the windows, because Steve and the other bad man might be circling the house, peeing holes in the snow to mark their territory, waiting to tear at us again and desecrate our fragile wholesomeness.

The Holiday Inn had "Welcome IHSA Speech" lit up in red letters on its outdoor sign, the first of dozens of touches designed to make state weekend feel like the Winter Olympics. On our stroll to the student union, Miss Schuette, who had freaked us out in the car by revealing that she was only twenty-three, relived her championship year. She dabbed her eyes when Mindy went into the portable photo booth and pulled the curtain, the official start to registration. While our mug shots were turned into laminated badges, we filled Bradley U tote bags with freebie decals and key rings from all the state schools, passes to historical sites, magazine offers, feather pens, and wall calendars. Officials and student volunteers congratulated us at every station, but I scarcely noticed. I wanted to see the program book.

It did not disappoint. The state seal was embossed in four colors on the silken royal blue and buff cover. The fresh-smelling, glossy pages were stapled along the spine, not in the upper left corner like the sectionals program. After welcome pages from Governor Thompson and the state legislature, there was a letter from the university president guaranteeing a speech scholarship to Bradley for each and every champion. I read it twice, putting off the parade of events for as long as I could bear it.

245

Legible proof of me was printed on page nine in two different typefaces.

The state program is one decent memory I have from high school. Another is the party they threw that night in the women's gym for the contestants. Each event had its own flagged station. Eric, Mindy, and I had barely hung up our coats when a pair of long, hairy arms grabbed my waist from behind.

Dina Demacopoulos, drunk on Hawaiian Punch, crowed in my ear, "Rick darling! You're here at last!"

I instantly sensed a different Dina, a Dina who wasn't going to flirt except in jest. Rolling right with her, surprising myself, I yanked her hands up to my lips and kissed a chunky wood bracelet. "Dina, you star!" Eric's jaw dropped.

We strutted to the D.I. station. Dina's hair had grown out some since I'd seen her in December and fell in a small wave just below her ears. Her parents had kept their word: the braces were gone. I said her teeth were so straight and white she should model. Dina's flip reply to the compliment—"I am a triumph over circumstance"—stayed with me. She made circumstance sound like a fence you simply hitched a leg over. She repeated it several times that night as she knit the eighteen dramatic interpers together with introductions, funny sayings, snippets from scenes, accents, imitations, and on-the-spot rhyming nicknames. Slick Rick, Dina Pina, Spacy Tracy, Mark Spark. Of the gorgeous and collected Veronica Schmonica who stood on the other side of me in the group D.I. photo, Dina whispered, "She's spite, and I am despite."

I laughed without really knowing what she meant, but as with her circumstance crack I understood what whistled behind her words. Dina Demacopoulos had learned to juggle the balls she had, and if I stuck by her she could teach me too. Before the tops were even off the pizza boxes we had traded phone numbers and were planning to move to New York together after high school. She'd seen *All About Eve* on the Late Show, and I knew an actress on tour who could lend us her apartment on Horatio Street. We were set.

As dances go, it was pizza and punch and the seventies hits that the normal kids bought at Wax Trax and listened to and made out to, but it was all the dances I would never attend. High on the feeling of belonging, I boogied down for the first time in my life, leaping behind Dina in a raucous all-state Locomotion line that held back the dawn.

Another brilliant touch at state was that the events were spread over the whole campus. Dramatic Interp was held in Westlake Hall, a cream-brick Ag Science building with crinkly turrets and a bell tower. As Dina and I walked down the packed hallway to Room 12, hardcore fans were checking their programs against our tags. "It's pronounced Dema-COP-oulous," Dina said to those trying to sound it out. "Accent on the third syllable. And this is Richard Lahrem."

"Rhymes with harem," I said jauntily.

"This is just like the Oscars," she whispered.

"California, here I come," I said, quoting the end of her D.I.

She swatted my butt with her purse. "Take that back, bushdog." The epithet "bushdog" was another piece of Demacopoulos nonsense I couldn't hear enough of.

We gave our names to the door proctor. As we entered from the top of a huge lecture hall our eyes popped at all the people—a couple hundred at least. At the bottom of the stairs the professor's lectern had been moved to the right, next to a chart showing the cross-section of a horse. Lamps had been positioned to project double cones of light on the floor in front of a blue curtain. The three judges' seats, placed midway down the slope, were fitted with tiny desk lamps.

As we descended Dina pivoted on a stair. She had picked out Nancy Corley, a contestant from Macomb, at the other end of the fourth row. Nancy Pantsy stood, and they blew kisses. Nancy fluttered her handkerchief at me, and I bowed back. I gallantly motioned for Dina to enter the row before me.

From the front row the timekeeper called for silence. A hush fell. The lights dimmed. At the sound of the judges breaking the seals on their tally envelopes, Dina started to tremble. I held her hand the entire round.

Out of the eighteen purveyors of pain in the group D.I. photo, six of us would keep going, but doing the Locomotion with my competitors made it harder to critique them the next day. Faced with an equation, the kid on the math team solves it or he doesn't. The speller at the bee recognizes the word or she doesn't. As I watched the other interps in my prelim rounds, I tried to convince myself that it would be okay not to make finals; I had a boyfriend, after all, and a ticket to *A Chorus Line* and two more speech seasons before I graduated. It was enough, wasn't it, just to show the other kids why Briarcliffe's triumph over circumstance had been invited to the dance? Even with its new, emotionally noisier ending, my piece was on the subtle side, so I was back to the riddles I began the season with. Is smothering your baby more dramatic than turning into a rhinoceros? Is screaming better than crying? Can a whisper be louder than both? How do you judge pain, rank pain, grade pain? I could interp the hell out of *The Boys in the Band,* but what about it, or me, or me doing it, might put me ahead of the rest?

For months my coaches, including Ned, had ducked from stating the obvious secret to my success, obvious to all but me when I began competing. Like the judges who down-ranked me on the "appropriateness" issue, Mr. Wegner was a coward who stopped short of acknowledging the truth in his typecasting. Beneath the surface of my performance was the unsavory threat, the phantom picture of what Carla had caught me doing. It had found me out, but the greater truth, far outlasting a silly telltale boner, was that I had found me out in it. By the time we got to state I was a sixteen-year-old telling my truth. Maybe the power of that truth gave my interpretation the edge it needed to outshine infanticide and regicide and more seemly animal hatreds.

Maybe the pride behind that truth was why I neglected to fight for my life. Around three-thirty that same afternoon, Eric and I were waiting in slaphappy lines of kids at a row of pay phones in the student union. Bopping between us with a bag of pretzel rods, Carla was overjoyed to have witnessed for the first time the power of her prayers: all three Wolverines had made finals. It was Mindy who had finally taken Dina Demacopoulos from my insufficient arms. Her mascara had stained my suit, and I hated myself for feeling relieved to have the new sport coat in reserve.

Miss Schuette zoomed through with dinner plans. Eric checked to make sure he would be able to catch the national news. We high-fived for maybe the tenth time, speech studs ready to hit an indoor pool in February.

Tracy Hilger, an intense girl from my second round, came

up with her program open to page nine. "Will you sign this, Richard?"

"Don't you mean Slick Rick?"

She tried to laugh. "Good luck tomorrow, Slick Rick. I'll be rooting for you."

"Me too me too me too," clapped Carla. "I can't stand it." She offered Tracy a pretzel.

"Tracy, this is Carla," I said, trying to scribble with a dead pen. "Spacy Tracy did an amazing *Gingerbread Lady*."

"Not amazing enough," sighed Tracy.

I asked Eric for his pen. "The judges made a mistake, because I thought you were great. There's next year."

"I'm a senior. This is my last year."

"Oh."

"Some colleges have speech teams," said Eric.

"I'm not going to college."

"Neither am I," I said, hoping to make her feel better.

"You could if you win it all tomorrow," said Eric.

As I reached for his pen, I noticed that Carla had dropped out of the excitement. The bag in her hand was hanging upside down. Pretzel rods had bounced and snapped around her feet, and her face had gone white. She looked at me with stricken eyes, then back at a figure standing thirty feet away in front of a ROTC poster. She kept going back and forth between us— wasn't this the same man who'd run past her upstairs?

Carla looked at me again, and I met her gaze. This moment was mine. I was signing a fan's program. Worst case, I was already the sixth best dramatic interper in the Land of Lincoln. If I chose to, I could share Carla's astonishment or horror or whatever else she had cooked up to feel at the second sighting of Ned Bolang. Or I could convince her it wasn't the same man. Or I could find us a campus chapel and convince her that I was still Teachable and Reachable; I could renew my vow to bind up sin and cast it away, and she could renew her vow of silence. Whatever I chose to do, I could convince her the way I'd convinced my judges to send me into finals.

Instead I got cocky, gave in to cocky. Instead I shrugged at life. Instead I lifted a brow. Instead I made a soft, noncommittal sound. Our eyes locked a final time. The man had moved on, a mirage if need be.

So that fans could watch several events, the finals were staggered Saturday morning. Extemp Speaking, Prose, and Verse were at 8:30 a.m. Eveready Eric left with Wegner at 7:00 to draw his topic. He declared himself psyched for any conflict but had a gut feeling he'd get Northern Ireland. He clicked the top of his lucky pen and put it in his jacket pocket. The curve of the watch chain across his vest, which he considered his secret weapon, followed a formula he had devised himself in calculus class. We shook hands. "Go Wolverine," we said to each other, and we weren't kidding around. He picked up his briefcase of news magazines and walked through the door like he was making a parachute jump.

Original Oratory, Dramatic Interp, and Humorous Interp were scheduled for 10:00 a.m. I had hours before Schuette was coming for me, but I couldn't fall back asleep. I showered, I watched *Jonny Quest*. With Eric gone I could spread my talismans out across my bed. Steve's cufflinks were going into my new striped blue shirt from Mark Shale.

I scanned my mother's latest scriptural passage, from Philippians. *Do nothing out of selfish ambition or vain conceit, but in humility consider others better than yourselves.* That made clearer

251

sense than her previous messages. I wished my opponents all the best.

There were only so many times I could check my part and pull my shirttails under my lucky underwear. I thought about a walk. Exploring the campus would help me visualize attending Bradley on a speech scholarship and might boost my chances for ultimate victory. On the other hand, a walk might take me into toilet stalls with telephone numbers, and I didn't want that kind of help. I wanted to stay clean and balanced.

I knew where to go. I carefully arranged my tokens in my jacket pockets. District and sectionals medals inside breast left, over my heart. Theater ticket and picture of Ned inside breast right. Presidents outside right. Scriptures outside left. Because I was afraid the elevator might break down with me in it, I climbed the two flights of stairs to Mindy and Carla's room.

Mindy answered, a towel pinned around her neck. She held her curling iron like a track baton as she accepted my good luck hug. Looking over her shoulder, I saw new heels standing at the foot of her neatly made bed. Carla's pajamas, hairbrush, and Bible were in a tangle on the far one. Mindy didn't invite me in.

"Can I talk to my sister?" I said loudly, so Carla could hear. She'd been silent and pale all through the dinner with Eric and Schuette and Wegner.

"She's in the shower."

I didn't hear any water running.

"I thought maybe we all could read some Psalms and Proverbs. You know, for luck."

Mindy waved her curling iron. "I still have hair and makeup."

"Maybe just Carla, then? Would you ask her to come to my room when she gets out of the shower?"

Down the hall a bellhop knocked on a door. "Room service," he said. Distracted, we waited for the mystery guest to answer. Veronica Satterwhite might just be glamorous enough to order room service. He knocked again. Mindy sighed.

"Okay," I said. "Could you remind Carla that D.I. is in Westlake Hall, Room 12?"

A funny look crossed Mindy's face: sad, then weirdly superior.

"What is it, Mindy? Is Carla okay?"

"She's fine, Rick. She's decided to watch the Doomsday Clock instead."

"Did she—"

But Mindy was closing the door, with a downright unfriendly reminder that the Word of God wasn't a good luck charm.

I listened to the echo of my feet in the concrete stairwell. I bought an oblong sticky bun from a machine off the lobby. This was my succulent fatted calf. I thought of squeezing it to death inside its bag, then cleared my head of the crazy impulse by resting it against the cold glass front of the machine.

I ate the bun, stale and wet, over the toilet. I sat on my bed and opened the Young Man's Bible. Esther. Job. Ezekiel. Acts. The words blurred, and I was afraid my fingers would tear the delicate pages. I had to talk to Carla. I called her room, intending to ask whether she'd mind if I started calling Carl "Dad"— an act of treason unthinkable any other morning before or since—but the line was busy. The rest of the Musical Kendigs were probably crooning "Blessed Mindy" over the phone to their little warrior. Or maybe she and Carla were talking directly to Jesus, holding the receiver between them.

The soothing velvet harmony of the Manhattan Transfer

singing "Operator" popped into my head but it was instantly usurped by the squeaky sound of girls starting "The Telephone Hour." I began to sing with them: *"Hi Nancy, Hi Helen. What's the story, morning glory? What's the tale, nightingale? Tell me quick about Hugo and Kim."*

The segue to *Bye Bye Birdie* led directly to revelation. I was going to try out that Monday for the musical, not for the chorus but for the part of Mr. McAfee. Who better to imitate Paul Lynde? Life would keep going after final round. I would share the stage with Joe and Beth and Mindy and Carla and the Campus Lifers. Cheering from the audience would be Marie and Carl and Lisa and my father and Julia and Bev and Cactus and Steve and Hannelore and Patty and Veronica and Dina and Ned.

So miraculous was this vision of room enough for all in the life to come that I knew I must pray for it to happen. I began at the beginning. Like beads on a rosary, I ticked off the songs from my Genesis: "I Hope I Get It," "I Can Do That," "At the Ballet," "Sing!" "Hello Twelve, Hello Thirteen, Hello Love," . . .

Then it was on to Exodus: "Overture," "All That Jazz," "Funny Honey," "The Cell Block Tango," "When You're Good to Mama," . . .

At the end of every B side—"Home (Finale)," "Pass the Cross to Me," "Finale," "We Go Together (Reprise)," "Being Alive"—I'd cross myself, and the next album would appear on wings. I moved in slow and solemn motion around the room, palms up to let them land safely. As the titles coursed through me, the rush of words on my lips was enough to restore the color to Carla's stricken face and resuscitate her smile of sisterly peace. Taking stage together, our lives would twine and bloom in the coming spring.

Schuette noticed the Playboy bunny cufflinks in my new shirt just as I was pulling open the giant oak door to Westlake Hall. An inspired eleventh-hour detail, she said. I was her classiest act.

Inside it was the movie premiere feel again, times ten: flashbulbs, whistles, applause, waving programs to sign, deposed gladiators in street clothes clapping me on the back, everything except searchlights and heralds blowing long thin trumpets. I was looking for Dina to see if she would sit with me. I needed her to call me a bushdog again. From a distance, I waved to the D.I. timekeeper in the doorway like he was an old buddy. He turned, tapped a ribboned official's shoulder, and pointed at me. Maybe I was the last contestant to arrive. I knew I wasn't late.

A second official stepped in front of the timekeeper and blocked my entrance to Room 12, saying that some people needed to meet with me. He escorted me down the hall. The first official wouldn't let Schuette come along and ignored her increasingly shrill demands for information.

Compared to the lecture hall, Room 18 seemed the size of our pantry. My mother was there. She looked awful. She was the color of ash, hair undone, no makeup, clothes thrown on. Her hands were twisting inside the opposite sleeves of her camel coat. My first thought was that Lisa had died. Then I saw Patty Puller. And then Wegner, his face a stone, with another IHSA bigwig. Chairs were pulled out around a seminar table, but no one was sitting. Patty's humungous Bible was on the table, in its blue leatherette case, alongside an imposing book of IHSA rules and regulations.

Doomsday was here. The Christians had ratted me out. Praying with Mindy before they went to bed, Carla had broken down and told her about the man in my room. Mindy insisted that Carla phone home with the information rather than try talking to me again. Carla called Marie, who conferred with Sister Patty, who served up a big helping of Leviticus and got in the car with her at the crack of dawn, leaving Carl in Wheaton with Lisa. My mother tracked down Wegner in his motel room, and he relayed his suspicions about a speech coach from another school.

And now, given that there was a clearly stated morals clause on page sixty-seven in the rule book, my mother was telling me that I wouldn't be permitted to compete in the final round at state unless I revealed the identity of the man Carla saw.

I couldn't speak, wouldn't speak in their noise of cross-examination. My mother kept saying please, please. Patty was gurgling hellfire in the corner, fanning the flames with puffs of yeasty denture breath. Wegner clicked a pen over and over. I refused to write down the man's name.

The official scratched a nostril, wiped his glasses, spoke. "Mr. Lahrem, there's very little time. We have reason to believe that the man whom your sister—"

"Stepsister," I interrupted. My voice stilled the room.

"The man whom your stepsister has identified as your . . . your . . ."

"Boyfriend," I said. My mother and Patty gasped. It would have been funny in a movie.

"Seducer," he said sternly. "This man, this seducer, we have reason to believe, is a speech coach from another school."

I shook my head no. I don't know why I thought stonewalling would help.

Schuette stormed into the room. "The boy must be allowed to compete if it's his wish. Do you want to, Rick?"

Having gotten nowhere with me, my mother took it out on Schuette. She grabbed her by the arm. "You are a *student* teacher, Miss Schuette. If you don't get out of here right now, I will make sure that you never graduate from teacher's college. I will have you banned from the profession for encouraging my son to perform this piece."

"You gave him your permission, Mrs. Schwob. You saw him perform the interp in the fall, at Wheaton Central—"

"I didn't know then what I know now," said my mother, shaking Schuette hard. "Look what it's led to."

"It's taken him all the way to the state finals."

"It's taken him all the way to Sodom and Gomorrah," thundered Patty, with a dramatic lift of her Bible.

Schuette was the last to know. She was told about Ned, in more clinical terms, and hung her head. But I could tell from the way she was gnawing off her lipstick that she wanted me competing in front of that crowd in Room 12. In the end, she sided with my mother, but for different reasons.

Mr. Wegner mentioned the time. My mother, still on a tear, threatened him and School District 200 and the IHSA with a lawsuit for giving me *The Boys in the Band*. That was when the official suggested a clearing of the room, since this had become a strictly parental issue. On her way out, Patty tried to anoint my head again. This time I smacked her oily thumb away, sank my hands into her fat flanks, and pushed.

"Get out of here, you witch," I said. I slammed the door.

Physical exertion had burned off a little of our tension. I tried guessing what subject was taught in Room 18, but the walls were blank. My mother saw me look at the clock. It was 10:04. She started over.

"Honey," she said. "So much of this is my fault, believe me, I know. I should have stopped your interp as soon as I found the Lord, but you were so happy, and I was so proud of you,

257

and so worried about what Carla was up to, that I didn't stop to think about the content when I should have. I could have given you the time to change pieces, found something more appropriate. I should have been paying more attention—"

"That's right," I said. "You weren't paying attention, and now it's too late. All you care about now is God and Jesus and Patty and Psalms and Proverbs! Last week you and Patty were praying for me to win today, you know you were."

"I'll have to ask you to forgive me for that."

"Shut *up*, Mom. I'll never forgive you if you don't let me compete."

"Then you have to tell me who that evil man is."

I tried to stay calm. "He isn't evil. He's nice to me, nicer than anybody. *He* pays attention."

"Evil attention! He is a sick, sick, evil homosexual. He'll die in the fiery pit for what he's done to you."

"Then I'm sick. I'm evil."

"No! You're my son, my only begotten son. You're just a confused boy. When you come to know God like I am coming to know Him, He will save you from this confusion."

"I don't want to be saved. This confusion is who I am."

Her voice was starting to get throbby. "God knows you, Rick. He knew you from day one. He formed your inmost being and knit you together in my womb—"

"Gross, gross, shut up, please please shut up—"

"He'll save your life, like He has mine, like He has Carla's, and even Carl—"

God was the tougher opponent, but she really ought to have remembered that Carl was an even bigger red flag. I heaved a chair against the wall to make her listen.

"No! Don't you get it? Carl is just playing along with it! Carla told me."

"Carla told you what?"

"That he's faking it. She said that Carl is going to church and doing this Marriage Encounter crap just so"—I paused before I exaggerated Carla's claim—"just so you'll go down on him."

The term confused her. "Go down on him?"

"Don't be stupid, Mom," I yelled. She knew what sex was. I threw the chair again, but it still wouldn't break. "He's pretending to be a Jesus freak so you'll blow him."

"Blow him? What—"

"So you'll suck his dick! Do you want me to draw it on the blackboard?"

Until that moment, I would never have thought myself capable of hurting her deliberately. My betrayal, and its meaning for her life, took time to sink in, but when they did she fell into a chair like I'd punched her in the stomach.

I walked along the blackboard and snapped every piece of chalk in the sill. I watched the sweep hand on the wall clock jerk from second to second. I was preparing to take it all back, tell her that I was lying, tell her anything to stop the racking sobs I'd caused, when something worse, something that had been crouched and waiting inside me, broke free and tore its way out.

"How can Jesus be more important to you than I am?"

Asking it was admitting it. Admitting it was so embarrassing, and so naked, and true, that I sat down too, put my forehead on the edge of the table and started bawling my own eyes out.

That was it for words. Eventually I heard her shift in her chair. She reached to cover my hand. I laced my thumb inside hers, curled my fingers around. I turned to look up at her. She tilted her chin to mirror the angle of my head. Faces streaming with tears, blood beating in the ball of our hands, we watched one another and spoke our hearts.

Oh, baby, He isn't. How can He be?

I miss you. I need you.

Mommy knows. Mommy always knows.

I love you. I want you back.

I know. Mommy loves you.

Will you come back?

And there we were, as we'd been before there was God and Ned, before there was Carl, before there was my father; there we were, as we'd been in the golden time, after I was knit in her womb and before a request for mustard made me intelligible to others.

Please, son.

Please is a plea. How could I deny her?

I reached into a pocket with my free hand. Madison clinked against Taft. Wrong pocket. I concentrated on the exact location of my charms. Finally, from inside my right breast pocket, I withdrew the Polaroid of Ned and me at the Shubert Theatre. I slid it to her, face down.

She turned it over on the table and stifled a cry. Her eyes searched my face to see whether I was that boy in the picture or the boy in front of her wiping his nose on a cashmere sleeve.

I nodded, attempted a smile for bravery's sake, and became the boy she craved. We released our hold.

She fished a handkerchief from the pocket of her cardigan and waited while I blew my nose. Perfectly Richard held the door open for his mother and turned to avoid catching the photo handoff in the hallway.

⌒12⌒

So many mistakes. It was a mistake for me to believe that Marie would or could renounce her attachment to the living God, just as it was a mistake for her to believe that my turning Ned in meant I wasn't going to be gay. Though made in good faith, our silent promise in Room 18 was bound to unravel. My mother had left and was never coming back, and I would have to learn not to scream about it.

A mistake as well to believe that details and ugly distortions of what had happened in Peoria wouldn't travel back and circulate through my high school. Wheaton-Warrenville had time-tested procedures for the oppression of designated pariahs, and my physical safety swiftly became an issue.

Given the deteriorating home and school environments, Family Court stepped in and let me choose where to live. I suppose it was a deliberate tip of the scales on my part to confess that the Nazi dagger found in my closet had been acquired in an attempt to protect myself from a violent stepfather. Only I knew I hadn't enough gumption with a blade to scratch side B of an *Oliver* album.

Finally, it was a mistake to believe that I would be able to kill the people one more time. That last round officially began, just ten minutes late, the second the proctor closed the door behind us. Marie took the first available chair in the last row. I stumbled down a few more rows, sick and sweaty with fear, and took an aisle seat.

I tried, but I really couldn't imagine what winning state might mean to me now. How would this first-place trophy squeeze into the life of a room that was gone? Having cast my lot with my first love, I reached into my left jacket pocket and took counsel from Marie's last smiley-face message: *Do nothing out of selfish ambition or vain conceit, but in humility consider others better than yourselves. Philippians 2:3. I love you, Mom.* Miss Schuette would have died to read it, but it was good advice.

So I watched us come and go, with humility.

Peggy Spero, *Picnic*. A spinster schoolteacher begs her boyfriend to marry her.

Tim Pool, *All My Sons*. A son confronts his father over defective airplanes he manufactured in World War II.

Dana Davidson, *The Visit*. A rich old lady bribes her hometown to murder the man who jilted her when she was a girl.

The proctor called my name. Descending the stairs, I pressed the rabbits in my sleeves. Steve Hendrie, there at the beginning, traveled with me to the very end. I apologized to the poster of the cross-sectioned horse for taking his spot. I pivoted front and hitched my shoulders up. Before uncorking my eight minutes of pain, I focused briefly on the splashes of reflected light on the tips of my polished shoes.

I looked up and out. Of course he was there. In the third row, slightly to my left, leaning forward, coat folded across his lap, Ned smiled, but not too broadly. Proud of his boy, but proper. My mother was high up and to the right and illegible. Focal points, but too far apart to be of technical assistance.

I fluttered my fingers at my sides, took a breath. Because I had ceded her everything else, at the last split second I began my intro with that mildly controversial modifier. "*Some* homosexuals are sad and lonely young men." One infinitesimal word was all I could offer in thanks and farewell.

Richard Lahrem, *The Boys in the Band*. A man attempts to convince an old college friend that he isn't homosexual.

I did my best, but it wouldn't be wrong to say that very recent events had dulled my competitive edge. I went fourth, and I got fourth place. The ordinal symmetry of it pleased me at the time, and in hindsight, was utterly fair.

Veronica Satterwhite, *This Property Is Condemned*. A little girl walking along a railroad track remembers her dead sister Alva.

I was sitting near enough to a judge to watch him wipe an eye at the end of Veronica's interp. Fair enough. What made Veronica a killer, and a champion, was her refusal to cry at the end of "My Blue Heaven." She pulled back and made you cry.

Skip Cunningham, *Long Day's Journey into Night*. One brother confesses to another that he loves him and hates him.

The timekeeper stood and led a final round of applause. Getting up, I felt surprisingly hungry for a six-hundred-year-old teenager. I mumbled thanks to the good wishes of those around me and kept my eyes on my shoes. My mother and Miss Schuette were waiting in a grim truce at the top of the stairs. Neither mentioned my performance. Marie held my arm tightly. Schuette tried but failed to distract me from the sight of two campus police officers checking the crowd. From the corner of my eye, I saw Wegner playing backup. A corner of the Polaroid was pinched between his thumb and forefinger, a dead mouse hung by its tail.

I pushed myself into the cold. Hiding my face from the sun, I trudged back to the Holiday Inn. Gray puzzle pieces of sky came through the cracks at my elbow. My mother's false cheer, as she weighed lunch options, struck my ears like a hammer; I let her talk for both of us.

Marie turned my room into a scripture library not long after it became clear that I would never visit for more than a meal. Before they retired to a trailer in Apopka, Florida, where I understand Carl is now a lay deacon at the True Temple of God, Lisa and I cleared out what was left of our stuff from the ancient Andover. My trophies and programs had gone to New Jersey with me, but in a musty trunk of old papers, games, birthday cards, and Presidents Washington through Nixon, I found a folder holding other traces of those four months on speech team. In its left pocket was a clipping from the *Wheaton Daily Journal* headlined "Speech Rivals Bury the Hatchet." Veronica Satterwhite's hair wings in the photo are the size of orange-juice cans, and my puffy bangs make me look like a mushroom. Under the feature, its top sheet tattooed in orange by the leached chemicals of the old newsprint, was my cutting from *The Boys in the Band*. I found I could still recite it by heart. Lisa, dear to me as ever, laughed at my solemn rendition of its opening lines. "Mickey, I'm leaving." "Stay right where you are." Schuette was right: some things you really do never forget.

In the right pocket of the folder were the schedule sheets. The play titles and doodles on the third of six pages caught my eye particularly. Under "Dramatic Interpretation, University High School, November 12–13, 1976," careful circles picked out 11A from five matrices. Beside the second block of numbers were three little skeletons, two of them in skirts. Anne Boleyn from *Anne of the Thousand Days*. Thomas More from *A Man for All Seasons*. Joan of Arc from *The Lark*. My Death Row round. A room with an astronomy moon, Ned Bolang waiting on the other side of the door.

They may not have particularly wanted me there, but my father and Julia did their best during the time I lived with them. I graduated from Ridgewood High School in June of 1979, a quiet transfer student with no activities. For someone who didn't go to college, I consider myself very lucky. Practically my first call in New Jersey was to Reed Goodkin. He took me to my first Broadway shows and gave me my start with sugarless gum. As I matured, I moved on to soft drinks, suntan lotion, hair mousse when it became fashionable for men, shaving gear, pain reliever, liquor, and now, finally, financial products. My face, my voice, my interpretative skills inspire consumer confidence, especially in Malaysia and the Czech Republic, where I'll admit to something of a following.

Residuals paid for and maintain my handsome surroundings overlooking Central Park. In my own way, I tithe. A portion of my money and energy goes to a foundation whose mission is to promote understanding of, and provide safe spaces for, gay and lesbian teenagers. The need is immense. Mindy Kendig Sanders makes a meaningful annual contribution, and Carla, who fell off the Jesus wagon almost immediately after high school, tends to tuck a twenty in the appeal envelope. She grooms horses in Arizona and is raising two kids on her own. I hear about her through Lisa.

I like to believe I perform smaller acts of charity as well. As I've grown older, and weary of air travel, and have learned through other, less painful triumphs over circumstance that each meal will not be my last, I have made it a policy to offer my dessert to any young people sitting in my row. They always accept, and I always turn away. The truly free pieces of cake in life are hard to come by. Today, the airlines get by on peanuts, but I make the gesture anyway.

I never saw Ned Bolang again, and Reed Goodkin discreetly knew never to mention him. Without question I ended his teaching career, but that era was less punitive toward that sort of offender. I could google him, but I'm not prepared, not yet anyway, to learn of his death or an incarceration.

The oracular Patty Puller, long gone to the bone orchard, was wrong on many counts, but she was especially wrong about hell. Hell is not hot. Hell, when I visit, is a cold, barren plain where mistakes are permanent and mothers and lovers go missing.

Acknowledgments

"When am I going to get another story?" asks my cherished circle of first readers: Judy Dennis, Lillian Groag, Pebble Kranz, Kennie Pressman, Catherine Weidner, and Jaan Whitehead. Their faith in and attention to my sentences keep me at the laptop.

Many friends, writers, editors, and showbiz collaborators encouraged and abetted my impulse to attempt fiction after years in the theater: Irene Lewis, Jean McGarry, Kathleen Hill, Rhona Bitner, Walt Wangerin Jr., Susan Birkenhead, Henry Krieger, Ed Ku, David Schweizer, Nancy Hoffman, Margaret Hunt, Jill Rachel Morris, Charlotte Stoudt, Tim Vasen, John Lanasa, Paul Hildner, Catherine Sheehy, Jeannette Festa, Dudley Clendenin, Peter Hagan, Wesley Gibson and Charles Flowers at *Bloom,* and Janet Horn. My gratitude and affection to one and all.

A portion of *Sugarless* was written at the MacDowell Colony, where wonders happen, especially in winter. Colonists Amy Bloom, James Cañon, Kelly Link, Margo Rabb, and Lisa

Shea were unstinting with their lovely selves and liberal with their professional advice.

The nonpareil Michael Mayer came through for me yet again, this time leaving a copy of the manuscript in the elevator for his neighbor Nicole Aragi. Her generous read led me directly to my agent, Katherine Fausset, whose efforts to keep my spirits up and *Sugarless* in play over the long haul were extraordinary and deeply appreciated.

I'd like to thank Raphael Kadushin, Nicole Kvale, Adam Mehring, Andrea Christofferson, and the entire team at University of Wisconsin Press for their enthusiasm and care.

I am especially grateful to Dick Scanlan, who spotted a more compelling story in an early draft and insisted that it must be told, and to Joy Johannessen, whose editorial lapidary helped bring it out. Finally, a lunch with Kathy Shapiro can turn my worst days around, and David Nolta sets the bar for comedy, prose, and friendship.

And then there is my partner, Steve Bolton, the happy ending to every story and every day.